Alfred the Great; King's Revenge

(Book #2 of the King Alfred Sagas)

(Book #8 of the overall series)

By Bruce Corbett

Dedication

To Beverly Wilfrid Corbett,
a gentleman and a great father.
He taught me what selfless love is.
Thank you for everything.

FOREWORD

This is the second book in the King Alfred Sagas, and the eighth book in the Ambrose historical adventure series. The previous novel covered a time when England came very close to becoming a Danish kingdom. In this novel, Alfred's long-term plans are finally coming to fruition. His plan to build fortified towns and a navy is underway. The end of this war will see Wessex spread to the north of the Thames, and control much of Mercia. His sea thanes, his garrison troops, and his summer and winter army are all part of a master plan to give Wessex a fighting chance against the savage Viking invaders.

The titles of the books have changed, since the main character in the last two books is Alfred the Great, though Ambrose, Polonius and Phillip will continue to play a major part in the war against the pagan Danes.

Some years before this story begins, in 876 AD., King Guthrum of the Danes invades the Anglo-Saxon country of Wessex. Trapped at the town of Wareham by Alfred the Great and his West Saxon army, the Viking agrees to a truce, but, instead, slips out and retreats to Exeter. After a Viking fleet is destroyed in a storm, Guthrum is forced to sue for peace and retreats to East Anglia, a country that he and his ravaging Vikings have already conquered.

Just before Christmas 877, Alfred, whose army was disbanded for the winter, is caught by surprise by a second invasion of Guthrum's army. The Saxon king is forced into hiding in the forest of Selwood. Eventually he finds his way to Athelney, an island surrounded by marshes. From there, he organizes a secret gathering of his fighting men. Meanwhile, to the west, one of his ealdormen,

Odda, destroys a second Viking army newly arrived from Wales and led by Ubbi Ragnarsson.

A single major defeat could mean the end of Saxon Wessex. All of the Angle, Saxon and Jute kingdoms north of the Thames are reeling or have already fallen under the Viking onslaught. Alfred's army manages to gather in May, however, and they meet the Vikings at Edington. Alfred is victorious and the Vikings flee to Chippenham. After a two week siege, Guthrum agrees to be baptized and signs a peace treaty with Alfred. Wessex is saved. This story is told in **Alfred the Great; Viking Invasion**.

In 885, Wessex is threatened by a new enemy. Another Viking army, fresh from France, lands in Kent and besieges the town of Rochester. This is where **Alfred the Great; King's Revenge**, begins. Guthrum and his powerful army are bound by treaty to stay out of the fight, but his men are ever hungry for more land and adventure. The territory north of the Thames River belongs to Guthrum. If the Viking king joins his forces with the Danes from France, Wessex may finally be overwhelmed. Alfred arrives with his army before the city falls, and the combined Saxon forces rout the Vikings, who flee precipitously, even leaving behind their entire horse herd.

The Anglo-Saxon Chronicles say very little about what actually happened between this attack and the eventual peace treaty between Alfred and Guthrum, although they report Alfred attacking a Viking fleet in the mouth of the Stour River. Alfred's fleet wins, but is subsequently defeated by an avenging fleet sent by Guthrum. Why was Alfred's fleet sent so far north; into Guthrum's home waters? How exactly did Alfred take London, and why? Did Guthrum attempt to defend it? The details I use in this story are fictitious.

Although regaining a strong base on the north bank of the Thames seems a good strategic move for Alfred, it was counter to the treaty he had signed with Guthrum. I have to assume that Guthrum must have been involved in some way in the hostilities at Rochester. Statements in Asser's biography of Alfred bear this out. Asser states that the king takes the city of London 'after . . . burning cities and the slaying of the people.' I mention Bishop Asser, but at the time of this story he was actually a newly arrived monk at Alfred's court. He was not made a bishop until the 890's.

I have made the assumption that Guthrum came south to defend London and the north bank of the Thames. How Alfred took the city, and the battle that ensued, is strictly a figment of my imagination. The terms of the subsequent treaty, however, are accurate. (See Appendix III)

This was a critical time for Wessex and all England. The Danish tide had rolled over all but the one southern Anglo-Saxon kingdom. If Wessex had fallen, English history might have been very different. I hope that you enjoy the story. *Words in italics generally have special meaning and the details may be found in Appendix I.*

The author,

Bruce Corbett

CAST OF CHARACTERS

Alfred: The younger brother of Ambrose, Ethelbert, and Ethelred. He was an intensely curious man who unexpectedly became king at the death of his brother, in 871 AD. A great general, he drove King Guthrum, leader of the Viking Great Army, out of Wessex, but was almost taken captive in a surprise winter attack. Hiding first in the forests, and then at his island base of Athelney, he started to strike back at the hated enemy. When his men rallied to him in the spring, he was able to defeat King Guthrum. Surprisingly, he treated Guthrum generously and became his godfather. In this story, he is forced to once again take up arms against the Danish ruler who conquered Essex and East Anglia. In the end, he defeated the Viking king and took vital land north of the Thames.

Ambrose: (Fictitious) He was an Anglo-Saxon bastard prince of Wessex. Kidnapped by Viking slavers as a boy, he was taken to Denmark, and then fled to Norway and Sweden. Chased by the Danes, he joined Gunnar of the Rus Vikings, who sent him and his two companions, Phillip and Polonius, to trade on his behalf down the Russian rivers. Ambrose set up trading posts in Novgorod, and then Kiev. Finally, he traveled to Constantinople as an emissary for the Kiev leaders. From there, he eventually returned to England to help his father and brothers fight against the Viking raiders.

   He and his friends became a legend when he first joined the Danish Great Army as Canuteson, stole a princess from a Viking stronghold in Ireland and, as Hamar, spied a second time on the Danes, at Chippenham. In this story, he rode to Guthrum in an effort to keep him out of the upcoming fight, returned home in time to fight at Rochester, and then spied on the Vikings from France. Finally, he participated in the taking of London and the defeat of King Guthrum's army.

Anwell: (Fictitious) He was the Ealdorman of Cornwall who had previously made an alliance with the Danes in return for nominal independence.

Askold: He, with his cousin, Dir, were the Rus leaders who left Novgorod to settle at Kiev, a city they felt was ideally situated to control the Russian-Byzantine river trade. Under their leadership, the Dnieper River region came under Varangian control, and they participated in an attack on Constantinople itself. After the attack, in an attempt to end the hostilities, they appointed Ambrose to negotiate with the Byzantine Emperor.

Asser: He was a Welsh monk who was invited to Alfred's court around 885, though he actually arrived in 886. Eventually, in the 890's he was made bishop of Sherborne. He is best known for writing the story of Alfred in the Life of King Alfred. I thus have him at court, and promoted somewhat early.

Byram: (Fictitious) A ship officer aboard Alfred's **Leaping Stag**, he was the thane sent as temporary captain to the prize Alfred captured on the Stour River.

Cedd: (Fictitious) One of the crewmen aboard the Thames ferry.

Dag: (Fictitious) The Viking ruler of Wexford, he was mentioned when a Viking minstrel sang of Ambrose's rescue of his fiancé after she was kidnaped and enslaved.

Dir: See ASKOLD.

Ealhswith: Wife of King Alfred.

Egbert: He was an ancestor of Alfred's. He ruled Wessex as king from 802 to 839 AD.

Egil: (Little): (Fictitious) A Danish warrior, he was earlier mentioned in the story of when Ambrose and his comrades joined the Viking Great Army. Thrust unconscious under a tent and then wounded in combat against Ambrose, he was the butt of many Viking jokes. Egil recognized Ambrose when the Saxon prince traveled north as Alfred's envoy. He first threatened Ambrose, and then tried to assassinate him. Declared outlaw by his own king, he raided south of the Thames, where he was captured.

Ethelred: (of Mercia) The nobleman conquered western Mercia from the Dane's puppet king, and eventually married Alfred's daughter. In this story, he joined Alfred and swore allegiance to him just before his final battle with King Guthrum.

Ethelwold: Alfred's nephew and Ealdorman of Dorset, his father was Ethelred, older brother of Alfred. Ethelred had been king of Wessex from AD. 866 to 871. Ethelwold questioned the wisdom of Alfred taking the fleet north against the Francian Vikings.

Galar: (Fictitious) In this story, he commanded the queen's escort and rode with her from Winchester to Rochester.

Gauti: (Fictitious) He was Alfred's Frisian navigator on the king's flagship, the **Leaping Stag**.

Giric: (possibly along with Eochaid) was the king of the united kingdom of the Picts and the Scots.

Gretchen: (Fictitious) Was the daughter of Osmond, Ealdorman of East Anglia, and distant cousin to the royal family of Wessex. Previous to this story, she first met Ambrose at the Wessex court, and then nursed him back to health when he was wounded during his earlier escape from the Danes. They were betrothed, but Gretchen was first kidnaped by Welsh, and then Viking brigands. Ambrose traveled to Ireland to free her. After many adventures, they were married. A wilful wife, she risked her safety by following Ambrose to Rochester.

Godric: (Fictitious) The young warrior (Dreng) who guarded the path to where Phillip had seized a Viking long-ship on the south bank of the Thames

Guthred: A Viking recognized as king of York in 883, he was a potential adversary of King Alfred.

Guthrum: A Dane who was king of East Anglia, Essex, and part of Mercia. He attacked Wessex, was bought off, and then attacked from Mercia at Christmas of 878. After signing a treaty, he returned to East Anglia. In 885, as this story starts, he broke the treaty with Wessex by allowing his men to go south and join some Vikings from France besieging the West Saxon city of Rochester. Alfred went north to punish the attackers and seized Viking ships at the mouth of the Stour River. In response, Guthrum attacked with every ship he could muster, defeating Alfred. A second treaty was signed after Alfred seized London and defeated Guthrum in battle.

Halfdan: He was elder brother of Ubbi and Ivar the Boneless. He was one of the three original leaders of the Danish Great Army in England. His father was Ragnar Lodbrok.

Hamar: (Fictitious) Was the name Ambrose used previously when he pretended to be a Swedish trader in King Guthrum's camp some years before.

Halig: (Fictitious) Was the young warrior raised up to take the place of Thane Pyt, who had failed to have his long-ship ready to join Alfred's fleet.

Ivar The Boneless: The brother of Halfdan and Ubbi and one of the three original leaders of the Viking Great Army. His father was Ragnar Lodbrok and his son was Sitric Ivarsson, a friend of Prince Ambrose.

Jokul: (Fictitious) The Frisian captain who lured the Vikings towards Alfred's fleet and then led a raid on the East Anglian coast.

Kuralla: (Fictitious) She was a Slav chieftain's daughter whose village defied Bothi, a Rus nobleman settled near Novgorod. Bothi ordered her father tortured and killed, and she was about to be given to his warriors when Ambrose purchased her to save her life. Polonius married her before they returned with Ambrose to England.

Matilda: (Fictitious) Was the flaxen-headed and sharp-tongued wife of Phillip.

Odda: The elderly Ealdorman of Devon, he had served four kings faithfully and killed Ubbi Ragnarsson when his army invaded Wessex. In this story, he was a stalwart supporter of Alfred.

Penrith: (Fictitious) One of the crewmen aboard the Thames ferry.

Phillip: (Fictitious) A giant of a man, he was the free-born guardian of Ambrose. Often called the weapons-master, he had trained several generations of West Saxon noblemen in the military arts. Wherever Ambrose went, there was Phillip. His great goal in life was to protect his prince.

When he spied on the Great Army in 868, he called himself Edgar.

Polonius: (Fictitious) He was born to noble Byzantine parents and given an excellent education. When his family had financial reverses, he and his sisters were sold into slavery. He was taken to Lombardy, France, and eventually Frisia. There, he chanced to meet Ambrose and Phillip. Together they embarked on a series of adventures that took them to Norway, Sweden, Novgorod, Kiev, and eventually Constantinople itself. An expert linguist and knife-thrower, he returned to England with Ambrose, and, as Nicholas, helped him spy on the Danish Great Army. Soon thereafter, he helped steal Gretchen back from the Irish Vikings. He taught Alfred to read, and in this story he acted as the king's military advisor and spy master.

Pyt: (Fictitious) Thane of Alfred's Personal Guard, who arranged to hang the Viking hostages at Chippenham, Given 300 hides of land as a reward, he was expected to supply and crew one ship. Because he had assigned his carpenters other tasks, the ship was not completed when Alfred needed it.

Radnor: (Fictitious) Was a loyal thane to **Odda**, the Ealdorman of Devon.

Raedan: (Fictitious) He was the Ealdorman of Kent who sent his men into Rochester before the Vikings could attack. In the following spring, he brought Alfred's main army, by a southern route, to Wallingford.

Ragnar Lodbrok: A powerful Danish chieftain who invaded England and France. Legend had it that he was killed in Northumbria by being thrown in a pit of snakes. His three sons were Halfdan, Ivar the Boneless, and Ubbi.

Rinc: (Fictitious) The inn keeper and Saxon spy in Lundonwyc.

Rodor: (Fictitious) The priest of the village in Essex on the north shore of the Thames, he arranged to get Ambrose and his friends across the river.

Ryscford: (Fictitious) Thane of a little marsh village near Athelney, in this story he brought the news to Ambrose of an attack on a Kentish village.

Sigenert: (Fictitious) A gaunt villager who captured Ambrose and his two friends soon after they crossed the Thames River from Viking-ruled Essex.

Sitric Ivarsson: The son of Ivar the Boneless, he previously met Ambrose at the Wessex court, where he was a spy with the identity of a Frisian peddler named Harold. Phillip rescued him from brigands, and they shared adventures together in Ireland. He did not join his uncle on the attack on Wessex. By 883, he was king of Dublin. In this story, he trapped Ambrose's ship, but let the prince escape.

Stearc: (Fictitious) The young assistant to the Anglo-Saxon innkeeper in Lundonwyc.

Sun Tzu: A Chinese strategist who wrote **The Art of War.** This text was written some time between the fifth to the third century B.C.

Theomund: (Fictitious) Commander of Ealdorman Raedan's army. (Kent)

Ubbi: He was younger brother of Halfdan and Ivar the Boneless. Ubbi was killed by Odda's fyrdmen when he brought his army into Wessex in 878 in support of Guthrum.

Wade: He was a master blacksmith who served with the Wessex fyrd.

TABLE OF CONTENTS

PART ONE

"In the year of our Lord's incarnation 884, which was the thirty-sixth of king Alfred's life, the aforesaid army (Viking army in France) divided into two parts; one body of them went into East France, and the other coming to Britain entered Kent, where they besieged a city called in Saxon Rochester, and situated on the eastern bank of the river Medway."

.............Asser's Life of King Alfred.

CHAPTER 1

Vikings Land at Rochester

Polonius entered the room and approached the table that Ambrose and Alfred were sitting at. The king looked up and smiled. "So there you are, Polonius. I was wondering where you were hiding today. Your turn is next, Scholar. Just as soon as I finish this game with my big brother here, I will show you how well a king can play this new-fangled game you call chess.' He watched as Ambrose took his castle and grinned wolfishly. 'You see - even now Ambrose foolishly sacrifices his horse for my fortress . . . Scholar, what is the matter? You look pale and you are out of breath."

"Majesty, a messenger has just arrived. The Vikings we have had watched in *Francia Occidental* have finally moved."

"And?"

"Their army has split into two."

"You have my attention, Polonius. Where are the two pieces going?"

"One is pushing upriver into *Francia Orientalis*."

"That should be a major concern for our friend Charles the Fat and his Franks, may God help them. And the other?"

"They have landed on this side of the channel."

Alfred brought his head up sharply. "Those are not words I like to hear! You said there was a good chance they would try Britain after they finished stripping the Frankish coastal provinces bare. Whose kingdom must face their onslaught this time? All that is left for the heathens to devour is the lands of the Scots and Picts, or the Welsh. Perhaps we will be lucky enough to see them tear at Guthrum or Guthred. That would be divine justice."

"There is also us, Sire. They have landed in Kent."

"By the beard of sweet Jesus! I had hoped we were done with the devil's spawn. We already have bloody Guthrum in East Anglia and this Guthred strutting about in Northumbria, not to mention your friend Sitric ruling in Dublin! Will the devils never stop coming?' The king took a deep breath. 'Okay, Polonius, how many and where?"

"The messenger reports that some fifteen ships headed up the Medway River and then beached near Rochester."

"And what have the Vikings done since they landed?"

"They immediately marched on Rochester."

"And?"

"And they have besieged it."

"Rochester . . . It was not yet on our list of *burhs* to fortify, Polonius, nor have we yet assigned it a garrison. Still, with its old Roman walls properly reinforced, it would be a bitch to take back from the heathen Vikings."

"There is one bit of good news, Sire. The ships were spotted approaching the Medway River and *Ealdorman* Raedan, your old comrade-in-arms, sent in both supplies and some of his men to reinforce the town before it was forced to close its gates."

Alfred looked up suddenly. "You mean that the burh has not fallen?"

"It was still holding out when the messenger started his ride to here."

"Well, by the bones of all the saints, may God bless Kentish stubbornness! How long can they hold out for?"

"Unknown, Sire. The old Roman walls are pretty substantial, but they are not in great shape. Raedan and the remainder of his sworn band are skulking in the forest and doing their best to harass any Viking raiding parties, but the messenger reports that his ealdorman's forces are very limited. Many of Raedan's best men are inside the city, and the local people are panicked. They are too busy fleeing with their families to answer his call to arms."

"That can only mean that the Vikings are up to their old tricks, spreading out in all directions and terrorizing the population."

"Exactly, Sire. Raedan is not capable of standing up to the Viking army without serious reinforcements."

"He can best defend his people by constant and ruthless attacks on each and every raiding party that sets out from the main Viking encampment. You and Ambrose taught me that, Scholar."

"Sire?"

"That the Vikings only respect strength and firmness. You told me once that, to a Viking, Christian charity is nothing more than a weakness to be exploited.'

"We also hid on the island of Athelney when Guthrum caught us with our *breeks* around our ankles, Sire."

Alfred looked up sharply a second time. "We attacked, and we won, Polonius! You have a short memory."

"We fought and won in the spring only after you had managed to secretly gather a strong force of your best warriors, Sire. Raedan is only doing what we did. He is attacking when he can, and then slipping away into the forests before he and his men are butchered. The Vikings apparently brought horses from Francia, and, of course, they are stealing more as fast as they can find them. It makes the Viking army frighteningly mobile. Remember, too, Sire, we have had relative peace for some eight years now. Probably over half of Raedan's fyrdmen have never experienced a real battle. He is leading inexperienced warriors against battle-hardened veterans who managed to hold off several Frankish armies for years."

"So what are you telling me, Polonius?"

"Raedan's only real hope against fifteen shiploads of warriors, Sire, is the West Saxon *fyrd*."

The king looked at the chess board and sighed again. 'Well, that Rochester is holding out is good news, and I am relieved that Raedan is still alive and organizing resistance of any sort. Where is the messenger?"

"He literally fell off his horse when he arrived. I sent him to the kitchens for some food. He had ridden without pause for more than a *night*. Shall I send for him?"

"No. Let the man rest. I have the information I need to make some decisions . . . Ambrose, your inevitable capitulation tonight will have to wait. I have another job for you. Brother, please be so good as to call up my scribes and any of the priests who are capable of writing a sentence. Don't forget Bishop Asser. He has a nice script. Tell them to bring parchment, quills, and ink. My kingdom is at war, and I want the war arrows to be sent from Cornwall to

Kent - this very night.

Polonius, get me my maps of southern *Angleland*. Phillip, pray spread the word to my Personal Guard. I want them fully provisioned and ready to ride in less than two nights. Send riders to recall any *thanes* who are within a night's ride.

⚐

Ambrose looked over Alfred's shoulder at the large map stretched out on the king's table. "Polonius' *Frisian* spies had warned us, brother, that, there were almost two thousand Vikings ready to leave Francia's coastal region."

Alfred nodded. "The question is, how many Vikings can you cram on to fifteen ships? Are other enemy ships cruising our coast, and, perhaps most important, what is bloody Guthrum up to?"

"You are worried that Guthrum might bring his Vikings across the Thames, Brother?"

The king drew his *sax*. The long dagger traced a route on the map. "Ambrose, look here . . . Here is our road to Rochester. From Winchester we will follow the old Roman road south as far as Portchester, but then we move north and east until we hit the Thames.

The king stared at the map indicating the ancient Roman roads snaking across his domain. Suddenly he stabbed at the spot of ink that represented the island's ancient capital. "And here, brother-of-mine, is God-cursed London. Worse, from there to Rochester, our road is perilously close to the river and Guthrum's territory.

"Then you do think that Guthrum will come south, Alfred?"

"He signed a treaty of everlasting peace at Wedmore, Ambrose. Let us hope that my Viking *godson* plans to keep his word. London itself is a ruin, particularly after Guthrum seized it as part of his Mercian conquest several years ago. Its small Viking garrison is no threat to us, but the old city itself is still the center of the entire island's road system. Mounted men can move quickly on the old Roman roads. If Guthrum sends sufficient men down from the north, they will be posed like a dagger just above my line of march.

If he crosses the Thames in strength, he could easily cut off our supply line and probably even make us turn back from Rochester. We cannot let him rampage through our heartland while we sit in Kent.'

Ambrose pointed at the map. "We could try strongly reinforcing Southwark, brother. From there we can literally watch London."

"For what purpose?"

"Then once Guthrum crosses the Thames, he would have a choice. He could bypass Southwark, leaving us in a position to cut off his supply line, or he could stop and try and take it, giving us time to return, and probably preventing him from doing much damage to our heartland."

Alfred suddenly turned and faced Polonius. 'Scholar, you have been heavily involved in surveying our *tuns*. I know that Southwark is one of the ones we designated as a defensive burh, but what shape is it currently in?"

Polonius sighed. "Not good, Sire. There is a small fort there, probably constructed originally to defend the ferry site after the Roman bridge collapsed. The fort was built long ago, however, and it was built of wood. The dry moat is largely filled in and what palisades there are, are rotten. With a garrison and a little work, it might be able to hold off a small band of marauders, but it could not possibly hold out for long against the likes of Guthrum's army."

"By the robe of our Savior! That's just the way I remember it. I had hoped that there had been some recent changes for the better."

Polonius spoke. "To be fair to the local thane, Sire, it was just recently designated as one of our defensive burhs. He is a good man. He just hasn't had time to do much yet."

"Write the orders, Scholar. As of today, I expect Southwark to be his main priority. Ambrose is right. If it is strong enough, it would cause considerable trouble for Guthrum. No, wait. Send an order for the thane to report personally to me. I will impart to him myself just how critical Southwark is to the defense of Wessex. And now, Scholar, to my original question - just what numbers of fyrdmen can we call up?"

Polonius spoke from memory. "You have a couple of hundred of the young warriors - the *drengs* - in your Personal Guard and slightly less than seven thousand *duguos* on the rolls who hold land in your name, Sire. Your thanes and *shire* ealdormen, in turn, may bring an equal number of fighting men in their own ranks. Most of this latter, however, are neither well armed nor trained in large-formation battle. They could never hold unaided against a Viking shield-wall. The Viking *skjaldborg* would simply cut through the retainers like a hot knife through butter. Only your veteran fyrdmen with battle experience can stand and battle it out man to man with any hope of victory . . . Do you want to call up both your summer and winter fyrd, Sire?"

"It is tempting, Polonius, but if I call up the winter fyrd now, we will have no force once the summer fyrdmens' service time is up. When they go home, the kingdom will again be left unprotected for the winter. I don't ever wish to be caught again with no army. It was only with God's grace that we survived Guthrum's last winter attack. No, I fear that we will have to make do with only the summer fyrd."

"From that number I just gave you, Sire, you must deduct the men assigned to garrison the new burhs and man your fleet. At four men for every five and a half yards, the new garrisons tie up a vast number of men, and the more ships you build, the less mounted fyrdmen you have at your beck and call."

"But as you yourself told me, Scholar, the fyrdmen will only march willingly if they know that their wives and children were safe back home. It takes walls and garrisons to provide that protection, Polonius."

"Yes, Sire . . . a lot of men. And then there is the matter of *Bookland*."

"We must support Holy Mother Church in any way we can, Polonius. It is our God-given duty."

"I did not say that to support Mother Church is a bad thing, Sire. I merely wished to point out that your very generous grants of Bookland to the church leaves you with less land available to assign to a fighting thane, nor does the land ever revert to your control when the fyrdman dies or is killed. The Bookland the church currently holds costs you the equivalent of several thousand fyrdmen."

Alfred held his stomach and grimaced. "How many can I call up, Polonius?"

"Sire, you do not look good. Do you want a sip of my elixir?"

"Soon, Scholar, soon. First the numbers."

"If you wish to move east without any long delays, you could field a mounted force of somewhere between one and two thousand sworn men."

"Plus what fighting men meet us on the march, Polonius. I don't think I can count on many fyrdmen from Kent. They are already fully engaged, fleeing with their families or dead . . . And my sworn men might bring as many more of their own armed followers."

"Though not all will be armored or mounted, Sire."

The king rubbed his stomach. "Well, at least our plan for two armies will pay dividends. We will call together enough fyrdmen for a summer campaign, but, come the winter equinox, for the first time ever I will not be defenseless when my summer fyrd goes home for the winter . . . Let it be so, Scholar. That, along with any *churls* we can round up in Kent, should be more than enough to crush fifteen boatloads of the Viking devils."

"Unless Guthrum comes south, Sire."

"Aye, that is the rub. Unless my Viking godson decides to come south with his entire God-cursed army."

Ambrose spoke. "We need to know, brother. If he comes south when we are in Kent, he could - make it difficult for us. It is obvious that Southwark will not be defensible for some time."

King Alfred nodded. "Polonius, put the scribes to work! Send word to all the defensive burhs across the country. I want all burhs fully provisioned and all garrisons at full strength. Further, in the North, I want the people to start moving to the centers . . . You were right, Scholar."

"About what, Sire?"

"You told me of the need for secure havens for my people years ago. I have to admit it - you were right. My fyrdmen are afraid to leave their home shires unless they know that their families are safe, particrly with the ruthlessness and mobility of these God-cursed Vikings. The burhs and their garrisons have solved my greatest problem, whatever the cost in fighting men to my army. At least the ones I have don't keep trying to go home on me. I only wish I had a few more years to get the whole system properly organized. Many of the burhs we have selected so far are only half completed, and we still have to select more. When I am through, Scholar, I intend that no man in Wessex will be more than twenty miles from a burh and protection."

"Even as they are, Sire, they give the people security. The Viking presence will also give the people an incentive to hurry the repairs."

Alfred smiled. "Yes, I guess there is always that. There is nothing like a little fear to spur construction along."

Ambrose spoke. "Alfred, I have been thinking - we really do need to know what Guthrum is up to. We can handle one front, but we could be crushed if Guthrum took this opportunity to come south while we are in Kent."

Alfred stared at his brother. "Just what do you propose, brother-of-mine?"

"How about if we sent an important emissary north?"

"I assume you mean to Guthrum and not that upstart, Guthred of Northumbria."

"Guthred is busy trying to swallow Strathclyde and going up against Giric and Eochaid of Alba. Polonius tells me that the Scots and Picts are pushing right back. I don't think the Vikings of Northumbria are going to be a problem right now."

"Ambrose, do you really think Guthrum will just tell us his plans?"

"He is a direct man. He just might, and, in any case, we are within our treaty rights to ask him to send men to support us."

Alfred laughed. "You are an optimist, Ambrose! What are the odds of Guthrum sending his fighting men to fight their own cousins?"

"I suspect - very little. We just might, however, talk him into neutrality. Equally important, we can take the opportunity to see for ourselves just what exactly is happening in East Anglia."

"Brother, do you really wish to play the spy again? It almost got you killed last time."

"This time, Alfred, I go as the official emissary for Wessex. Even the Vikings accept the sacred status of an emissary. It is unlikely that any Dane would dare interfere with me."

"And you would take Phillip and Polonius with you?"

"Only if Matilda and Kuralla agree. Long ago, Polonius made a promise to Kuralla to never leave her side again. I just hope that she has forgiven me for the last five or six times I took her husband away from her and into danger."

Polonius looked surprised. "I will explain the situation, Master, and she will agree. She tells me that she fears for your life if I am not at your side."

Alfred smiled. "As do I, Scholar. Phillip?"

"Matilda has borne six children, Sire, three living and three dead. I do not think she is eager for a seventh. She will agree just to get rid of me for a while."

Alfred turned back to his brother. "And Gretchen?"

Ambrose grinned. "I am not so foolish as to not ask permission, but Gretchen will agree. She knows that I have pledged my life to the defense of Wessex.' He shrugged. 'Sometimes even princes have to risk their lives for what they think is important."

"Well, the three of you have my blessings to go in an official capacity, but I leave your wives for you to deal with. Even a king should not stand between a husband and his wife.' Alfred sighed. 'God knows, we need as much information as we can get our hands on."

CHAPTER 2

Ambrose Talks with Gretchen About Going North

Ambrose blew out the lone candle and slipped into his bed. A soft shape moved close against him. Gretchen murmured. "Mmm. Could there be a strange man in my bed?"

Hands groped Ambrose's naked body. "No. No, I think I know this one . . . I thought that you would never get here, husband-of-mine. Were you beating your brother at chess again?"

"I was, but we had to call off the game. Alfred called an emergency council meeting tonight. There is big trouble."

"Husband, I heard a courier ride in two turns of the hourglass back, and several leave at a gallop not more than two 'glass marks ago, but I decided to wait for you to come and tell me what is happening."

"A good thing, my sweet. If you had come as you are dressed now, you would very definitely have distracted more than your husband!"

"How do you know what I am wearing, light-of-my-life? It is very dark in here."

"I can feel your soft twin protrusions poking my chest, and if I reach down here . . . I can find your love-button . . . Ouch!"

"You have strayed from the topic at hand, oh lord and master. You must wait for any further treats or explorations until you have finished explaining just what is going on."

"It is you who was attacking me with your heavenly globes, love-of-my-life!"

Gretchen rolled on to her back. "Then I will take my heavenly globes out of your reach until you finish telling me what has happened. Why were so many riders galloping off into the night?"

Ambrose sat up in the darkness. "That is because Wessex is at war, my love."

Gretchen gasped and Ambrose could sense her sitting up. "Oh, no! What has happened, husband?"

"Part of that Viking army we saw in Francia years ago took to their ships and invaded Kent."

"Did not Polonius warn us they might move to Britain some time ago?"

"Yes, he did. They have stripped the coastal provinces bare. There is little gold or silver left in the country with which to pay *Danegeld*. The Vikings who stayed behind have moved inland in search of more plunder, but Charles the Fat and his magnates keep putting together armies almost as fast as the Vikings can crush them. Even with the casualty ratio exceeding ten to one, the Franks must eventually win through sheer attrition. Sadly, Polonius' assessment of the situation in Francia was quite accurate."

"So what happens now?"

"The couriers you heard are the first of many messengers carrying the war arrows from one end of the empire to the other. The entire summer fyrd has been called to arms."

"What exactly are the Vikings doing in Kent?"

"You mean aside from raping and pillaging?"

"I know what they do to the people, husband! One group visited Mercia, and their *Norse* cousins enslaved me. If you will remember, we met because my father came to court to borrow the money from your brother to pay the Vikings their cursed Danegeld."

"I am sorry my love. I did not mean to sound flippant. We both have worn a Viking slave collar. The answer is - they are besieging Rochester as we speak."

"Then they haven't managed to seize a stronghold?"

"Not yet, although they apparently built a rough fort near Rochester."

"Then that means that Alfred must move at once!"

"You are right, my love. If Alfred can arrive before Rochester falls, the Vikings will be in a very precarious position."

"Then the fyrd marches as soon as it is assembled?"

"Most of it, yes. Three extraordinarily handsome advisors have been given a special assignment."

Ambrose felt a small hand seize his. "And do Kuralla, Matilda and I know these handsome advisors?"

"Intimately, my love."

"And what are these extraordinarily handsome advisors supposed to do?"

"Take the sacred white shield of an emissary and ride north."

"Not to York, surely? Guthred is no friend of yours and Sitric is far away in Ireland. Guthred's commanders hate you for what you did to Halfdan and Ubbi. The Saxon and the Angle *scops* still recite ballads about how you fooled the Viking commanders."

"I won't be going that far, my love. Alfred needs to know what Guthrum is going to do. If he comes south when the army is in Kent, Wessex will be in very big trouble."

"Then you are going to Guthrum as official emissary from Alfred?"

"Exactly, my love, but only if my wife agrees."

"You actually told Alfred that?"

"Word for word."

Gretchen giggled. "And what did he say?"

"He said that even a king should not come between a husband and wife."

"I am the wife of a warrior, husband. You will go where Alfred needs you. That is your sworn duty. Go and do your duty - with all my love!"

Suddenly, Gretchen was in Ambrose's arms. She squeezed him tight.

"What is all this about, wife-of-mine?"

"In the morning, you belong to the king and will do your duty. Tonight - you belong to me!"

CHAPTER 3

Pigeons

The tun of Winchester was a beehive of activity. Armorers built their fires high and pounded on their anvils. Wagons were loaded with tents, food and the million other items that would be required to keep Alfred's army in the field. Messengers galloped off in all directions, and little groups of mounted fyrdmen trickled into the tun.

In the midst of the organized chaos, Ambrose, Polonius and Phillip hugged their respective wives and children one last time and then went to the stables to complete their preparation and head north.

King Alfred strode into the stables just as Polonius was putting a last pigeon into its little traveling cage. He watched in puzzlement.

"If you would like to take some live food with you, I will find you a couple of plump chickens. There is an entire flock just outside that you may choose from."

Ambrose smiled as Polonius closed the cage door. "That is very kind, brother, but we need pigeons. These are special birds."

"I can see that. They are very fine, if a little thin for my taste. Are you sure you wouldn't prefer a couple of plump chickens?"

"Brother, chickens cannot deliver messages."

"And you are saying that these pigeons can? They must be very special indeed."

"They are. Did I never tell you how Hakim of Alexandria used pigeons to beat all his business competitors?"

Alfred stared at the birds. He sighed. "How could I not be interested in learning how your merchant friend taught Egyptian pigeons to excel in commerce? I can only hope that Saxon pigeons are as intelligent, but, alas, I have seen little evidence of it . . .

Okay, how did Hakim use pigeons, bright as Egyptian birds must no doubt be, to beat his competitors?"

"It was easy, brother. When one of his caravans arrived in a small town some ninety miles from Alexandria, Hakim would sell off the rest of his goods to the city merchants at a discount. The merchants would eagerly snap them up, only to find that, a few days later, the market was glutted by the arrival of another caravan full of the same goods.

Alfred smiled. "And just how did Hakim know when to lower his prices?"

"That is what the Alexandrian merchants all wanted to know. His rivals watched his house for hard-riding messengers, and even posted their own messengers on fast horses in the outlying settlements, to alert them as the trade caravans approached the city. It was all to no avail. Hakim always knew when to sell well in advance of the fastest riders."

Alfred looked puzzled. "How did Hakim's messengers consistently manage to beat the fastest rival riders? Why were they never spotted?"

"That was his great secret. His messengers had wings and could easily out-distance the fastest horse or camel. His pigeons told him when to sell."

"I think that you are teasing your king. You have told me much of Hakim and his business acumen, but not once did you tell me he could speak to birds. How could his pigeons tell him when to drop his prices?"

"Brother, what happens if I take these birds and throw them into the air?"

"Why, they would fly in a great spiral."

"And then?"

"They would eventually fly back to their coop. It is hard to lose a pigeon."

"And what about if I released them several miles away?"

"They would fly about in circles, but they would eventually return to their coop. Pigeons are famous for it."

"And if I took them to Guthrum's encampment and released them?"

"If they didn't get lost, I guess they would eventually show up at their home coop."

"And if a light one meant peace and a dark one meant war, could I send you a message from there?"

Alfred paced for a few moments. "So if Hakim found a pigeon in his coop that had been released by an agent in a town on the caravan route, he would know his caravan was approaching and it was time to sell off his stock more cheaply."

"Exactly, brother. He even told me that his man could send a brief note tied to the pigeon's foot."

"Brilliant! He would consistently have knowledge no one else was privy to. The pigeon could easily beat even the fastest rider. And now to us. If I find a dark colored pigeon in the coop here, then I will know that Guthrum is coming south. A light colored one will tell me I can push on to Rochester. This much I now understand. Why have you packed two of each coloration, however?"

"Whatever the message, we will release two birds. One might be taken by a hawk or get lost, but at least one of the two should make it back."

"And the other two birds?"

"They will help provide us with dinner, so there is no possibility of a mistake or misunderstanding."

"I will arrange that when the message arrives here, couriers can ride the road to bring word to me, wherever I am."

"Exactly, brother. The birds will cover the distance within hours and the couriers, riding in relay, should be able to catch you fairly quickly. We will ride hard, but from East Anglia, it will take us quite a few days to catch up with you."

Alfred hugged his brother. "It is an excellent plan, brother-of-mine! In one step you have alleviated my greatest fear. I was afraid that I would have to leave a third of my mounted fyrd to guard the road to Wessex and protect the supply column. That would force me to go east slowly and wait until I had gathered adequate forces before I dared approach Rochester. All that would take some weeks, and I was worried Rochester could not hold out."

"And now?"

"As soon as sufficient mounted fyrdmen have gathered, I will take them east. If I receive a dark bird from you, then I will send a third back towards Southwark, but I fear the consequences of doing that."

Ambrose nodded. "Agreed, brother. A dark bird will mean danger to Southwark or the supply convoy. A white bird will mean that you are free to push on . . . I do have another pair of concerns for your ears, Alfred."

"Speak, big brother."

"Cornwall and Dorset."

Alfred sighed. "Go on, Ambrose."

"The ealdorman of Cornwall has no love for you or the West Saxon Empire, Alfred. His predecessors have raised the sword of revolt before, and Cornwall allied itself with a Viking army back in 838. We only prevented them from joining Guthrum's last attack on you by kidnaping the ealdorman's sons and holding them hostage."

Alfred smiled. "Kidnapping is a harsh word, brother. We merely helped his boys report to their king for their military duty, as they were, in fact, sworn to do."

"And Ethelwold of Dorset?"

"I know my nephew feels he should have followed in his father's footsteps and been named king by the *Witan*. He was only a child at the time of his father's death, however, and the councillors felt a more mature king was needed. I swear to you that I had no idea that the Witan would choose me. I did not seek the honor."

"Be that as it may, Alfred, it was only fear and Odda's army on his frontier that kept him from open revolt the last time Guthrum invaded Wessex."

"I know that Ethelwold betrayed me several times over and deserved to die, brother, but he is of the royal blood and has many supporters. His execution could have rent the kingdom in two at the very moment of our greatest challenge. Don't forget that Northumbria fell to the Viking hordes only because two rival kings refused to coordinate their efforts until it was too late. Our own sainted father left a usurper on the throne and accepted the division of his empire when he realized that the alternative was for the entire country to be embroiled in a civil war."

"I understand the politics, Alfred, and am not questioning your decisions. The question is - how are we going to make sure that these two don't betray us again?"

"Both have sons of military age. Both sets of sons have been granted many *hides* of land each - in my name."

"I wondered why you rewarded the sons of traitors with land, Alfred."

Alfred grinned. "In exchange, they had to swear allegiance to me personally. For good or ill, they are now part of my sworn men - available to be called up when I wish. I will dispatch two special bands of warriors to escort my sworn men to my side. My Personal Guard has need of such fine young men. Further, if they do not report promptly, I will consider their fathers to be in open rebellion and have the excuse I need to get rid of them. The Witan will order their deaths, however, not me."

"Thank you, Alfred. I was worrying about those two issues all last night."

Alfred hugged his brother. "Go with God, brother, and come back safely!"

CHAPTER 4

Ambrose Rides North to Guthrum

Ambrose stood on the shore, looking northward. London's ancient city walls could be discerned to the west and east of their location, while the river bank across the Thames had the remnants of a much lower wall. Just to his east were the remains of a stout Roman bridge. While it still spanned the river, the central arch had collapsed, making it unusable. Instead, the prince stared at a ferry sitting tied to its dock on the opposite bank, where the river wall had almost totally disappeared. Ambrose and his companions had stood on the spot and yelled, for over an hour. The ferry crew lay indolently on the grass of the northern shore.

Phillip called out again in a stentorian voice. When his words were ignored, he drew his giant broadsword, held it tight against the river-spanning guide rope, and started a sawing motion. The ferry crew reacted instantly, leaping to their feet and rushing to push their crude flat-bottomed boat into the current. Within a short time, the ferry slid along its tether and nosed into the little wooden dock that was its southern home.

The tall emaciated-looking captain looked angry, but, realizing that he faced not merchants, but well-armed warriors dressed in very expensive armor, he spoke softly. "If we 'ad known that ye fine gentlemen were waitin' sirs, we'd a bin over straight away like!"

Phillip was still angry. "You saw us, you sniveling little toad! You just decided to ignore us!"

"Now, sir, there be no call to shout. It be God's truth that we would a come if we seen ye!"

"Then it's very strange that you were able to see me right after I started to cut the ferry rope, ferryman!"

"Sir, I caught a wink o' yer sword and that did kind of wake me up. Now that we're here, I know ye to be eager to cross to t'other side. Let's see. Ye be three riders an' three 'orses. At a shilling apiece, that's six shilling for the lot o' ye. If ye would just pay up, we would be on our way. We'll 'ave ye safe and sound on the other bank quicker than a wink."

Phillip approached the man until his nose was just inches from the man's face. "Are you hard of hearing, man?"

The captain looked confused. "Me wife says so, but that's just 'cause I don't usually want to 'ear what she got to say. Me ears generally work pretty good, stranger. Why do ye ask?"

"Did I say I want to buy your tub? I said I wanted the three of us to be ferried across the river."

"That be London o'er there, stranger! It be Viking land. This be a dangerous place to run a ferry service. I 'ave to pay me people danger pay. If'en I take the risk, then I 'ave to make a modest profit, an' the Vikings squeeze every penny from me that they can. The fee for ye lot be six shillings, stranger - and with yer attitude, I fear 'at we'll 'ave to 'ave it all in advance."

"You'll take six pence, and like it!"

"Oo the 'ell ye think ye are, mate?"

Phillip stared down from his lofty height. "I am weapons-master to King Alfred, and my companion is Prince Ambrose, brother to the king of the land you are standing on!"

"Sure ye be, stranger. I have 'eard the tales of this Philip, and even I know that he be the size of an oak tree. Besides, if'n good King Alfred was 'ere, 'ed gladly pay six shilling for the crossing. Unlike ye, sir, 'e be a generous man oo would understand the crushing taxes and the danger I face every day of me life."

Phillip glowered at the man. "For six shillings, I can buy a live pig, get a sheep thrown into the bargain, and have enough silver left over to buy your tub . . . Speaking of money, have you paid your fees to the king's reeve for running this service?"

"Ah, no. Ye sees, sirs, I don't need to."

Phillip spoke in his sternest tone and put his hand on his sword. "You dare tell the king's brother and royal advisors what you need to pay and not?"

The sweat broke out on the captain's face. "I wouldn't do that, sir! I would surely pay if'n I lived on the south bank. But ye sees,

I 'appen to live on the north bank. I already pay the Danes."

Phillip turned to the thin Byzantine scholar at his side. "Polonius, this man ties his rope to a stout tree growing in Wessex. He tells me that he does not swear allegiance to King Alfred, yet he lands, on a daily basis on the king's shore! Advisor, what do we normally do to Guthrum's lackeys who land in Wessex without permission from good king Alfred?"

"The king's rules are very clear, Weapons-master. They are to get six feet of earth and a length of hemp rope."

Phillip frowned. "Then let's hang the blackheart, here and now."

"Wait, Weapons-master, perhaps he did not know the law. In any case, hanging him will not get us across the river. I suppose we could ask the king to consider waiving the sentence if the man offered to pay a shilling fee for each time he had set foot in West Saxon territory. "

"Then for this weasel of a ferryman that would be, say, ten landings a day, for a minimum of one year. I guess I could round that off to three thousand shillings."

The tall man just spluttered.

"And then there is the rest of this fine crew. We would have to charge something for each of them, too. They are not the king's subjects."

The sweat poured down the captain's face. "Sirs' since ye be messengers for the great king of Wessex, I would deem it a great 'onor if ye would let me run yer across for free. We be going that way anyway!"

Ambrose spoke. "You will get your six pence, Captain, but as long as you land on King Alfred's shore, you will follow King Alfred's regulations. Are we clear on that?"

The man wiped the sweat from his brow with the back of his hand. "Oh, aye, Great Lord!"

"Hear me, ferryman! If I find out that you attempt to fleece honest travelers in the future, I will come back and hang you personally."

"I will remember yer words, Great Lord! If'en ye'd like to get yer 'orses on, sirs, we will be on our way!"

As the ferry nosed into the northern bank, Polonius spoke to the captain. "You! Where can a prince of Wessex find shelter for the night?"

The captain inspected the bank for a moment before answering. He spat on the ferry's deck. "Well, 'onoured sir, there be lot's of room in London, but I would not stay there if'n I were ye."

"Why not, Captain?"

The thin man crossed himself. "It be haunted, sir! Few Saxons care to live there. The buildings be amazing structures, but they be crumbling. It be not safe to go into the ancient buildings."

"Why is London haunted?"

"It be filled with the souls of the ancient pagan Romans, sir. They were immortal giants, sir, but something even greater than them came and killed 'em all.' He leaned closer and fingered the cross he wore around his neck. 'At night, sir, ye kin sometimes hear the ghosts moaning in the wind. I would not spend a night in the old city for a gold piece!"

Polonius spoke. "Don't the Vikings live in the city?"

"Oh, aye, sir, they live in an ancient stone fort called Cripplegate, but they be pagan and their souls already belong to the devil. They don't care."

"Then where will I find suitable lodging for the prince here?"

"'ead west sir, along the shore. The first road ye 'it will take ye direct-like to Ludgate on the western wall. Keep going through the gate until ye cross the Fleet River. From its western bank ye kin see the Saxon town - name o' *Lundonwyc*."

Here are eight pennies, Captain. Just remember what Prince Ambrose told you. You will not be welcome to land in Wessex if you try and cheat innocent travelers."

The captain tapped his head with his hand. "Oh, aye, sir, I will not forget - Cedd! Penrith, get those planks down for our fine passengers."

As Ambrose watched the two men carefully placing the planks between the decrepit dock and the ferry, he noticed a full dozen Saxons approach. They were not armed with swords or spears, yet each man carried an oar, a fishing gaff, or some other implement that could be used as a weapon in case of need. Ambrose turned to Phillip and spoke quietly in the Slavic tongue that they had both learned in far-off *Kiev*. "String your bow, Weapons-master. I do not like the look of the captain's new friends."

The big man moved behind his horse and then replied tersely in the same language. "Target, Prince?"

"The captain goes first. Pin him if he tries to leave."

The prince took two steps closer to the captain and put his hand on the pommel of his sword. "You have more friends approaching than I care to see, Captain. I would hate for you to have a serious accident after all that we have been through together."

The thin captain looked very nervous when he saw where the prince's hand was resting and then saw what Phillip was holding. "No, no, great Prince! They just be here to make sure that you pay my rightful fee."

"Well then, I guess that it is a good thing that we already paid. Tell them to go away before you bleed all over your fine ferry."

The captain looked at the three warriors and sweat broke out on his brow. "Aye, that be a good idea, sir! We would not want some kind of accident to 'appen now that we be friends."

"See to it, Captain, or it will be your blood that flows."

"Aye, Great Prince. I will ask 'em to drop their weapons. I do need 'em to take the ferry out of the water for the night."

As the captain spoke, he sidled nearer the planks and the inviting shore. He turned to face the land, when an arrow suddenly pinned his cloak to the railing.

Ambrose smiled. "Another step, Captain, and you will be joining the ghosts wandering around this city."

The captain turned back to face Ambrose. His eyes widened when he saw that Phillip had a second arrow drawn and aimed at his chest.

Ambrose smiled. "The weapons-master is using a type of bow used in some parts of Wales. It is so powerful that it can drive an arrow through the stoutest armor. Now Phillip here, he made his much stronger than the average Welsh bow. Only a few men can even draw that bow. You can hide behind a tree, and it will not matter. The arrow will go through the tree and still transfix you. He can also hit you four out of five times at a hundred paces. Think carefully about what you do next, Captain."

The man licked his lips nervously. He stared from Phillip to Ambrose. "What would ye like me to do, Great Lord?"

Ambrose smiled. "I think that the ferry will stay in the river overnight, Captain. It will cost you your life if those men come any closer."

The thin captain called out to the approaching men. "You men! This great man beside me misunderstands yer intentions. He seems to think that ye be 'ere to rob him, and 'e is 'olding me 'ostage. Drop what ye're carryin' an' return 'ome before something bad 'appens to me!"

As the men dropped their makeshift weapons and backed away, the captain spoke angrily to Ambrose. "Prince, yer man there ruined me new cloak! It will cost me a shilling to get a new one."

"That cloak was old in your father's time, Captain. The two extra pence we gave you will buy you a fine new one."

"Prince, I protest! Why are ye cheating an 'onest man?"

Ambrose tugged at his chin before he replied. "Captain, I think that you just might be right. I will tell you what I will do."

"What is that, Great Prince?"

"We will ask God to decide the right of your case."

"Ask God? Just how do we do that, Prince?"

"It is simple, Captain. Choose a weapon, and the king's weapons-master here will meet you in fair combat. I will even lend you my sword if you wish."

The captain gasped. "Fair combat!? This weapons-master of yours be a giant! I've heard the scops sing the ballads about 'im! 'e will carve me limb from limb."

"Are you a Christian, Captain?"

"Aye, Prince. God is me shepherd."

"Excellent. Then you know that if your case is fair in the eyes of God, then the Almighty will guide your sword-arm. Captain, you must have more faith in the righteousness of your case."

The sweat poured in runnels down the captain's face. "Lord, you be right. Now that I look again, it be a minor rent. Me wife will have it fixed up in a jiffy!"

"Captain, take your men and move a hundred paces up-river. If you or any of your men get in our way, we will kill them for the dogs that they are. You, of course, will be the first to die. Do I make myself clear?"

"Crystal clear, Great Prince."

"Then draw that arrow from the rail, drop it gently on the deck, take your two crewmen, and run, captain, before my friend here uses your worthless carcasses for target practice!"

"Aye, Lord!"

After the captain and his friends had moved a hundred long paces up-river, the three friends led their nervous horses along the planks thrown down by the crewmen before they had retreated. As they mounted their horses, Polonius spoke to Ambrose. "Prince, this is Guthrum's territory. I think you might want to uncover the white shield."

"Do you think we will meet Vikings so soon, Polonius?"

"Don't be fooled by his simple manners, Prince. Guthrum has a first-rate spy system. I have no doubt that the Vikings know we are here even as we speak, and if they don't yet, then you can be sure your new friend there will be reporting your presence just as soon as he can."

"Now that I believe. That captain would sell his own mother for a copper penny."

Ambrose sighed and stripped the cloth covering from the shield that rode on the back of his saddle. The fresh white paint gleamed in the sunlight.

"I hope that you are satisfied, my Greek scholar."

As he spoke, Polonius stared at the crumbling ruins that surrounded them. "I am, Master. You know, this is the first time I have actually seen the former capital of Britain. This was once a reasonably large city."

"You can say that after living in Constantinople, Scholar?"

"Constantinople probably has more citizens than you have people on the entire island. It is the capital of an empire of millions."

"And Rome?"

"Rome is a crumbling vestige of what was once the greatest city on earth. As in London, the present Romans now live in mere corners of that once majestic city. Still, London must have been, at its height, a major city, with all the amenities of an imperial Roman provincial capital."

Phillip spoke. "It has been many years since I was last here. On my last visit, it was the capital of a free Mercia."

"A free Mercia that fell before Guthrum's Viking onslaught, Weapons-master."

The big man replied. "King Burgred of Mercia was a fool. He should have let us crush the Vikings when our two armies had them trapped in Nottingham. He thought he could buy peace with silver and gold instead of good steel."

Ambrose nodded. "He at least died safe in Rome. He did better than poor King Edmund."

"Prince, Edmund stood up to the Vikings. He chose death over being made into a Viking puppet."

"True, Weapons-master, and one day he might even be made a saint for the manner of his dying . . . What do you remember of this city?"

"The road we are on will take us directly to the old forum. A little to the west of that, you will find the old Roman amphitheater."

"And the fort - what did our lazy captain call it? - Cripplegate?"

"In the north-western corner of the city."

"Is it a serious fortification?"

"All Roman fortifications are serious. The ancient Romans built solidly. The walls were collapsing when I was here last, but they were still formidable."

"And the Vikings have had a few years to repair them. I will assume that Cripplegate could not easily be taken . . . My friends, let us put a few miles between us and the Saxon boatmen back on the river-bank. Their stench is still in my nostrils."

⚑

As they approached the south-western gate called Ludgate, a patrol of ten mounted Danes, coming from the north, intercepted them. The patrol leader spoke in bad Saxon. "Hold up there, strangers! Where you going?"

Ambrose stared at the squad. They carried their weapons casually, but they were well armed and looked ready to use them if necessary. The prince replied to the man in perfect Danish.

"And good afternoon to you, Commander."

The man looked puzzled. "You speak the Viking tongue perfectly, yet you come from south of the river. It is not healthy for Vikings in Wessex, sir! Their king makes it a practice to hang any Danes he catches."

"Only those who come with hostile intent, Commander. Alfred welcomes Viking traders who come in peace."

"And which are you, strangers?"

Ambrose reached behind him and hooked his arm through the support for his shield. He pulled it free and swung it in front of him. The white-painted shield spoke for itself.

The patrol leader nodded. "By your sacred white shield, I assume that you are Wessex born, but sent north with a message for my king."

Ambrose smiled. "I carry a message direct from King Alfred to King Guthrum."

"Then ride north, Emissary. Our roads are free to such as carry a white shield. If you take the main eastern road as far as Chelmsford, you will be directed to wherever King Guthrum is staying. What will you do for tonight?"

"I have never been to Lundonwyc. I thought I would explore it a little and then find lodging for the night."

"Then may *Odin* guide you quickly to King Guthrum, Emissary."

The trio rode across the intact Roman bridge that crossed the Fleet River and continued towards the little Saxon tun surrounded by a wooden palisade. The tun's defenses were minimal, and Ambrose was puzzled.

"Scholar, these walls couldn't keep out cattle thieves."

"I suspect that is the way the Viking overlords like it, Master. If Guthrum is smart, there will be no secure forts north of the

Thames that are not held by Viking garrisons."

"Aye, I suspect that you are right. Guthrum would want no place that could stand against him and his army. It is much easier to control a population if they have no defensive positions."

As they talked, they rode through the open gates of the Saxon tun of Lundonwyc. No one tried to stop them. Instead, the townspeople looked sidelong at them, but would not meet their eyes. The townspeople all looked to be Angle, Saxon or *Jute*, but they were dressed poorly and seemed dispirited. Ambrose looked around. The town itself was a typical *Angelisc* settlement, constructed almost entirely of wood. They rode down the single main road until they found an inn. It was not hard to find. Although there was no sign outside the building, it was the only building with a large stable attached. The three friends tied their horses to a post in front, and then pushed through the open doorway. A large fat man in a leather apron greeted them immediately.

"Welcome, strangers! It is always good to see some customers, but are you sure you are not lost? This now be King Guthrum's land, and free Saxons are rarely welcomed north of the river."

Ambrose smiled back. "Thank you for the warning, friend, but we are West Saxon emissaries on the way to Guthrum. We carry the sacred white shield of peace and a message direct to the king. I would be very surprised if any Viking decided to interfere with us."

The fat man beamed. "Excellent, then you are doubly welcome.' He looked slyly at his new customers. 'You will no doubt need food and a private room for the night. My wife will cook a veritable feast for you."

"Aye, we would appreciate the food and a room . . . and someone to take care of the horses."

"Done, great lord!' The innkeeper turned and yelled at a boy huddled near the fire pit. 'Stearc! Get your lazy body out that door and take care of the horses out front! Mind that you rub them down proper and give them a good measure of oats, and fill the water trough for them.'

The boy jumped to his feet and scurried out the door without a single look at the guests. The innkeeper spoke again.

"He is a useless pup, foisted on me by my own sister, but he will take proper care of your horses or he will not be able to sit down for a week! Come now, Great lords. Come, sit down, and let me pour you a little of my famous ale. It has been a long time since I have had the pleasure of any Saxon gentry."

CHAPTER 5

The Ferryman Returns

The sun was just setting and Ambrose was filling Polonius' horn with mead when the inn door burst open. A full dozen Saxons stood in the doorway and jostled for space, each armed with a spear held at the ready. At their head was the thin ferry-boat captain.

The man grinned, exposing his bad teeth. "We meet again, Prince 'igh and Mighty, and this time yer overgrown friend doesn't have 'is bow at the ready!"

Ambrose spoke. "What do you want, Captain?"

"Me friend 'ere saw yer purse when ye paid yer fee. I would 'a settled for the six shillings, but 'e 'as convinced me to relieve ye of the entire purse. Ye sees, ye 'urt our feelings really bad back on the shore, and I 'ave to buy a new cloak."

"Captain, did you not see my white shield? Your masters consider the white shield sacred. You are attacking an official emissary of King Alfred, so recognized by King Guthrum. Do you think that Guthrum will be amused by your actions? Both the Saxon and the Viking laws say that a man who interferes with a royal emissary is to be put to death."

The man grinned again as he hefted his spear. "Now, that were not a smart thing to remind me of, Saxon prince. What yer telling me is that I kin leave no witnesses."

"Then you plan to do more than merely rob us, Captain?"

"I 'ave no intention of 'anging, stranger. Whatever 'appens, I be relieving ye of yer gold and silver this very night."

Ambrose looked at Polonius and spoke quietly in Greek. "Scholar, I will screen you for a moment. When you are ready, kill the Captain and start on the closest men. Phillip and I will draw swords and attack in the confusion."

Polonius replied in the same language. "I assume that you

wish yet another demonstration of my prowess with the throwing knives."

"If you attempt to use your sword, my scholarly friend, we are all dead!"

"Didn't I teach you that fighting is always last on the list of options? You make a poor student, Prince."

"Do you think you can talk these men into going home?"

"I have to admit - I don't think writs or words are going to help us much here. I will not lose sleep over this one's death."

Ambrose stood, and reached slowly for his purse. "It appears, Captain that you give me little choice. Here is . . ."

As Ambrose spoke, he dropped the bag onto the table and, as he picked it up again, he momentarily blocked the captain's view of Polonius. As the prince moved back to his original position, a flying dagger caught the thin captain in the throat while a second sprouted in his chest. The man immediately on the left and right met the same fate. The three men screamed and fell.

Before the three men hit the ground, Ambrose and Phillip drew their blades in one quick motion and charged. Spears in the close confines of the room were a disadvantage, and the thieves were disconcerted by the suddenness of the collapse of their front rank. Phillip's giant blade tore into the thicket of spear points, and only one man stepped forward to face the onslaught. One of Polonius's daggers plunged low into his abdomen and the man screamed like a child. The rest broke. Within moments, the doorway was empty, except for the four men who had fallen. Two were dead, and two lay on the ground moaning.

The innkeeper left his fire pit and gawked at the fallen men. He turned to Polonius. "Sir, you killed two of them, and the other two probably won't live to morning. If'n I hadn't seen it, I wouldn't have believed it."

Ambrose spoke. "They came to rob and kill us, Innkeeper. The cowards brought a full dozen men against three."

"Aye, what you say is true, stranger. Guthrum's minions will probably still hang you, however!"

"I already told you that I am an emissary from King Alfred on my way to Guthrum, Innkeeper. I will tell King Guthrum myself what I did this day."

The portly innkeeper looked out the door onto the street. "I am not sure you are going to get a chance to do that, Emissary. There be some three dozen towns' folk gathering outside, and they are all armed."

Polonius, in the act of retrieving his throwing daggers, suddenly spoke. "Alfred for *Bretwalda*!"

The innkeeper started. He stared down at the slim Byzantine. "Just who are you, stranger?"

"It is not who I am that matters, Innkeeper. It is what I carry."

"And what is that, sir?"

Polonius opened his hand and the man peered closely at the piece of gold coin that Polonius held. The man stared, but finally spoke.

"Aye, I have seen its like before."

"I think that, if your name is Rinc, son of Penda, of Lundonwyc, you have more than seen one before, Innkeeper. Do you want to see if it fits against your own?"

"No, lord! That is not necessary."

"I am Polonius, the holder of the gold coin."

"Lord, I did not know. What do you want me to do?"

"Convince the people outside to go home, and then make these bodies disappear."

"It shall be done, Spy-master!"

As the stout innkeeper harangued the crowd gathered outside, Ambrose stared at Polonius. "I thought that you had never been here before, Scholar."

Polonius smiled. "I haven't, but a lot of your brother's gold has flowed into this town. My broken coin matches the silver one he wears around his neck. My gold one identifies me as the spy master."

"Then that explains what he called you."

The stout innkeeper returned with six unarmed men, who hung their heads differentially. "Sirs, these men will take the bodies down to the riverbank after dark and make sure that they are discovered and returned to their loved ones tomorrow morning - a little after you have left Lundonwyc."

Polonius nodded. "Good. And what about the people

outside?"

"They are going home, Spy-master. I explained that you three are true friends of the Saxons and they will not touch you. I do suggest an early start in the morning, however. The former captain has some more unsavory friends who just might decide not to listen to me."

Polonius shook the man's hand. "Thank you, Innkeeper, we are grateful."

"Don't thank me, Lord. Just beat the God-cursed Vikings! I want to live in a Saxon land again."

CHAPTER 6

The Emissaries Leave London

At first light, Ambrose and his companions had their horses saddled and ready to ride. The stout innkeeper joined them in the stables as they strapped on the last of their baggage.

"Here is some food for your journey, sirs! May the Good Lord keep you all safe."

As Polonius swung into the saddle, he spoke. "Any suggestions, Innkeeper?"

"Aye, I would suggest that you cut north to the Newgate road. None of the thieving bastards who man that ferry will be expecting that."

"But won't that will take us close to Cripplegate Fort?"

"Aye, sir, but that is to the good. Even the most murderous Saxon won't take action against you if there are Vikings about. For the most part, the Vikings just leave us alone - as long as we pay our taxes. If we break a Viking law, however, then the heathen devils butcher not only the culprit, but his entire family, down to the youngest baby."

"Thanks again, Innkeeper. Keep the faith!"

"May Alfred soon be Bretwalda, sir!"

Polonius smiled. "Alfred as over-king of all Britain. That is a dream worth fighting for. Amen to that, innkeeper!"

The three riders exited the Saxon settlement at a quick canter. Cutting cross country, they moved north and eastward until they hit the Newgate road. Within a short time they were again inside the walls of the ancient ruined city of London.

Ambrose nodded towards a large building on his left. "That looks like the baths, Scholar."

"Aye, I think so, Prince. I cannot tell you how much I wish they were functioning and we could stop to wash the grime off us."

Ambrose laughed. "I was corrupted in Constantinople, Scholar. I admit I grew to love the warmth of the water and the feel of a good scraping. It is not something that my people cherish."

Phillip spoke. "Hold, Prince. If this is the western corner of the forum, then we are to cut north right here. That will put us on the Bishopsgate Road."

Ambrose reined in his horse and stared at the immense building just ahead and to his left. "This must be the forum, Phillip. Even in ruins, it is an imposing space."

The three friends reached the north gate of the city less than an hour after dawn. The gates, however, were wide open. Ambrose spoke.

"They are trusting devils. No one even guards the gate."

Ambrose smiled. "To what purpose, Master? The only army likely to threaten London is ours, and it is in an all-fired hurry to get to far-off Kent. Who else would dare threaten Guthrum?"

"You have a point, my friend. There are few enough enemies left. What about the Vikings of York, however?"

"If Wessex fell, Wales, and then the land of the Scots and Picts, I do not think it would take long for the two rival kingdoms to go for each other's throat. As long as there is a free Saxon army, or land to conquer - they are more likely to remain allies."

∽

The two *long-ships*, propelled by current and long oars, swept majestically down river. Ambrose watched them go by and then turned to his two companions. "That makes three ships in one hour – on a very minor river, and the Frisians reported that Guthrum's main fleet is up the Stour river system."

Polonius nodded. "The message is pretty clear. Guthrum's men are on the move – right in the midst of the planting season."

Phillip growled. "This does not bode well for Rochester."

∽

The first Viking riders closed on them as they neared

Chelmsford. While one armed group waited on the main road, others appeared from the woods Ambrose and his two friends had just passed through. Ambrose realized that they were very neatly trapped. He slid his arm through his shield strap, and, prominently displaying the gleaming white shield, led the small group steadily toward the Danes waiting on the road.

He spoke in their language as they neared. "Greetings, warriors. Well met. I have a message for King Guthrum, and I hope that one of you can escort me to him."

"Who are you stranger, that we know you not, yet you speak our language so well?"

"My Viking name is Canuteson, for I am an adopted son of Canute of the Danes. You may know me best, however, as Ambrose, Prince of Wessex."

A huge man, almost the size of Phillip, spoke up. "Aye, I know of you. Even the Viking *skalds* sing ballads about you. You stole a shipload of noblewomen from Dag of Wexford. Before that, you were a spy in Halfdan's camp. I was there. We chased you half way across East Anglia and into Mercia. I caught up to you in Mercia and you stuck your blade in my gut for my troubles!"

Ambrose stared. "I do vaguely remember an overgrown warrior called Egil the Little. I think you were mad that we stuffed you under some old tents."

"You made a fool of me, Saxon!"

"We let you live since you and I had no quarrel. It would have been much easier for us to just cut your throat. We did not, Egil the Little. Then, a day later, you tried your best to kill me."

"You were lucky that day, Saxon, or I would have!"

"It was three to one when you attacked, Egil, and I defeated all three of you, with a little help from my friends."

"You left me to die, Saxon!"

"You were chasing me, Viking, and your friends put an arrow through me."

The giant was furious. He spat on the ground and glared at Ambrose. "You are an admitted spy and thief, Saxon, and here you are again on Viking land. Here the Saxons bow to Viking masters and they ask our permission to ride the roads. You have not received permission, Canuteson. Tell me why we should not just hang you from the nearest tree."

"I fought three of you in open combat, Egil, and you were the first to go down. I stole my betrothed back from Dag, and I bow to no one but my king, but I will answer your question. First, our two nations are at peace. Second, you owe me hospitality in the name of my adopted father. I am brother to your king's godfather. If you are not capable of understanding that, then I will just say that I carry the sacred white shield of an emissary. I carry a message directly from my king to yours, so it would be very foolish for you to interfere in any way with either me or my comrades."

"You crow like a cock, little man."

"My sword, *Victory-Maker* is already familiar with your gut. It is eager to teach you manners, Dane, but, alas, I am not allowed. I am sworn to deliver a message; not cut you down a second time."

"Beware, little man! You go too far."

"No, warrior. You go too far. You are threatening a messenger sent, in friendship, to your king. By your own laws, it is you who will be taken to the grove and sacrificed to Odin if you dare interfere with me!"

The big man put his hand on his sword hilt. "Draw your weapon, little man, and we shall see which of our gods is greater."

The commander spurred his horse in front of the angry Viking. "Nay, Egil, he is right. Our duty is to escort him to King Guthrum, and as quickly as possible."

"But Olaf!"

"Obey, Egil, or I will pay your blood price and leave you hanging from the nearest tree!"

CHAPTER 7

Ambrose Meets Guthrum

The Viking king himself came out of his *long house* when he heard the party of riders arriving. He stared at the new arrivals for several moments before he spoke. "Could it really be Prince Ambrose, Phillip and Polonius, or should I say Canuteson, Nicholas and Edgar . . . or is it Hamar? I am never sure what to call you three. You are far from your lands, Saxons."

Ambrose looked down from the height of his horse. "Greetings, King *Athelstan*. Hamar? So you enjoyed the Rus warrior's juggling that day?

"It was well done, *Atheling*. It is only when you disappeared so completely that we finally realized who you were and what you had done. The information you took with you that day may have cost me two of my best allies."

"It did, King, but today I come in friendship, and would just like to be Ambrose. Your godfather has sent us to you with some urgent concerns. I hope that we are welcome in your camp."

"Even aside from the sacred white shield that you carry, the brother of King Alfred is always welcome at my court, as are his companions. Amongst my people, however, it might be best if you call me Guthrum. Come, Atheling, dismount and enter my humble abode. You are in luck. You have arrived in time for the *Sigrblot* and we will be having a feast tonight - excuse me, Prince - I forgot for a moment that you lived for years with the Rus Vikings and well know our ways. Tonight, after the feast we will imbibe in '*Kvasir's blood*'. I have an exceptional skald that I want you to hear. Perhaps I will ask him to tell the tales of Canuteson and his adventures. He tells me that you are becoming known in our lands as the 'Dane-slayer.'"

"Sire, my companions and I only ever kill Danes who foolishly invade the peaceful land of Wessex. To sing our ballads is hardly necessary."

"Nonsense, Prince. My people know the tale and will enjoy hearing it again - in your honor. We Vikings always respect bravery - in ourselves or our enemies."

"I hope that I am not one of your enemies, King."

"Not tonight, Prince. Tonight you and your friends are my guests! Come now.'

As Guthrum took his place on his elevated seat-of-honor, he waved at the mass of warriors who preceded him into his long house. 'Make way for three emissaries, my faithful wolves . . . Sit you down, my friends. The food is being cooked as we speak, but I would be a poor host if I did not offer my honored guests a horn or two of good Danish ale - No, wait! Better yet, we will broach a keg of fine Frankish wine in your honor. A large quantity happened to come my way just recently. And for you, Polonius, I have a very special apple-wine. I remember how much you enjoyed it at Wedmore."

The king turned to a young female slave standing near him. "You! Get each of our esteemed guests a clean drinking horn. Run now, if you want to keep your hide intact!"

After several beautiful women brought the drinking horns and served the Frankish wine and the apple-wine, Guthrum smiled at his guests. The Viking king asked about all the members of Ambrose's Royal family. Ambrose was impressed at the King's memory as he asked, one by one, about several dozen ealdormen and athelings. Several horns of wine were served before Guthrum finally steered the conversation back to Alfred's message. "Prince, you mentioned that King Alfred had a message for me."

"Yes, Sire."

"Then, pray let me hear the words of my learned godfather."

"I assume you know, King Guthrum, that a strong Viking force landed near Rochester and proceeded to besiege the town."

"I know it, Prince, but you must know, in turn, that the Army is from Francia and has nothing to do with the Danes of either East Anglia, Northumbria, or Dublin.' Guthrum smiled suddenly. 'Your brother is a man I have great respect for. I have not broken my Christian oath to him."

"King Alfred knows that you have not broken your sacred oath, and for that he is grateful."

"You and your brother treated me with great respect, Prince Ambrose, when you had an opportunity to crush my army. You are therefore always welcome in my camp, but I must admit to being curious as to why you have ridden so far."

"Your godfather wants to thank you for honoring your oath, King, and hopes that he can continue to have friendly relations with you. In fact, he hopes that you will join him in Christian fellowship and march with him against our common enemy."

Guthrum stroked his beard idly with his right hand. "I have sworn friendship with Alfred, Prince, but I am not ready to go to war against my own people."

"My brother wants you to know that if you stand against the invaders, then he will formally recognize you as the legitimate ruler of East Anglia and Essex."

Guthrum smiled. "I **am** the ruler of East Anglia, Essex, and much of Mercia too, Prince. Although I do not in any way wish to slight the words of the greatest Saxon king in all Britain, both Alfred and I know that my legitimacy lies in the strength of my right arm."

"But my brother offers you the chance to be accepted by all the island's kings, not as a usurper, but as a legitimate ruler. If you do this thing, the king of Wessex will also swear, in turn, to stand at your side in friendship if you are ever threatened by any invader."

"Prince Ambrose, there is no ruler in all Christendom that I would rather have at my side than your brother, but I cannot do it. I have let the Christian priests into my land as I agreed at Wedmore. I am no longer burning the churches and I allow the conquered people to worship the Christian God. I wish to live in peace, but I am still a Dane. No Christian baptism can remove that from me."

"Then, Sire, Alfred would like to know what you intend."

The king smiled again. "I assume you are asking if my men are about to ride south and drive into the Wessex Heartland while Alfred is away fighting in Kent."

Ambrose smiled in return. "Not diplomatic, King Guthrum,

but quite accurate."

"I am a warrior, Prince, not a diplomat. I prefer a sword in my hand to wagging my tongue. Tell King Alfred this - my army will not attack Wessex."

"It is time for honest talk, Sire, and before our two great peoples once again face each other across a battlefield."

King Guthrum glowered. "I have just told you that I will not invade Wessex, Prince. What more do you want me to say?"

"Alfred is nervous, Sire. You have reinforced the garrison in London. On our journey here, we saw several ships heading south for the Thames. Unusual ship movements have been reported all along your eastern coast."

"The Frisians are both shrewd traders and have sharp eyes, Prince. You know as well as I do, however, that a long-ship is not likely to head out in the dead of winter."

"Nor, generally, in the planting season, King Guthrum."

Polonius spoke for the first time. "And what of Kent, King Guthrum? Your ships appear to be moving south. It makes me wonder if you consider Kent to be part of Wessex."

Guthrum's infectious grin returned. "I have honored the oath I swore both to the Christian God and on my sacred armband, Polonius, and I will continue to do so. Now that you have asked the question, however, I would have to say that I would consider Kent to be far from the heartland of the West Saxons. I will personally hang any West Anglian *jarl* of mine who invades Wessex, but I am quite unable to stop my young men from looking for adventure and a little loot in faraway Kent.

And while we are talking of provocations, do not think that I have not heard that your new . . . what do you call them . . . burhs . . . along our common frontier are also having their garrisons reinforced. Entire villages are on the march, down to the chickens and the dogs. This, Prince, is an unfriendly act that troubles me greatly. It is nothing less than preparation for war, and you know as well as I that it is not aimed at the Francian Vikings."

"Do you expect us to do nothing, King? Our land has been invaded and there is a hostile fleet at the mouth of the Thames!"

"I would not mind if you raise and arm every man in Kent! By *Thor's* hammer, I would expect you to. I, however, am not involved in this conflict. Reinforcing your new northern fortifications is an act of aggression against me!"

"Sire, my brother specifically enjoined me to tell you that he will not be the one to break the treaty. The garrisoning is purely a defensive manoeuver designed to protect his flanks. His main army is going east to crush the Danes at Rochester. You know that is well as I do."

"Then, Prince, perhaps you could explain your own ship movements. My spies tell me Frisian mercenaries are being hired by the hundred, and dozens of Saxon ship crews are being called up. Your brother is conjuring up an entire fleet where before there was none."

"Alfred has maintained a fleet for years. I seem to remember savaging one of your fleets when you were ensconced in Exeter."

The king scoffed. "Your memory is poor, Prince. You took one ship, but then found your flagship was too unwieldy to catch my other long-ships."

Ambrose smiled. "But the other captains were forced to turn back, with the supplies and reinforcements you needed so desperately.

Sire, the Frisians my brother hires are only in Wessex because your countrymen are devastating their homeland. You do have good spies, however."

"As do you, Prince.' He smiled at Polonius. 'I am honored to have Wessex's chief spy-master and strategist sitting here at my own table."

Polonius spoke. "You honor me, Sire. I am a mere student of history."

"You have, no doubt, fooled many with your cloak of humbleness, Polonius, but I know better. I still wait for my answer."

Ambrose became serious. "The Saxon fleet will sail towards Rochester. With luck, they will destroy the enemy ships even while the Saxon fyrd crushes the warriors on land."

Guthrum nodded. "I reiterate, Prince. My warriors will not attack Wessex. The Danes are my people, however, and it would be impossible for me to forbid cousins from joining cousins in Kent."

Ambrose frowned. "Then your men will cross our borders, King, and if your men do, then you may rest assured that Alfred will take the same liberties to catch them, wherever they go, in order to have a decisive victory."

"Alfred may pursue the *Frankland* Vikings to the gates of your Christian hell if he pleases, Prince, but he is not to pursue a single fugitive across the Thames without my express permission."

"But you have just said that your warriors may sail their ships to Rochester without restraint."

"I just said that I did not send them, Prince. I will not restrain them."

"Then I fear that we will have a serious problem, for Alfred intends to utterly destroy any and all pirates who land in his country. Your warriors will not be spared if their feet so much as touch West Saxon land. On this, my brother will not bend."

"Pray tell me how it is in my interest to see my own cousins and possibly my own men, slaughtered?"

"They would not be slaughtered if you forbade their presence south of the Thames, Sire, but to answer your question, you made a pact with a Christian king. As a result, your southern border is secure. You rule a country and your warriors have fertile land to till. The Wessex fyrd respects your boundaries. Your children can live in peace and harmony, or you can suffer the same ill effects we did when you arrived. New invaders mean strife, Sire. Do not think that your lands will be immune to invasion from your own cousins to the north. The Norse cruise the western coast of Britain, and they hold little love for their cousins the Danes. The Picts and the Scots, no matter how many times they are driven back, keep spilling over their own southern borders. Alone, you just might be defeated. We are willing to stand at your side. Frankly, we need each other. Wessex can be a powerful friend."

Guthrum spoke. "Atheling, I am very aware that Polonius here has been busy strengthening Wessex's defenses. You are right. Wessex is a formidable friend and I have no wish to have my own godfather as a sworn enemy. I will tell you what I will do. I will meditate on what you have said and discuss it with my jarls in council. I think I should tell you now, however, that it is unlikely we will change our policy. Tonight, however, you are an honored guest. We will feast. Tomorrow, you may return to your king with my final answer."

King Guthrum clapped his hands twice, and the serving *ambats* marched in loaded down with food. The first platters were of freshly baked bread, along with large chunks of cheese, and right behind were wooden platters holding heaps of steaming meat.

King Guthrum waved his hand magnanimously. "Eat, emissaries. A noble horse was sacrificed today to the gods. It is fortunate that the gods let us keep most of the meat! Next will come the salted fish and the pork."

The burley warriors of the Viking king's war band ate with much laughter and noise. No serving wench dared complain when she was grabbed and openly fondled. Course after course was brought out, and the men called constantly for more mead. Finally, when all the meat and fish had disappeared, the *thralls* brought out more bread and large bowls of honey.

King Guthrum was flushed with all the wine and mead he had taken. When he spoke, however, he sounded quite sober. "Bring forth the skald!"

The storyteller raced into the open area near the fire pit. He spoke. "What is it you would have me recite, Great King?"

Guthrum looked at Ambrose and grinned. "I want something different tonight. Do you know the ballad of Hamar and the theft of Dag's royal princesses?"

The storyteller bowed. "I know all the ballads sung about this Ambrose and his two magical companions, Great King, though they are not the tales I would normally recite to a Viking host. Are you sure that you wish me to tell them in front of your men?"

"The heroes of the tale, Prince Ambrose and his two companions sit before you in this very chamber, Skald. We will honor them with the telling of the tales."

The storyteller bowed again. "It shall be as you wish, Great King."

As the skald started to tell how Egil was tied up by Ambrose and thrust under the tents in the *Great Army's* encampment, Egil, more than a little drunk, staggered to his feet. "My king, I challenge the Saxon Dane-slayer to single combat!"

The crowd suddenly hushed and Guthrum growled in reply. "You will not start a blood-feud here, and tonight, warrior. Sit down!"

"Then, Great King, I demand the rite of my Norse cousins. I demand to be allowed to meet this prancing puppy in a *holmgang*. Find us a little island and leave us alone for an hour and I will show you who the real warrior is!"

Guthrum rose to his imposing height and no one dared stir. The ruddy light flickered over the bearded face of an angry king.

"You dare to challenge an emissary in the presence of your king!?"

"I have the right to call out any warrior I choose. I call upon *Ull* to give me victory over this puppy. It is the way of the Vikings, a sacred right, and even you cannot stop me, king!"

Guthrum seemed to loom ever larger. His deep voice resonated the length of the chamber.

"The fact that your feelings were hurt because you were too careless to look behind you and got hit over the head does not give you the right to demand single combat against an official emissary from my own godfather! You overreach yourself, Egil."

"Then I will just hack the little Saxon to pieces here and now. " Drunk, the warrior groped for his sword. When he found that he didn't have it, he headed back to his seat to retrieve his weapon.

Guthrum glared at the drunk. "Ambrose, what is the penalty in Wessex for a warrior who draws his sword without permission in the king's presence?"

"Under the laws of Wessex, if anyone draws his sword or fights in the king's presence, it is to be the king's judgement as to whether the man lives or dies."

"Egil the Little, you have heard the Saxon law. The Viking law is the same. If you draw your sword without my permission, in my presence, you will be executed on my orders. That is my right to declare, under our ancient laws."

The drunk paused, his sword half out of its scabbard. Even as he stared at the king in owlish surprise, four burley warriors standing behind the king lowered their spear tips and started forward.

Guthrum spoke again. "Return your sword to its scabbard and my guards will escort you to a quiet place where you can sleep off your mead. Disobey me and you die here and now."

Throwing a last glare of hate at Ambrose, the big man shoved his sword back into its scabbard. He staggered towards the door.

"I can find my own way out, King. Keep your jackals at your side. One day you may have need of them."

Guthrum growled. "The day I need another to fight my battles is the day I am no longer king! If you wish to face me in a holmgang, just say so! We will find a quiet little island and I will split you head to crotch."

Egil backed drunkenly toward the door. "You are king. I cannot fight you!"

"Then you have my permission to retire Egil. I will tell you when you are again to be allowed in my presence. Now out with you!"

Two warriors came shortly after sunrise to summon Ambrose and his two companions back to see Guthrum. Hurriedly dressing, the three friends followed their escort back to the king's long house. While Ambrose could barely open his eyes, Guthrum, looking fresh and alert, sat on his seat-of-honor and smiled when the three emissaries were led in. He spoke.

"Good morning, emissaries! Prince Ambrose, I hope that you slept well."

Ambrose tried to stand straight, although the effort caused considerable pain. "Your wine was superb, followed by an excellent mead, King Guthrum, although I fear that I may have drunk more than my share."

"Nonsense, Prince! You showed us that a Saxon can drink almost as well as a Viking!"

"Thank you, Sire. I remember many of the things we discussed, but I do not remember if you changed your mind about helping King Alfred. I do not wish to misquote you, Sire. Much depends on your exact words. What, exactly, do you wish me to tell Alfred?"

Guthrum smiled. "Hmm. You may tell my godfather that my army will not cross into Wessex, but I will not prevent my jarls from independently visiting their cousins in Kent."

"Even if that means war?"

"A wise king recognizes and accepts the consequences of his actions, Prince Ambrose. I do not feel that this policy breaks my sacred oath to your brother."

"Then there is nothing further to be said. I will take your words to my brother just as you have said them. With your permission, we will start south."

"Of course, Prince. You and your friends are welcome any time. May Odin grant you a safe and speedy journey home."

"I hope that all your people feel as you do, King Guthrum."

"What do you mean, Prince?"

"On my way north, our friend from last night was ready to hang me from the nearest tree, in spite of the sacred shield I carried."

"Yes, Olaf reported that to me. Egil the Little has a lot of pride, Prince, and last night was not the first time that his companions ridiculed him for letting himself be stuffed under an old tent and then losing the fight to you.

As I told him last night, however, I do not want any misunderstandings. The emissary's shield you carry is sacred to our people. No man will raise a hand against you while you carry it, or I will personally cut it off. I will tell you what I will do, Prince Ambrose. Take this ring.' As Guthrum spoke, he removed an ornate ring from his left hand. 'If any of my people trouble you, tell them that you received this from my own hand, and you may be sure that no Dane will dare lift a hand against you."

Ambrose held the ring in his hand. "I do not know what to say, King Guthrum."

"You may have it with only one proviso, Prince."

"And what is that, King?"

"You promise to return it to me in happier times."

Ambrose grinned. "It would be my pleasure, King Guthrum."

As Ambrose tied his pack on his horse, Polonius spoke quietly in Greek. "What message would you like to send King Alfred, Prince?"

"What do you think, Scholar?"

"I have seen no single massive gathering of Guthrum's warriors, but it is pretty clear to me that individual ships and their crews are heading south. It is equally clear that Guthrum has no intention of stopping the crews from crossing the Thames and trying to reinforce the Danes at Rochester, probably before we can even get our army together and march east."

"Phillip?"

"I think we will soon be at war, Prince. King Alfred will never accept Guthrum's answer, nor should he. Guthrum is just splitting hairs."

Ambrose spoke. "But should Alfred send back a third of his force to Southwark? That is the critical question."

Polonius nodded. "For the moment, we must assume that the ships are heading for Rochester, and, if so, that is where the king must concentrate his forces."

Ambrose looked at Phillip, who nodded his head as well. "I agree."

Ambrose smiled. "Then, Polonius, perhaps, in your clumsiness, you might accidentally knock open the cage door of the white birds. We can eat the piebald birds for dinner."

Polonius reached across to tighten a strap and suddenly bumped a cage door. Two white pigeons, startled, leapt into the sky. The Viking warriors standing nearby laughed, and the man who hated Ambrose so much stepped forth. "I think that you have just lost part of your dinner, Greek!"

Polonius watched the two birds as they spiraled into the sky.

"Aye, I think that you are right, Egil the Little. I am pretty sure, however, that those two were my friends' portion of the meal."

"Follow your pigeons and ride south quickly, Saxons, before king Guthrum decides you are spies after all and decides to honor you by making you a sacrifice to Odin."

Ambrose spoke. "Stay north of the Thames, Egil. I have no wish to kill you and your men."

The man grinned. "We shall see when we next meet, adopted-son-of-Canute. We shall see who lives and who dies!"

CHAPTER 8

Assassins in the Night

The three companions rode at a mile-eating trot, only pausing to give their weary horses some breaks. Once they hit the old Roman road, the going was much easier. The road had been so well constructed that it continued to be relatively level, in spite of a century or more of neglect.

The emissaries rode past only occasional settlements, where dull-eyed Saxons and Angles looked up fearfully, and then went back to their back-breaking labors. Few smiled at the strangers.

Ambrose spoke to his two companions. "The folk here do not seem very happy."

Polonius replied. "How could they be? The free-born men now till what was once their land for barbarian rulers. Many have been reduced to slavery and now wear the thrall's iron collar. Guthrum is no fool, however. Already, many of the youngest and strongest of the people have sworn allegiance to him and fight in the Viking army. By ruling part of the land through puppet noblemen, he is slowly gaining the allegiance of many of the conquered. A growing portion of his army is apparently made up of our friends and cousins. In a generation, the population here will be loyal to their Viking rulers."

"I am surprised, Polonius. It is not the Viking way."

"Prince, it is not the Viking way in their homelands. When Dir and Askold arrived with their fleet at Kiev, they joined with the Slav leaders. It got them a city, and eventually an empire. Slavs fought side by side with the Rus from the day of their arrival."

"The Rus also ruthlessly crushed Slavic opposition, Polonius. Kuralla's mother, father, and brother were all victims of a Viking ruler."

Polonius shrugged. "A few thousand Viking warriors

conquered probably a half-million Slavs. They used the carrot and the stick on the Slavs."

Ambrose looked puzzled. "How so?"

"For those who bent their knee in submission to the Rus and their Slav allies, the Vikings gave life - if a hard one. Thousand of conquered Slavs were called upon to join the Rus army of retribution against the Byzantine Empire. Most of those same Slavs went back up the Dnieper with more gold and treasure than they could have imagined. Within a few months, hundreds more villages voluntarily agreed to join the Rus federation."

"That is the carrot."

"You saw the use of the stick. Thousands of other Slavs were butchered, down to the youngest children, because their leaders refused to submit to the new rulers."

Phillip slowed his horse and spoke to his two companions. "I have the distinct impression that we are being followed."

Ambrose frowned. "I have seen no one, Weapons-master."

Phillip replied. "I know. That is what worries me."

Ambrose scanned in all directions before speaking. "Could Guthrum have sent an escort to make sure we don't see anything he doesn't want us to?"

Phillip frowned. "It is possible, but if so, they would do much better to just escort us openly. They do not have to be secretive. They certainly weren't on the ride from Chelmsford to Witham."

Polonius spoke. "It will be dark in less than a single turn of the hourglass. Does this mean that I get to huddle in a bush again all night while a log gets to sleep in my comfortable bed again?"

Ambrose smiled. "It will be an Anglish log this time - not an Italian one. And besides, it was your idea last time, Scholar. You were the one that made me sleep in the bushes on that damn hillside in Calabria."

"And?"

"And because of that, I have to admit, we were able to take on a dozen assassins, and survive the experience."

Polonius sighed. "Then I guess it is settled. I will shiver in the bushes yet again. I will be very upset, however, my master, if nothing happens all night."

"Then you collect the branches to fill out our beds, and I will scout out some secure hiding places."

&

Five of them appeared just as the moon rose over the horizon. They had spears in their hands as they crept towards the three shapes draped in bedclothes. The biggest and leader, Egil the Little, held a wicked-looking spear-point against one blanket-covered figure while two of his companions did the same for the other two. The man's grin was lit up by the nearby campfire. He spoke loudly.

"Wake up, Saxon filth! Your betters are here to teach you a few lessons in manners."

Ambrose spoke from his hiding place. "You will have to try harder than that to catch Saxons asleep, Egil the Little. You will all drop your weapons, or you will die where you stand!"

The giant and his men desperately scanned the surrounding vegetation. "Where are you, little man? Show yourself!"

Ambrose stepped out of the brush he had been using for shelter. His bow was drawn and the arrow touched his cheek. "You disappoint me, little Egil. I knew you to be a bully and a poor fighter, but I did not expect you to be a coward and a fool."

"How dare you, Saxon!"

"It took barely a five-count for me to cut you down the last time we fought, Egil, and now you have led your friends into a trap that could yet cost all of them their lives."

The big man darted glances at his four companions. "There are five of us and only three of them. I say we attack on my command!"

One of his companions, cadaverous in appearance, dropped his spear. "They may be three, you moron, but we don't even know for certain where two of them are hiding. If the other two also have their bows drawn, they will cut us down before we even locate them."

"They cannot kill all five of us, fools. At best they hit three!"

The man spoke again. "Bravo, Egil. Then the two remaining can take on their three, assuming that they cannot shoot fast enough to get more than one of us each, and assuming that we even locate the other two."

Ambrose's arrow did not waver, but he spoke. "These are bodkin arrowheads, Egil, long and elegantly tapered - carefully designed to easily pierce chain mail. Attack or flee, and we will drop you in your tracks."

The fifth warrior, hardly more than a boy, spoke in a high and nervous voice. "Sirs, will you let us withdraw with our lives if we lay down our weapons?"

Egil was furious. "Coward! You are not fit to be in mens' company!

The man flared back. "I do not intend to die just because you want to redress some real or imagined slight you suffered at this man's hands some ten years ago!"

"I almost died from my wound, and they still sing of blind Egil under the tents in his damned ballad! Is that an imagined slight?!"

"You chased him all night, and then he defeated you in open combat, Egil! Accept the hand that the gods have dealt you!"

"No man makes a fool of Egil the Little and lives!"

Ambrose spoke. "Egil, I have always respected the Vikings. I was once held as a slave, and was fortunate enough to be adopted by a great Danish warrior. I traveled the rivers through far-off lands and fought as a Rus warrior. I learned a lot about Vikings. You are cruel and brutal to the weak. You do not understand the concept of Christian compassion, but see it as a weakness to be exploited. My people see you as sent by the devil, inhuman creatures who eat the souls of little babies.

What I learned in my years amongst the Rus, however, was very different. I watched brave warriors willingly sacrifice themselves to protect a companion. I watched men with the courage to tear off their clothes and charge naked into battle, and I found men who lived with the strongest code of honor of any warrior I have met anywhere. I fought shoulder to shoulder with brave warriors whose honor was much more important than their lives."

Egil shrugged. "All of this I know, Saxon. I am a Viking!"

"You are a Viking who has betrayed your king! You may as well charge this arrow, for in my eyes, and your friends beside you, you are dishonored - you have betrayed your king and your code of honor."

Egil looked nervously at Ambrose and then back at his companions. "By Odin's balls, what are you talking about, Saxon?!"

"Did you tell your fellow assassins that I am an official emissary carrying the sacred white shield and bearing a message direct from your king to mine? Did you tell them that your king accepted me as a friend and invited me to return anytime? Did you, perhaps, neglect to mention that my brother is godfather to your king? Did you not tell them that I am a Dane by adoption and count many Rus amongst my best friends? Last but not least, did you not tell them that your king took his own personal ring off his finger this very day and gave it to me in friendship?"

Egil looked about very nervously. "I told them that you were a spy and a thief, Dane-slayer. That is all brave warriors need to know. As you said, a Viking's honor is more important than his life."

"Then you are tricking brave warriors into giving up their lives for your petty revenge! You know that King Guthrum ordained that I was a sacred emissary and, as such, untouchable. I think that you deliberately misled these men, Egil-with-no-honor."

The other three men dropped their spears with a sudden clatter. The youngest one spoke again. "I did not know that you were protected by King Guthrum, stranger. Egil just told us that you were spies who needed to be stopped at all cost."

Ambrose replied. "I thought as much. If you drop your weapons-belts and one of you fetches your horses, then the four of you can walk away with your lives and your honor intact."

Egil now stood alone as his four companions complied. "What about me?"

"If you have a shred of honor left, you will charge my arrow and see if your gods will protect you."

Egil's spear finally clattered to the ground. "I am forced to accept that you are a sacred emissary. As you point out, to attack you would be to betray my king."

"In that case, you will leave both your weapons and your clothes on the ground in front of you. You may leave as soon as you are as naked and defenseless as the day you were born. In future, it may be that you will be known as both blind and naked Egil."

"You take my pride. You may as well just kill me, Saxon!"

"Phillip, do not kill him this time. The next is to his heart."

An arrow over a yard long thudded into the tree next to the Viking with enough force to drive deep into the dense wood.

Egil hastily dropped his weapons belt and started to remove his clothes. Even his waiting companions laughed as the big man stripped off his clothes.

After Polonius had stepped forward to collect the weapons, Ambrose spoke. "Go back to Guthrum, Vikings, and tell the truth of what happened here tonight."

"King Guthrum will hang us all, Emissary!"

"Tell him that Prince Ambrose does not in any way hold you responsible for what happened. I only blame Egil the Fool."

CHAPTER 9

The Saxon Priest

As the three rode south along the ancient Roman road, Polonius spoke to his two companions. "Well, my friends, we have to make a decision soon."

Ambrose looked at the Byzantine. "And just what is that, Polonius?"

"We can hurry to London, or we can leave the Roman road and turn left in a couple of miles."

"And why would we do that, Scholar?"

"There is a trail coming up that takes us due south."

"Polonius, due south is the river, and, not far away, the Francian Viking fleet. We have no way across the Thames, and if you did manage to find one, we run a serious chance of bumping into an enemy long-ship."

"I can arrange the boat. The question is - do we take the risk?"

Phillip spoke. "It's true that it would save three or more days of hard riding."

Ambrose replied. "I wouldn't mind that part one bit! I would hate to meet any unfriendly Vikings at this point, however."

Polonius started stroking his chin. "Prince, you carry both the sacred shield and also Guthrum's ring. We were not restricted to any single path back to the border."

"I guess that you are right - we should be safe enough if we are stopped by Guthrum's men. I am not so sure about the Francian pirates, however."

Polonius nodded. "It is your choice, Prince. An extra four or five days in the saddle, or a midnight crossing of the Thames."

"Polonius, my friend, you are a very persuasive man. When you put it that way, then I guess we take our chances on the river."

The little group rode into the sleepy village on the north bank of the Thames. Many eyes followed their progress, but no one barred their way. At last a priest stepped out of the church and spoke to the three strangers. He struggled with the Viking tongue.

"We are but poor fishermen, honored sirs. We have nothing for you here."

Polonius spoke in Saxon. "On the contrary, good priest, if you are Father Rodor, then you have a great deal for us."

"You speak Saxon, stranger."

"My two companions are Saxon. This is Prince Ambrose, brother to King Alfred, and Phillip, weapons-master to the king."

The priest looked unimpressed. "We are honored to have such distinguished visitors, but I warn you that there are sporadic Viking patrols through our village. We will all be in a great deal of trouble if you are caught here!"

Polonius smiled. "Note the white shield my companion carries. We are official emissaries and carry King Guthrum's personal ring to ensure our safe-conduct."

"You are fortunate then, stranger. I ask you again, however, why you are here. You may be protected, but we serve stern masters."

"Father Rodor, my name is Polonius."

"Polonius? That is not a common name in Britain, sir."

Polonius reached out and dangled a thin chain on which was strung half of a golden Byzant. As he did so, he muttered a cryptic phrase. "Alfred for Bretwalda."

The priest stared at Polonius as if he had never seen him before that moment. At last he replied. "Your coin is of gold, sir, but it seems to have been mutilated."

"Perhaps you could compare it to the silver coin you wear around your neck, Father Rodor."

The priest reached deep with his shirt and extracted a similarly cut coin. He placed the two together, and, except for the metal, they were a perfect match. He looked up.

"It is cut the same, Lord Polonius, but yours is the wrong

metal."

"There are many silver coins, Father, but only one gold one."

"Then you are truly King Alfred's spy-master! Blessing be to God that you have made it this far, Spy-master! What can I do for you?"

"King Alfred waits for us not far from here, but on the south bank of the Thames. We need to get across as soon as possible."

The priest smiled. "Widows and orphans in this village eat, Spy-master, because of your generosity. I will have to do a little persuading, but you should have a boat and crew this very night."

"We would be grateful, Father Rodor."

As Ambrose watched the villagers uncover their boat and drag it down to the riverbank, he turned to his Byzantine friend. "Polonius, old friend, do you personally finance every village north of the Thames?"

"You would be surprised just how much of your brother's gold goes north, Prince."

"We are defeating Guthrum by bribing innkeepers in Lundonwyc and priests in coastal villages?"

"Right now, Prince, they spy for us. Eventually they may form into an army that will help us drive the Danes from London and perhaps Mercia. At the very least, they are our eyes and ears."

"I thank the Good Lord that you have found so many friends north of the river, but why, Polonius? Is it all worth so much gold?"

"Prince, a victory can be obtained just as surely with a thousand little cuts as one big one."

"What exactly are you talking about, Scholar?"

"I have told you before, Prince. Diplomacy is the best way to win a victory. War should only be the last resort, after everything else has failed."

"I have been brought up to fight for what I believe in, Scholar."

"And I do not disagree with that sentiment, if nothing else works first. My ancestors, led by a barbarian king from Macedonia, conquered much of the known world. The Greeks, with their phalanx, were unbeatable for centuries, until another race of warriors came forward who figured out how to outmaneuver the Greek formation. Do you know who they were, Prince?"

"I assume you mean the Romans, Scholar."

"You are correct, Prince, and after conquering most of the world, they took a tiny village on the Bosporus and made it into the wonder of Constantinople today."

"With a little help from your ancestors, the Greeks."

Polonius smiled. "True. The Greeks soon regained their rightful places as masters of the East. Byzantines know how to fight, Prince. They have had much experience and have made a science of it. Nevertheless, they try everything else in their quiver before they send out their very efficient armies."

"Who, as we saw, are mainly foreign mercenaries anyway . . . Then tell me, Polonius, how our friend Basil would handle the Danes."

"Probably much as Michael handled the Rus. Through us, Michael made a trade offer to the Rus that they would have been foolish to refuse. He punished the few minor officials who had so offended the Vikings as proof of his sincerity. He tied the tribes to him with the lure of trade. Mark my words - Basil will soon be recruiting the Rus tribesmen to his army. He will soon be using the northern barbarians to fight the other barbarians circling the rich lands of Byzantium."

"And using the rich profits from the trade with the Northmen to pay them their wages."

Polonius smiled. "Precisely. Meanwhile, your friend Michael the Emperor, just in case the Rus were not open to reason, entered into secret negotiations with the *Khazars*. The *Khagan* himself sent us word of the Byzantine intentions. If we had not paid their fair share to the Khazars upon our return upriver from the attack, and more besides, you may be sure that we would have found our way south blocked at the Dnieper River cataracts come spring.

Ambrose spoke. "So that is why Dir and Askold were so liberal with their hard won treasures. I thought they were being unusually generous."

"Exactly, Prince. The Khazars controlled the river, and so the

Rus bought their favor."

"I wonder who advised them to do that?"

Polonius looked modestly at the ground. "I am but a humble advisor who may have whispered a word or two into Dir's ear."

"And what would Michael have done if we had not signed a treaty and the Khazars had refused to turn against the Rus?"

"Don't think for a moment that the Pechenegs could not have been bribed. A judicious offer of enough gold would have brought entire hordes west to attack Kiev. Remember, bitter as our struggle was, we faced only one small branch of the Pecheneg nation."

"But it would have cost Michael so much gold. Would it have been worth it?"

"Prince, you are sending mercenaries to do your fighting. If they win, you can probably pay them at least partly from the spoils. If they lose, you have no grieving widows amongst your own people, you still have an intact army, and, in any case, there are not so many mercenaries left to pay."

"And what about if the Khazars and the Pechenegs both refused to cooperate?"

Polonius shrugged. "Michael may have tried the Magyars, or he might have decided to send his own troops north. The famous Chinese tactician Sun Tzu once said that "he will win who knows when to fight and when not to fight." There is a time, Prince, when you risk your own army."

"But that would be the very last resort."

Polonius smiled again. "Exactly, Prince."

"So how are we applying this Byzantine thinking to the Vikings of Northumbria and East Anglia?"

"You have mentioned two different kingdoms. Each is being treated differently."

"How so, Scholar?"

"We have already made an effort to bind Guthrum to us. Our priests are ostensibly in East Anglia in order to minister to the Angelisc Christians, but they are making inroads, slowly, with a few of the Danes. We encourage Guthrum to trade with Wessex, and the letter you carried to him offered him a formal military alliance. If he had accepted it, then he would have been seen as a traitor by the Danes of Northumbria. We just might have had the Danes fighting against Danes."

"But he did not accept the alliance."

"He would have been foolish if he had. Since he said no, we attempted to keep him out of the war while your brother crushes the Francian Vikings."

"Did we succeed?"

"If he does not call up his entire army and fleet, then, yes, I think that we have succeeded."

"What is your greatest worry, Polonius?"

"That Guthrum and this new king of Northumbria, Guthred, join with the Francian Danes. I am not sure that we can hold the West Saxon Empire together if there are three separate Viking armies rampaging through it at the same time, especially if they find local allies."

"You are thinking of Cornwall and Dorset again."

"In a word - yes. For that matter, how loyal is Kent?"

"My brother is marching to its aid even as we speak!"

"True, Prince, but Kentish subjects often see their best warriors sent west to fight in other shires when they themselves face the brunt of most of the Viking invasions, and we take a long time to move to their aid when they are threatened."

"Only the time to takes to gather enough fyrdmen to defeat our mutual enemies, Polonius!"

"Possibly, Prince, but, because of their location, they are very vulnerable, while we must gather men from as far away as Devon and Cornwall. Remember, they have seen Essex abandoned to the Danes by your own brother."

"It was north of the river and indefensible, Polonius."

"Nevertheless, the Kentish thanes just might decide to appoint a local leader and keep their young men at home."

"So what else are we doing with the gold, Scholar?"

"A lot, Prince. Guthrum knows that the priests and Frisian traders report to Wessex. What he does not know is how many of his Saxons currently obey Alfred."

Ambrose nodded. "And further north?"

"The Scots and Picts have been savagely mauled both by the Dublin Vikings and Guthred's host, but the stubborn bastards still harry Northumbria regularly. The Danes of Northumbria are very busy putting down rebellions and guarding their northern frontiers. With luck, the unrest just might keep the Northumbrians too busy to join the Francian Vikings."

"Now that, I concede, would be a major victory."

"And without the death of a single West Saxon, Master."

Ambrose looked at Polonius with surprise. "And we are responsible for the attacks?"

"The Picts and the Scots would fight the Vikings without our instigation. The Saxons rise out of anger and desperation. Our gold and supplies just allow them to be more successful."

"And there is more?"

"Of course. Ethelred of Mercia can not hope to take on Guthrum, but he has hit the Welsh so often and so hard that several of their leaders are considering recognizing Alfred as Bretwalda, on the condition that he brings Ethelred to heel."

"And can we do such a thing?"

"Ethelred understands that his little corner of Mercia will not survive Guthrum's next onslaught."

"But Guthrum has left western Mercia alone since King Ethelred killed his Saxon puppet ruler."

"Prince, Guthrum is but consolidating his position in Essex, East Anglia and eastern Mercia. When he feels secure in the east, he will invade the unconquered territories. Ethelred knows that. His only hope is to have some powerful friends. We are his natural allies. Both your wife, and Alfred's, are Mercian. He is Alfred's son-in-law. If Ethelred does somehow survive Guthrum then, in a weakened condition, he could end up facing Guthred, who wouldn't mind a piece of the fertile west Mercian real-estate. Ethelred would rather rule a province than find his wife and children in the hands of Arab slavers. You do not have to worry. He is a loyal vassal of Alfred's."

Ambrose looked at Polonius. "Will the Welsh really accept Alfred as their Bretwalda?"

"Let's just say that the seed has been planted. Exactly what will grow remains to be seen."

Ambrose laughed. "You are truly Byzantine, Polonius. My

head spins with all the ramifications. It is an exciting and complicated game you play."

"And the best part is, with God's grace, it will not cost the lives of a single West Saxon warrior."

"Unless we have to rescue Ethelred from Guthrum."

Polonius sighed. "There is that, but that is a battle that will come eventually, whatever we do. Wessex is the last free Angelisc kingdom on the island. The Vikings simply cannot afford to leave us independent. If we fall, the island is more-or-less subjugated."

"But we will be fighting in Mercia instead of Wessex, and, we should only be facing a single enemy."

Polonius smiled. "Exactly, Prince, and with battle-tested allies who are fighting for their very existence."

᚛

The tubby fishing vessel wallowed in the waves until the rowers managed to build up speed. Soon the boat was heading directly for the southern shore. Polonius spoke to Father Rodor.

"You do not even carry a mast, my friend."

"To be seen is to die. We may be loyal subjects of King Guthrum, but we are not allowed the right to sail at night. We will depend on the oars. The mast only makes us more visible."

"Are you sure you can get back and get the boat hidden before dawn, Father?"

"It is no problem, Lord Polonius. Don't worry. The biggest fear you should have right now is that a stray long-ship might be resting nearby and one of the crew spots us crossing the river. The Vikings are like dogs after a stag. They love to give chase just for the thrill of the hunt."

"I see the shores of Kent fast approaching, Father. You have made good your promise and delivered us safely into friendly territory."

"Be careful, Spy-master! The heathen are raiding far to the east of Rochester. You may be in for a rude surprise if you are not careful."

"Thanks for the ride and the warning, Father Rodor. May God

be with you."

"And with you and your companions, Spy-master. May He keep you safe always . . . Be ready now to jump as we near the shore. We do not intend to land."

Ambrose and his two companions leapt for the darkness of the land as the crewmen shipped their oars and let the left side of the ship briefly kiss the shore.

The three men walked for hours, until the dawn's gentle light illuminated a palisaded village on the river bank. Ambrose spoke. "Well, my friends, we have finally found one of those vills that Father Rodor described. Maybe we can buy horses here and considerably speed our journey."

Phillip replied. 'It may not be possible, Prince. This area has probably been stripped pretty bare by the Danish raiding parties out of the Viking fort near Rochester. If not, and the people are smart, they will have long ago followed your brother's command and left for the nearest fortified burh. Perhaps a few of the men remain - skulking in the woods."

When they walked into the little vill, Ambrose realized just how accurate Phillip's prediction was. Not a single hen clucked, no dog barked, and no cat slunk across the path. The pasture lands were denuded of cattle, sheep, pigs and horses. Not a single urchin howled at their approach.

The prince turned to the Weapons-master. "You are right, as ever, my big friend. Except for a few twittering sparrows, I don't see or hear a single live animal."

Polonius spoke. "Perhaps we should make for the forest. We are sitting ducks as long as we walk openly through the fields or along the road."

Ambrose nodded as he led the trio away from the village and towards the beckoning trees. "I am disappointed that we have found no Saxons, but I do think that that is good advice. I would hate to be caught in the open by some Viking raiding party."

Polonius spoke with sudden urgency. "I fear it may already be too late. Drop to the ground - now!"

The three dropped as one, into the long uncut grass. Ambrose dared to raise his head just enough to see what had so worried Polonius. It did not take him long to see the Viking raiders approaching along the ancient Roman road. He counted almost a hundred riders before he dropped his head again. The riders were nearing, and the grass was but poor protection from a man sitting high on a horse.

The riders trotted past and Ambrose lay with his stomach in his mouth. It seemed that the Vikings were blind, however, or just busy with the cattle they had stolen. The animals, lowing mournfully, ambled by at a walk. The Viking riders rode by without bothering to scan the open pastureland. At last they all disappeared into the east.

The three companions lay still for another ten full minutes, until Polonius spoke. "I think that we might consider making for the woods, and quickly! We will have no hope of escape if we are spotted, and I am not at all sure that Guthrum's ring will protect us on this side of the river."

Ambrose replied. "Then let us trot, my friends. That was too close for comfort!"

As the three men entered the forest, they ploughed through the dense underbrush until they reached the prime forest. The low dense vegetation disappeared, replaced by towering oaks and maples. The canopy was now high above them. Ambrose stopped to mop his brow and catch his breath, when suddenly two dozen men stepped from the shelter of the forest giants and rapidly surrounded them.

"Drop your weapons or you will die where you stand!"

The words were in Saxon, and Ambrose grinned even as he undid his sword belt. He faced a dozen men who held their arrows at full-draw. Most of the men wore only leather armor, and they were armed largely with axes, spears, and various farm implements.

Ambrose spoke, even as he raised his hands over his head. "Peace! We are not your enemy. We are Saxons on the way to meet King Alfred."

A gaunt man with a wicked looking barbed spear spoke. "You

are not from around here. How do we know that you are not spies?"

"If we were Vikings, would we have hidden from the raiding party that just went by?"

The man thought a moment. "Aye, you might. Greeting them would have let us know that you are really Vikings."

"You were well-hidden. We did not know that you were hiding here. Besides, would Danes be wearing Anglish clothes and speaking Saxon?"

"What else would good spies wear?"

"Good sir, my name is Prince Ambrose, and my companions are Phillip, Weapons-master to King Alfred, and Polonius, Chief Advisor to King Alfred."

"Ah, we have you now, spies. We have heard the ballads about Ambrose, Polonius and Phillip."

"And?"

"And you three do not even come close."

Ambrose looked at the man in exasperation. "Just what did you hear about us?"

"Them. Phillip is a tall as a tree and carries a sword as long as he is tall."

"Look at this man! Is he a midget?"

The gaunt man looked Phillip up and down dubiously. "He is a big one, I'll admit."

"Then look at his sword. Can he draw it?"

"Aye, but slowly. We hang spies in Kent. I don't want you three to die of arrow poisoning."

As Phillip drew the huge blade and Ambrose continued. "Is that the blade of a midget? I am telling you, this is Phillip of Wessex . . . What else did you hear about us?"

"That Prince Ambrose is a direct descendent of the ancient kings of the Durotriges."

"Ah, and how did this Ambrose prove it to the Irish?"

"Why he had a birthmark in the shape of an oak leaf."

"Where?"

"Umm. By one of his nipples, I believe."

"Left or right?"

The Saxon grinned. "It matters little. I do not know my left from my right."

"And if I had that birthmark, would you believe that I am Ambrose of Wessex?"

The man looked thoughtful. "I suppose there can not be too many spies with the birthmark of a royal family. Show me, spy."

"Tell your bowmen to stand down and I will be pleased to prove it, stranger. Their arms are wobbling from the strain of holding their bows drawn, and I would not like an unfortunate accident to happen now that we have finally made it back to the safety of Wessex."

The gaunt stranger nodded. "You are not safe yet, stranger, but I will tell my men to lower their bows . . . Stand down, my friends."

Ambrose removed his chain-mail shirt and undershirt. The Saxons stared at the birthmark with great curiosity.

"And now if you will stand over by that tree, I will ask Polonius to show you what he can do with his throwing knives."

"No, that is not necessary. I am convinced that you and your friends are who you say you are. I am sorry, Prince, but we had to be sure that you were not spies."

"I understand, stranger . . . I do not even know your name."

"Sigenert, Prince. I am commander of Cooling in my thane's absence, or, at least I would be, if there was still a tun called Cooling."

"What do you mean, Sigenert? I know your tun well."

"The God-cursed Vikings surprised us. Mounted on fine horses, they swept down on us in overwhelming numbers. We were leaderless, but many brave men stood and tried to defend their families. Most of them were quickly cut down.' He suddenly hung his head. 'The rest of the survivors, broke and ran blindly for the deep forest."

"You said you were leaderless. Where was your thane, Sigenert?"

"He had answered the king's summons, Prince, and took with him our strongest and best-armed young men."

"Sigenert, I will pray for your dead, and my brother King Alfred will do his best to help rebuild your tun and ransom your loved ones, but at the moment, we badly need your help."

"Ask, Prince. We will obey."

"We urgently need three good horses."

"I will send my swiftest runners for them, Prince. The rest of our little force, along with a few surviving women and children, is hidden in the forest some two miles to the south, along with a half-dozen horses."

"I thank you, Sigenert. If you can hide and survive for a few more days, then Alfred will be here and you can join the West Saxon army of retribution."

"Prince, nothing would give me greater pleasure than taking fire and sword to the heathen devils."

$$\rightleftharpoons$$

The three riders spotted sunlight reflecting off metal far ahead on the road. Phillip spoke.

"Someone ahead! Do we make for the woods?"

Ambrose replied. "We have seen no sign of the Vikings for hours. We must be nearing Alfred's lines."

Polonius craned his neck. "While you two argue, our fate has been settled."

Ambrose was puzzled. "What do you mean, Scholar?"

"Look behind us. We are trapped."

Even as Ambrose turned, a squad of riders erupted from the woods behind them and started to ride after them. From the west came the source of the reflected sunlight - a second band of armored riders."

The force approached and its leader called out. "Who are you, strangers?"

Ambrose grinned. "As I live and breathe! Is that really you, Thane Radnor? If you are here, Odda can not be far behind!"

"Prince Ambrose! We knew you would be riding hard to catch up, but we expected you to come from the west. How in the name of God did you get past us?"

"We took a little shortcut, Radnor."

"I'll bet! Knowing you, it was right through the Viking army."

"Close, Thane, but we were not spotted by any of the Danes.

How is the old warhorse?"

"He is growing more feeble, Prince, but the ealdorman insists on riding to the king's summons. He would rather die in battle than in his bed."

"Well, Odda is one of the greatest warriors I have ever met. Where is the king's army?"

"Some three or four miles to the west, Prince. King Alfred will be thrilled to see you. He watches his back trail daily for your arrival."

"Then let us go find a king, Radnor!"

CHAPTER 10

Alfred Rides

Ambrose, Polonius and Phillip stepped through the doorway into King Alfred's command tent. Alfred quickly rose to his feet and hugged the three men in turn.

"Welcome back, my friends! I had feared for your lives."

Ambrose spoke. "Did our winged messengers arrive, brother?"

"Aye, Ambrose, just as you said they would. It was a neat trick. I was relieved that you sent the white ones. Does that truly mean peace with Guthrum?"

"He has sworn to not invade Wessex itself with his army, but we counted several of his long-ships heading down the Lea River, heading for the Thames. It is clear that, although Guthrum has not called up his full army or fleet, he has no intention of stopping individual warriors from sailing south and supporting the Francian Vikings at Rochester."

"Did you not tell him that I would find that unacceptable!?"

"I did, brother. I also told him that you would chase the Vikings, once you have defeated them, wherever they flee. He understands that you will not let East Anglia be used as a refuge against your vengeance."

Alfred paced the length of the tent. "And what did he say to that?"

"He said that 'a wise king recognizes and accepts the consequences of his actions.'"

Alfred paced some more. At last he returned to the map, stared at it for a full minute, then spoke.

"You know, this may not be as bad as I feared. We may yet be able to use Guthrum's position to our advantage."

Ambrose was puzzled. "How so, brother?"

"My greatest fear was that he would march south with his entire force, or sail his fleet to our unprotected southern coast. Once his army crossed the Thames, I would be forced to break off the attack against the Francian Vikings at Rochester. Unopposed, he could devastate our heartland and possibly even encourage a few of our unhappier western shires to revolt."

Ambrose spoke. "Speaking of which, has the situation with Cornwall and Dorset being settled yet, brother?"

Alfred shrugged. "As much as is possible under the circumstances, brother. The young men from both families have joined the ranks of my Personal Guard. I actually gave them little choice, short of their fathers ordering the murder of the warrior escorts I sent to bring them to me. The sons are being carefully watched. Their fathers know that I am holding the sons hostage and why. I expect no trouble, though I would almost welcome it."

Ambrose looked puzzled. "You want trouble, brother?"

"It would give me the excuse I need to cut out the rot within my own empire. Both Ethelwold of Dorset and Anwell of Cornwall are just looking for a chance to stab me in the back, yet to go after them openly could lead to civil war. I saw Northumbria fall into civil war, and then collapse when the Viking tide rolled over it. Our own 'dear' brother led a rebellion against our father that could have easily destroyed the power of Wessex if father had not been so forgiving."

"Alfred, father could have easily crushed Ethelbald if he had but sent out the call to his loyal fyrdmen, Alfred! God's vicar on earth supported his cause, and the people would have rallied to him."

"Don't be so sure, Ambrose. Many people were angry that father had declared his child bride to be our queen. He knew that doing so was against our laws, but his heart blinded his reason. He just couldn't say no to the wee girl. It had cost Wessex a great deal of gold to send father on his pilgrimage to Rome not once, but twice. Some of Wessex's bishops and several ealdormen openly supported Ethelbald in his claim to the throne."

"So rather than launch a civil war, father rotted in Kent as under-king of a remote shire within his own empire."

"Exactly so, Ambrose. The alternative was to put father against son and brother against brother, to the detriment of all. Truth to tell, our father wanted a religious life, not a military one."

"Alfred, what do you fear most about Guthrum and the Francian Vikings?"

"Brother, the two Viking armies together would just about outnumber all the drengs and duguos of my fyrd. If Guthrum brought his entire host south, then I would have the choice of fighting for northern Wessex while I lose Kent and maybe some more eastern shires, or stay in the east and have our heartland devastated. As it stands now, if Guthrum keeps his word, I should be able to crush the Vikings at Rochester, and, if I catch so much as one of Guthrum's warriors on our land, then I will have the excuse I need to take London and build a buffer north of the Thames."

"A buffer, brother?"

"Ambrose, I am tired of the Thames being a highway for the Viking fleets. By taking the north bank, and London in particular, we will close that particular route for good."

Suddenly Alfred turned again to his map of the West Saxon Empire. "Well, Polonius, how do we do it?"

"How do we do what, Sire?"

"Defeat the Danes, Scholar, defeat the Danes."

"Which ones, Sire? A moment ago we were talking of lifting the siege of Rochester, and suddenly we are attacking London."

The king smiled. "You are right. We should plan one conquest at a time. Let's start with Rochester."

Polonius stroked his chin before replying. "How big a risk do you want to take, Sire?"

The king grinned wolfishly. "I would like a total victory with no losses, Wizard."

Polonius smiled. "Calling me a wizard will not change your losses column, Sire. I repeat - what losses are you willing to accept?"

The king sat silently for a full minute before he replied. "Victory is more important than losses. We must teach the heathen devils a lesson. Guthrum of East Anglia, Guthred of Northumbria, their heathen friends in Francia, and even your friends in Dublin will be watching what we do. If we fail to act decisively, one or more just might decide to join in. Then we could be in serious trouble."

"So you are willing to risk the fyrd's defeat, Sire?"

"If the odds are in my favor, then yes, I must, Polonius. Did you not tell me that your old friend Sun Zoo once said 'unless you enter the tiger's lair, you cannot get hold of the tiger's cubs?'"

"He was hardly my friend, Sire. His name was Sun Tzu, and he died hundreds of years before our lord Jesus Christ was even born. You have, however, quoted him correctly. I assume that you are telling me that you are willing to take a large risk if the end justifies it."

Alfred smiled. "Exactly so, Scholar."

The thin Byzantine smiled back. "Sire, with all due respect, we are moving steadily eastward with only a small part of your army. We must make some more decisions before we reach the Vikings."

"What do you mean, Scholar?"

"Sun Tzu also said that 'if you set a fully equipped army to march in order to snatch an advantage, the chances are you will be too late. On the other hand, to detach a flying column for the purpose involves the sacrifice of its baggage and stores.'"

"So are we going to risk a small flying column of my best mounted fyrdmen in a lightening-fast thrust, as we did in Wales, or are we going to move ponderously eastward in a massive and slow-moving column, knowing all the time that Rochester could fall at any time?"

"That is the choice Sun Tzu was alluding to."

"Polonius, what if I told you that we will do a little of both."

"You have my attention, Sire. And I thought I was the wizard here. Just how is this magical feat possible?"

"First, I want assurances that all of the people along the Thames and in Kent have moved to the defensive burhs we have designated, along with the men sworn to protect them. If we want the army to stay intact, the men need to know that their families are safe."

"Returning messengers have reported that garrison troops are manning their walls. Most of the people in Kent who can, have long-ago fled to safety, along with most of the people along the Thames River.

"That is excellent news. Then order my vanguard to press forward as far as Gravesend. The men of Kent can meet us there."

"And the rest? You still have over a thousand fyrdmen on the road, some from as far away as Cornwall, and their retainers, and hundreds of wagons, loaded with most of our supplies, plodding in your wake."

"Let them gather at Greenwich. I would expect most of them to arrive within a week or so of me reaching Rochester. When the force is powerful enough, it can move forward to Gravesend. If all goes well, then we might not even need them."

"Because?"

"I am really glad that you asked that question, Polonius. You mentioned the attack on Carnarvon in Wales. I am thinking of attempting another *Long Ride*. I need to get there before Rochester falls. We just might surprise the Viking devils, and, at the least, my thanes can provide the needed backbone for the Kentish levies."

"Sire, you clearly do not remember the pain you felt when we last tried it."

The King grinned. "I remember all too well, Scholar! I think I even let you rub horse liniment on a King's regal bottom."

"And I was discreet, Sire."

"Very wisely so, Scholar. Now, as I was saying, in spite of the obvious pain we all suffered, the Long Ride was sensationally effective. We arrived without warning and actually took Carnarvon with only nominal losses."

"Sire, do you plan to take the Viking fort in the same manner?"

"I don't think that we are going to be able to force their gate open as we did in Wales, no. That took disguised fyrdmen guarding the roadways, men on the inside and total surprise. Even if the Long Ride doesn't give us entry to their fort, what I had in mind was to bypass any foraging or raiding parties and hopefully reach the fort before they can adequately provision the place."

"And when we get there?"

"We cut down any Vikings who are caught outside the gates. Perhaps we can get the men of Rochester to sally forth and lure the

Vikings out of their own fortification. We might even, with luck, find their fleet undefended and be able to capture or burn it. I know Ambrose is eager for us to take any Viking vessel we can. Once the fleet is neutralized one way or the other, we would be able to kill the heathen devils at our leisure . . . Why are you looking unsure, Scholar?"

"I am just thinking, Sire. I think it is possible the Long Ride will achieve surprise, but if we destroy or seize their fleet, the Vikings will have no choice but to stand and fight. I fear that that might cause a serious problem."

"And what is that, Scholar?"

"The Vikings are always reluctant to risk their entire forces. Their numbers are limited and reinforcements for them are very far away. As you know, Sire, they are brave men who will fight to the death if they must. To die in battle, in fact, is their only hope of being taken to *Valhalla*. I have known of dying grandfathers who asked their sons to carry them into battle so they can die fighting as a proper warrior. Should you destroy their fleet and trap them, they will have no choice but to fight to the last man."

Alfred spoke. "And I will be happy to see every stinking Viking corpse. What are your thoughts?"

"The arrival of your flying column will ensure that Rochester will not fall. Once that task is accomplished, your entire army, reinforced with your slower-moving infantry and supplemented by the Kentish greater fyrd, moves to the attack. If the Danes don't meet us in open combat, then we besiege their camp.

We make no effort to block the path to their ships, however. When they see the numbers arrayed against them and hunger starts to set in, they will simply sail away."

"That is not the message I wish to send to the world, Scholar."

"You achieve a victory, Sire, and it costs you few casualties."

"Except, Polonius, the Vikings are undefeated and may simply decide to land elsewhere in our territory. No . . . we let them flee, but our fleet is waiting for them and gives us the victory. We must have our fleet patrolling off-shore, Scholar."

Polonius looked suddenly grim. "It will not be quite that simple, Sire."

"Not that simple? What exactly does 'not that simple' mean,

Scholar?"

"There are delays, Sire, with the crewing of some of the ships."

Alfred's face went red. "Delays!? You told me just before you headed north that the recruiting of Frisian refugees was going very well."

"It is not the mercenaries that are the problem, Sire. It is our own people."

"The sea-duty thanes hold their farms or their tuns on the sole understanding that they will build ships and row them when I bloody-well tell them to! Tell the ship captains to record the names of those who are tardy. We will be levying fines and re-distributing land soon enough to those who fought faithfully for their king! . . . Now, how long?"

"I would estimate at least another two weeks before the fleet will be completely manned and gathered at Dover, but even then it will not be the entire fleet. Some ships that were promised have yet to be completed."

Alfred grew even angrier. "Rochester could fall in two weeks. The garrison is depending on us for relief, and the ealdorman's men are dying in the forests of Kent. Polonius, I was counting on the fleet to arrive just as we complete the Long Ride."

"Then you have answered your own question, Sire. You will have a powerful force of your best mounted fyrdmen at Gravesend within a few nights, ready and willing to make the Long Ride. Most of the settlements have already moved their families and livestock to the burhs, or are in the process of doing so. Your camp holds almost fifteen hundred well-armed fyrdmen and their retainers, Sire, as we speak. As many more should be on the way soon, though many of the rest will be churls following in the wake of their thanes. Most do not have a horse, but they do have wagons, weapons, and most of our food supply."

The king sighed. "And Kent?"

"Thousands fled the Viking arrival in panic, but word is that many able-bodied men are flocking to the gathering points. They should be already moving slowly towards Rochester."

Alfred broke his pacing in mid-stride. "I do not want the Kentish fyrdmen to close on the Vikings until we arrive. We both know that the Kentish greater fyrd would be torn to shreds by the Vikings in open combat, and such a defeat at this moment would totally demoralize my army. The Kentish fyrdmen need the leavening of a lot more heavily armored and trained warriors in order to survive against Vikings."

"They are doing well so far, Sire. They skulk in the woods and attack small bands of marauders any time they have overwhelming numbers."

"So how many ships can we have off the tun in a week, Polonius."

"If you had your entire fleet, Sire, then you just might be able to take on the crews of fifteen long-ships, but even then your ships would be no match for Guthrum's fleet. A set battle of the three fleets would likely shatter your new fleet and lose you crews that are utterly irreplaceable."

"It is a risk, Polonius, but if we have to, we can cut more trees and assign more men to a new fleet."

"Sire, the ancient Romans used to claim that it took five full years to completely train a legion. You can call up warriors who can sail in a ship in a matter of weeks, but to have men who can read the wind and the waves - that takes a lifetime of training. If you lose such men, Sire, you will not be able to replace them. There are few enough Saxons left who fish and know the ways of the sea."

"Then we hire more Frisians, Scholar!"

"We have hired many, Sire, but they are not an inexhaustible resource."

Alfred sighed. "Polonius, I am in favor of destroying every last Viking, whatever the cost. We must make it very plain that Wessex will never again tolerate Vikings on our soil. I understand your concern, but I am not sure that we should not take the risk."

"Sire, would you rather risk the fleet, or have the sailors on your shield-wall? Until the full fyrd catches up with us, we barely outnumber an enemy that is securely ensconced behind walls."

"I suppose we could use more good foot soldiers, couldn't we?"

"Yes, Sire."

Alfred sighed again and held his stomach. "Then send word

that the ships are to be tied up in Dover and the men are to ride for Rochester."

"There will not be enough horses to mount all the sailors, Sire."

"Then they walk, Scholar, but send word that I want them at Rochester within four nights! And Polonius?"

"Yes, Sire?"

"I think I need a few drops of your elixir. My stomach is on fire."

The Byzantine scholar stared at the King and then nodded. "First I will get the medicine and then I will issue the orders, your Majesty."

Alfred smiled. "And get a supply of horse liniment, Polonius."

"I will get a large supply of horse liniment, King, but discreetly."

Ambrose laughed. "Enough for four, my Byzantine friend!"

Polonius spoke to his king. "There is no word from the sailors, Sire, except that they are on their way."

"And Raedan and his men?"

"They have been bloodied, Sire, but Raedan has sent word that they will join the battle as soon as he sees you or hears the sound of battle."

"Excellent, then call the men to assembly. It is time to ride!"

Polonius bowed. "As you command, Sire."

Alfred faced almost a thousand of his sworn fyrdmen and slightly more than five hundred of their best mounted retainers. He spoke with a stentorian voice and then paused often so that his words could be relayed to the more distant men.

"Men of Wessex! Today we ride the Long Ride . . . Rochester is about thirty miles due east . . . Once we start, you will stop for nothing . . . If your horse is blown or comes up lame, then leave it and switch to your remount . . . If you fall behind, you will be left to catch up as best you can . . . Our task is to outrun any Viking spies, raiders or scouts who may be out there . . . I want the first hint of our presence at Rochester to be the appearance of your avenging swords and spears . . . Ignore raiding parties . . . Once we cut off the head and tear out the heart of this army, we will mop up the rest.

We ride for the fort . . . If we can enter and hold the gate, we will do so . . . Otherwise, kill any Viking you can find and head off any supplies heading for their fort . . . If you hear two long horn blasts from my signalers, you will ride for the fleet on the Medway River . . . If we cannot seize their fort, we will try and take or burn their fleet . . . We ride to the glory of God and for Wessex! Mount up!"

The huge column of riders, several miles long, swept along the old Roman road at a mile eating trot. Almost fifteen hundred riders, each armed, armored and with a spare mount, rode without pause for Rochester.

Several times, Ambrose could see the smoke from burning villages, but Alfred just cursed and urged his own mount on faster. The king spoke to his brother.

"Ambrose, somewhere over there my people are dying. It is hard not to stop, but I tell myself that it is better that we cut off the head than one small finger."

"Are you sure you do not want me to take a detail and hang some pirates, Alfred?"

"I would like nothing better, brother-of-mine, but I need the full force to strike against Rochester. As Polonius quite rightly pointed out, until our secondary force, the Kentish greater fyrd and the sailors all arrive, we are perilously close to being outnumbered by the heathen pirates. We know that some of Guthrum's ships have arrived with reinforcements, but we do not know the numbers. We could yet find ourselves outnumbered. Our biggest ally today is surprise, and every man counts."

As Alfred spotted the walls of Rochester, he signaled the columns to separate and the battle horns to be sounded. As a flood of riders poured off the ancient Roman road, the sound of dozens of horns echoed as far as the city itself. Hundreds of Viking heads turned as one.

Without any hesitation, the Angelisc riders spurred towards the ancient Kentish tun and the Viking fortification sitting impudently in front of it. Hundreds of Danes were harassing the defenders on the Rochester walls or were working in the open, secure in the thought that the men trapped within were too few to come out and hurt them. Herds of cattle accompanied by large numbers of Viking horses were calmly grazing under the watchful eyes of a few sentries.

Two of the three Saxon columns transformed into skirmish lines, and suddenly the scattered Vikings were facing a charge by a continuous wall of horseflesh. Alfred led his column of Personal Guardsmen directly at the fortress gate, while the other two lines engaged and cut down any Danes luckless enough to be caught outside the walls. Isolated, the Vikings were no match for the solid lines of hard-riding Saxon warriors.

Alfred's compact column easily punched through the scattered Danes as far as the approach to the gate, but a throbbing horn sounded, of a timbre deeper than the Saxon war horns. The gates swung shut almost in his face. He turned breathlessly to Ambrose. "Brother, we almost had the devils!"

"Let us fall back, King. The gates are closed and I see archers gathering on the wall."

Alfred held his sword high in frustration, but Ambrose knew his brother was a good enough leader to realize that he was endangering his best men if he stayed near the gate. No warrior of his Personal Guard dared retreat while his king faced danger. Cursing, Alfred turned his horse and retreated back to the little knoll where he had told his standard-bearer to wait for him.

The other two lines, sweeping wide around the Viking fort, continued to find and run down panicked Vikings. The attack was over within minutes, however. The Danes were either safely inside their fort, or dead. Alfred's well-trained forces started to regroup and return to the king's prominently displayed banner.

Alfred watched his riders returning to him, mixed in with jubilant warriors from Rochester. The ramparts of the Danish fort were now lined with armored warriors, each hammering his shield with his sword and calling, "Odin! Odin!" The moment had passed. The Danish fort was secure against anything Alfred had with him. The king turned to his companions. "How many heathens died today, Scholar?"

"Several hundred, Sire, and your column prevented any of the animals from being driven within their walls. We did not quite catch them with their breeks down, but I suspect their larder is pretty bare."

Ambrose spoke. "The men have re-grouped, brother. Shall we go after the ships?"

"Aye, brother! Signaler, blow two long blasts."

Polonius held up his hand. "Wait a moment, Sire! There is something happening."

Alfred spoke. "I see Raedan's men running from the forest to join us."

"Not that, Sire. Look towards the Viking fort."

The king scanned the fort anxiously. "What is it, Polonius?"

The Byzantine pointed. "There! I thought I saw a glint of armor just behind the Viking fort . . . right there. And listen, the men remaining on the Rochester walls are screaming themselves hoarse."

"I see it, Scholar. By the robe of sweet Jesus! It looks like the heathens are running for their ships. Signaler, blow the attack!"

The exhausted Angelisc warriors turned their horses again and rode hard after the escaping Vikings. The Danes were brave men, however, and, now that they had had time to organize, they retreated in a fighting wedge. There was little Alfred's warriors could do. The Saxon riders threw their spears and picked at the edge of the wedge, but the Vikings gave as good as they got. The fastest Kentish fyrdmen caught up to the escaping Vikings, but could do little damage. The fighting retreat became a war of attrition where neither side had a clear advantage. The Vikings were all veteran warriors from the Frankish wars, and the Saxons were not trained cavalrymen. Dozens died on both sides, but Alfred's warriors were unable to prevent the wedge from reaching the safety of the sturdy palisades that guarded the fleet.

The king roared in anger as his force neared the palisades.

"Dismount! Form the shield-wall! Forward, men-of-Wessex! Kill as many as you can before they escape!'

Alfred was furious. 'Look, Ambrose. The Northmen are escaping. Why, in God's name, did I leave the fleet at Dover?"

"Because, Alfred, without the men of the fleet and the warriors of Kent, your army is actually outnumbered by the Francian Vikings and their friends who are at this minute running. And then there is the little matter of Guthrum's fleet - we still don't know where it is."

"Well, my sailors are doing little good right now tromping down some God-forsaken road, and I know where a good part of Guthrum's damned fleet is! It is sailing away as we watch."

"And could our fleet have taken on those thirty vessels?"

"Well, perhaps not until all of our God-cursed ships showed up, and, even then it might have been close!"

"And that, brother, is why our fleet is at Dover."

"Ambrose, we must punish the pirates. We must set an example. Just chasing them away is not enough."

"What do you want to do, Alfred?"

"I want us to track them to their lairs and I want to burn their ships. Then I want to kill them."

Polonius arrived on a blown horse and dismounted. "Sire, I rode down-river and counted fifteen ships fleeing with the emblem of Guthrum prominent on their sails.

Alfred went red. "Then by your count, Scholar, fully half of the force I faced today was Guthrum's warriors! He will rue this day!"

Polonius nodded. "Make no mistake, Sire. We surprised and panicked the Danes, but they are masters of the sea battle and would fight like demons if they could reach our fleet. They are not yet crushed, and you may be sure that right now they are very hungry for revenge."

The king took two steps forward and lifted the thin Byzantine off his feet. "Ah, Polonius, what would I do without you and Ambrose? You are the voice of my conscience. Even if I do not appear to like your words, I command you to always tell me the truth."

Polonius gasped. "Only if you let me breathe, Sire."

Alfred put Polonius down and grinned. "You are right as ever, my friend. I would hate to turn a victory into a defeat and lose my fleet. We were just so close to breaking them."

Ambrose hugged his brother. "God has granted you a victory today, Alfred. The siege of Rochester is lifted. The Danish fort is abandoned, hundreds of Danes lie dead or wounded on the shore, and it seems likely that they were unable to carry much of their spoils with them in that fighting wedge. I suppose this is not a bad day's work, brother."

"You mean that the Dane's camp might still hold some of their treasure? God is merciful! It may be that we can return to Mother Church some of its looted treasures.

Phillip! Take two squads of my Personal Guard and assign men to guard both gates to the Viking fortress. I want no Saxons to enter until I give permission. Ambrose, Polonius, would you care to take a tour of an abandoned Danish fort?"

As they rode slowly back to the Viking fort, hundreds of riderless horses trotted by, caught up in the excitement. Ambrose grinned. "The herds of Francian horses seem especially fine, Alfred."

"Francian?"

Ambrose smiled. "There is no way that all of these mounts came from Kent. I think the Danes imported a fine herd just for you. I am curious to see what else the Danes left behind, king and brother!"

The first thing Ambrose noticed as he rode past the Saxon thanes on guard duty and through the now open main gate of the Viking fort was the odor. He had smelled it before, when the Cretan pirates had taken him to their slave quarters. It was an odor he would never forget, consisting of equal parts of sweat, despair, urine and feces. Hundreds of captives stared dully at him from behind wooden bars. They were mainly older children of both sexes, and adolescent or young adult women. There was a smattering of men, but Ambrose knew that most of the men would have died trying to protect their families. There were no babies or old men or women. The prince knew that these did not sell well in the slave markets, so they would have had their heads bashed open and been left to die where they fell by the callous Danes.

Alfred held his nose as he stared at the hundreds of captives. He sighed. "May God be merciful! Polonius, would you organize their release? They need clean sleeping quarters, food, and water to wash. A lot of water to wash!"

"I will arrange for them to use the Danish quarters, Sire, unless you have another use for them."

"No, that would be perfect. The army can be billeted in Rochester until our tents and other supplies reach us. Ambrose, let us go and seek treasure. I think that solid looking building by the command tent would be a good place to start our hunt."

Ambrose struck the lock twice with a borrowed battle axe, until it popped open. He then opened the doors of the solid building next to the Viking commander's tent. He and Alfred picked up a flaming torch each and stepped into the gloomy interior. Almost at once, the king gasped.

"Brother, look at the gold and silver! There is a king's ransom in here."

Ambrose stared and then sighed. "Merciful God! How many poor priests died protecting these sacred vessels? How many Kentish churches were gutted to produce so much treasure? In fact, either the Kentish churches were richer than I would have believed, or some may have come from Frankish churches, Alfred."

"Well Ambrose, we will return all we can to our own churches. As for the rest, we will make a generous donation to holy Mother Church and then use the rest to help defray our expenses."

CHAPTER 11

Alfred Wants to Hunt Down the Attackers

Alfred looked at his ealdormen and his advisers over the dying fire. "Warriors and nobleman, it is true that we have won a victory here today. To chase away the Vikings is not enough, however."

Ethelwold, ealdorman of Dorset and son of a former king, spoke up. His hate for Alfred was almost palpable as he spoke. "King, Rochester is safe, the Vikings are driven from our land, and you have won horses and treasure today. My father would have been content. What more can you want?"

"All that you say is true, Ealdorman. The Viking army escaped relatively intact. I do not think that they have sufficiently learned their lesson. If we do not punish them severely, they may be back, and, if they come with Guthrum's Army, then all Wessex will be in great peril."

Ealdorman Ethelwold nodded. "Today we have killed hundreds of the heathens, and even as we speak, your men are hanging over a hundred more wounded or captured. And just how, King, do you intend to punish Vikings who have sailed far away in ships that over-match our own, and are probably in safe harbors that belong to a powerful Viking king - one who has not even declared war on you?"

Alfred stood. "Ealdorman, I am glad that you have touched upon the subject of Guthrum. Today, just hours ago, we identified up to fifteen ships that fled with his insignia prominent on their sails. Guthrum, too, must be punished."

The ealdorman was not finished yet. "King, today you defeated a powerful enemy. It seems like you now wish to take on a second, even more powerful enemy. The man is your godson, and he did not bring his army south against Wessex. In spite of this, you wish to declare war on him."

"It is true that Guthrum did not bring his full force south, but he is probably about to harbor the Francian Vikings, and he allowed fifteen ships - fifteen ships, Ealdorman, to join the invaders. By Almighty God, that is fully half of the attackers! I find fifteen shiploads of his men attacking Rochester, and you preach forgiveness! Guthrum was feeling out our resolve - and make no mistake - if the attackers had taken Rochester, he would have come south. Guthrum has not prevented his warriors from invading my kingdom, and for this he must be punished!"

The Ealdorman of Dorset spoke one last time as he took his seat. "If you are so determined, king, then you will have to find out where the Francian fleet has gone. Then you will have to risk our precious fleet deep in Guthrum's territorial waters."

"Aye, you are right there, Ethelwold. That is the crux of the problem. We must locate and identify the Francian ships, and before they escape to continental waters.

Suddenly King Alfred rose to his feet again. After listening for hours to various suggestions and concerns from his councillors, he had made up his mind what to do. He started speaking quickly.

"Ambrose, send the fastest messenger you can find. Turn my crewmen around. I want them back in Dover and setting sail for Rochester within two nights. I want my fleet here as soon as humanly possible.

Polonius, send out your eyes and ears. Promise a little gold to our Frisian friends. I want to know where the Francian Vikings went to, and I want to know where Guthrum's ships went."

"Are you expecting either to return?"

"If the entire fleet is sitting in East Anglia, then that, along with considerable reinforcements, is a real possibility. If they split, then I think that we have won the day."

Ambrose stared at his brother. "Alfred, I have a thought. Do we not have any Viking long-ships in our fleet?"

Alfred looked at Polonius. "Scholar?"

Polonius spoke. "I have not seen them personally, but Odda reported taking a raider last year, and I think that one or two others were seized and now should be at Dover. Why do you ask, Prince?"

Ambrose stroked his chin. "Ethelwold had a point. In order to punish the Vikings from Francia, we have to know where they are. The same would also apply to Guthrum's men."

Polonius spoke again. "We have many eyes in East Anglia. Not many Saxons like their new masters. Our eyes and ears have a problem, however. They are not normally allowed to travel far. Our agents will ride north within a night or two, but it will take considerable time to spread the word and then get replies."

Ambrose smiled. "Exactly. But what would happen if a lost Viking ship headed north tomorrow?"

Alfred spoke. "I fear that we would lose a ship and many good men."

"Do we not have enough Viking speakers amongst our fyrdmen to man a single ship?"

"I do not think, Ambrose, that Guthrum will show mercy just because my warriors speak his language."

"But Alfred, they will be crewing a Viking vessel, wearing Viking clothing, and speaking the Viking tongue. They will be landing amongst much confusion, and they will have Viking trade goods. Why would Guthrum's men assume they are anything but what they seem?"

"I had intended to send our Frisian friends north as soon as possible."

"Alfred, you know as well as I do that Guthrum does not trust the Frisian traders. He knows they spy for us. We discussed it openly when I visited him."

"What I suspect you are telling me is that I can wait for Polonius' spy network to filter back information over weeks or months, or I can send my brother on another suicide mission."

Ambrose nodded. "The Francian Vikings will not sit in East Anglia long, brother, and Guthrum's forces may simply disperse and go home. You do not have long if you want to strike a decisive blow."

"Brother, after what you did in spying on Ubbi and attacking Dag's ships, I would be foolish to send you north again. The scops across the island still recite the ballads about you, and I understand that some Vikings are not amused by your doings. More and more they are calling you 'Dane-slayer.'"

"Alfred, it is your only hope if you wish to strike before the enemy force disperses."

"Ambrose, suppose I listened to your crazy idea for one moment - just how would you plan on fooling the Vikings?"

"The ship and men should not be suspect. The cargo should be easily obtained from the supplies left behind in the fort."

"But what story could you give that would justify your presence there?"

Ambrose shrugged. "Let's see - we are Swedish Vikings coming south to join the Francian Army. We were surprised to find that the force we intended to join has split. We tried to ascend the Seine River into Eastern Francia, but were attacked by an overwhelming force of Franks. Thus, when we heard about an attack on Rochester, we sailed across the channel to join in. After almost being captured by the terrible king Alfred, we fled north to the land of our Danish cousins."

King Alfred looked at his brother. "I do not wish to lose you, Ambrose. You have already risked your life too many times for Wessex."

"I will never rule, brother. I am a warrior sworn to the defense of you and Wessex. Warriors are called upon every day to risk their lives. I can do no less."

Alfred sighed. "You know that I want the information, brother, and I do not see any other way to obtain it. I want you to know, however, that my fleet will be close behind you."

Ambrose smiled. "I am counting on it. Then when can I leave?"

Polonius interrupted. "Prince, it is unlikely that Rus warriors would arrive in a Danish ship."

"What is different between a Rus and a Danish vessel, Scholar?"

"The construction is the same. I think the biggest difference would be the color of the shields and the sail."

Ambrose smiled. "So we paint the shields and have a new sail made up."

Alfred looked concerned. "That is a large task to complete in just a few days."

Ambrose spoke. "Alfred, the Rus sails are made up of

hundreds of triangles of wool. A hundred men working individually should be able to make up the triangles quickly enough. It will take some talented sewers, however, to put them together in a Rus pattern and then sew the triangles together."

Alfred looked thoughtful. "I will have some sailors take apart any woollen sails we have. If necessary, I will put the entire army to work on the sail. You will have it, brother, in a matter of days. Now to other things. Ambrose, did you send the messengers to the fleet as I asked?"

"Of course, brother. They left less than hour after you gave the command."

"Then the ships should arrive within a couple of nights."

Polonius spoke. "Why do I not send a mounted courier tonight direct to Dover? There should be enough late arrivals trickling in to man a single Viking long-ship. It could probably get here a night or two before the rest of the fleet."

Ambrose nodded. "Phillip, can I ask you to round up a full crew of sailors who speak the Viking tongue fluently?"

"It shall be done, Prince."

Alfred spoke. "Brother, put together a crew, but you will not sail until the entire fleet arrives and is readied for the expedition."

"Brother, I can go ahead and scout north as far as the Stour estuary. I can hardly do that with the Saxon fleet in tow."

"You are right in that, but I said I will be close behind you, and I meant it. We will go north when the entire fleet is ready, and not one night before."

"It may be weeks before the fleet has gathered and is properly re-vitaled."

"Then it will be weeks before you can go north, brother . . . No, don't argue with your king. On this I am adamant."

Ambrose nodded reluctantly. "You are king, brother. I will obey. While I am waiting, perhaps you will let me take a force of a few hundred mounted fyrdmen west along the coast."

"Of course, if you wish it. You have already done more than your share, however, brother. I can just as easily send a young commander who is eager to prove his prowess to me, or even the old warhorse Odda."

"Some of the Viking vessels were seen to turn west when they hit the estuary, brother, instead of east and the open sea."

"You think they may land upriver and raid, Ambrose?"

"I will watch for them, as well as take care of any raiding parties that have not yet made it to the north side of the river. Who knows - with luck, I may be able to add a vessel to your fleet."

Alfred sighed. "I hope you find another one of your *sun-stones*, brother. I know that is what you are hoping to find."

"I will try and find one if I can, but I will also escort the supply column here. I will still be back before the whole fleet arrives."

Alfred hugged his brother. "Go with God, Ambrose. May He look over you and protect you . . . Oh, and be sure to be back here in *seven-night*. I will make sure your ship, and the entire fleet, will be waiting for you, ready to sail."

CHAPTER 12

Guthrum's Men on the South Bank

Ambrose stared gloomily out of his tent door. It was early summer, but on the Thames estuary, it was both windy and freezing cold. The water was being whipped into whitecaps and the prince pulled his cloak tighter. Nearby, four hundred of his brother's sworn fyrdmen dozed, cooked, or repaired worn equipment.

The prince sighed. He knew that there would be more rain before noon, and they still had a long ride before the day would mercifully end.

Phillip suddenly thrust through the opening. "Good morning, Prince. Are you ready to ride?"

"I would rather sleep for a week and let my backside heal, but yes, after a warm meal, I suppose I can be ready."

"Polonius prepares it as we speak, Prince. What is our goal today?"

"The same as yesterday, Weapons-master. We search for any last remnants of the Viking raiding parties, watch out for any new raiders who might have crossed the Thames, and otherwise ride west towards Southwark. It now seems unlikely that Guthrum is coming south, but if he does and manages to get past Southwark, he will tear our supply column to pieces if we are not there to reinforce it."

Even as Ambrose spoke, a fyrdmen burst in. Ambrose looked up. "What is it, Thane Ryscford?"

"Prince, we just spotted two columns of smoke to the west!"

Ambrose looked at the thane. "A burning village or a signal pyre?"

"Don't know, Prince Ambrose."

Ambrose sighed. "Well, in neither case can we afford to ignore it. It looks like our hot meal will have to wait, old friend. No battle horns. Just tell the men to mount up quietly. If it is Danes, we don't want to alert them."

Phillip stood straight. "At once, Prince! Shall I tell the men to break camp?"

"No, leave everything where it is. If it is a real attack, then every second counts. If it is a false alarm, we can return and finish breakfast at our leisure."

Phillip soon had the officers rousing the men and sending them to gather their armor and weapons. The veteran fyrdmen were soon dressed for war and then they went off to find their hobbled mounts. In less than a half hour from when the smoke was sighted, the entire force was mounted and ready.

The column swept westward along the empty Roman road. The first column of smoke was indeed a signal pyre, put there to warn neighbors of enemy raiders. The men manning it waved to the column leaders. Ambrose rode close and then reined in his horse.

"I am Ambrose, Prince of Wessex. What is the purpose of your signal fire?"

"Sirs! We were praying that there was a Saxon force nearby! There is a little village on the riverbank less than a mile west of here! The villagers returned yesterday, having heard of good King Alfred's great victory over the Danes. Just this morning, however, a Viking craft beached before dawn and the heathen devils attacked the village. Please, Prince, hurry! The people are being butchered!"

"You! Swing up behind me. I want to waste no time finding the village. And you! Yes, you. Do you know where the ship landed?"

"Aye, Master!"

"Then climb up behind my big friend here. Phillip, when we get close, I want you to take sixty riders and attack the ship. Ride right up to it and kill the sentries before they can get the ship into deep water."

Phillip growled. "I well remember watching our fyrdmen standing idly on the shore while we were kidnaped by the Viking raiders, Prince. Consider it done!"

"And Phillip, I don't want it looted until I have had a chance to search it thoroughly."

"If there is a sun-stone aboard, Prince, I will make sure that you get it."

Ambrose smiled at Phillip for a moment. "I will keep searching until I find another one, old friend. Such a stone is beyond price. Now let's ride!"

Ambrose swept his hand in a forward motion and instantly the column of warriors started forward at a quick trot.

Realizing that the village was now very near, Ambrose signaled Phillip. As soon as the sixty men peeled off after the giant, Ambrose led the rest of the warriors at a reckless gallop. Following the instructions of his guide, he swerved off the ancient road and charged through an apple orchard. Suddenly, the stunted trees thinned and the village was before them.

Ambrose took in the situation at a glance. The village's defenses were rudimentary. The primitive palisade, without even a dry moat, had easily been overcome by the Viking raiders, and the Danes were in the midst of raping and pillaging when the fyrdmen arrived.

At heart foot soldiers, no matter how often Polonius tried to teach them cavalry tactics, the burly sworn men of Alfred's fyrd swung off their mounts and attacked on foot with relish.

Ambrose swung down with his men. Bodies of innocent villagers lay sprawled obscenely on either side of the primitive palisades. The men of the village had fought hard and died, but they had been unsuccessful in preventing the raiders from reaching their families.

The Vikings were shocked to see hundreds of armored fyrdmen pouring into the village, but they, too, were veterans. Isolated individuals dropped loot or released terrified captive women. They instinctively joined partners, and the little groups quickly became larger as warriors scrambled to join comrades. Within moments, most of the raiders were standing shoulder to shoulder with at least a couple of their companions.

It did little good, however. Three hundred very angry fyrdmen charged perhaps a hundred Vikings, some of whom were naked or drunk. The battle was over in seconds.

Ambrose closed on one giant warrior. Suddenly he recognized him. He cried out. "Little Egil! I am surprised that King Guthrum has let you live."

"You! I live in hiding, thanks to you, Saxon! I have to skulk in the woods when my own king rides by!"

"I am not surprised. A man of honor would have kept his clothes and charged my arrow. You betrayed your own king's hospitality. What are you doing in Kent, Viking?"

"You will no doubt be pleased to know that, since I was declared outlaw, Guthrum took my gold and silver and my land. I came south with a band of comrades to renew my fortune. It seemed only appropriate that I would take the gold from your land, Saxon!"

"Little Egil, I thought I told you to stay north of the river!"

"It is Egil the Little, Saxon. Your brother butchered some of my cousins at Rochester, Canuteson. We are going to repay you a hundred fold!"

"Not today, Viking. It appears that you have led yet another band of brave warriors on a suicide mission."

Egil growled as he swung his sword at Ambrose. The prince dexterously deflected the blow and spoke.

"So you are taking out your revenge on innocent villagers? I don't think this is your day, Egil. Surrender or be cut to pieces!"

The giant shrugged. "You hit me over the head and tied me up. You stuck your sword in my gut. Then you stole my clothes, my last sword, and my honor. You will never get this sword. If the gods are not with me, then today I join Odin in his hall in Valhalla. It beats dying in bed or being hung by you, Anglishman."

Ambrose fended off several more wild slashes, but with difficulty. The warrior was strong. The prince called out to Polonius in Greek. "Are you there, Scholar?"

"As always, Prince. Do you want me to kill the blowhard?"

"No, this is our old friend the would-be assassin. I want him alive. Can you do it?"

"Be prepared to attack when he drops his sword, Prince."

Three daggers suddenly hurtled past Ambrose. Egil was quick and he batted one aside while taking the second on his shield. The third, however, struck deep into the back of his hand and, cursing, the big man was forced to drop his sword.

"That is the best I can do, Prince."

"Little Egil, it looks like you have lost another sword after all."

As Egil's sword hit the ground, Ambrose swung **Victory-Maker** in a head cut. At the last second, however, he twisted the blade and it was the flat of the blade that struck hard against the man's helmet. When the warrior dropped to his knees in stunned confusion, Ambrose swung again and delivered a second blow that rendered the Dane unconscious.

"Polonius, my friend, can you tie this one up securely? It is the proof we need that Guthrum's men came south of the Thames."

While Ambrose's fyrdmen finished off the badly wounded Vikings and tied up the rest of the prisoners, the prince took a small detachment of a dozen men and rode down-river toward where he had been told the Viking ship had landed.

As he followed the winding shoreline, he suddenly came to a screen of trees. A disembodied voice called out in Saxon. "Who approaches?"

Ambrose recognized the voice as a young dreng from Southampton. He stopped the column with a raised hand and replied.

"It is Prince Ambrose, Dreng Godric. May we approach?"

"Uh, of course, Prince! I am sorry - I did not know it was you!"

"You do not have to be sorry when you are but doing your job, Dreng. Just tell your men to unnock their arrows. I do not want any unfortunate accidents today."

"Prince, if you stay on the little path you are following, and then take the fork to the left, you will see the long-ship in no more than another hundred yards."

Ambrose smiled. "Thank you, Dreng. Keep an eye on the trail and the bows handy. I do not want Phillip and his men to be unhappily surprised."

"You can count on me, Prince!"

"Good man.' Ambrose gestured with his right arm to his mounted followers. 'Forward!"

The prince led his little column along the path that meandered along the river bank. Where the path split, he went left. As the path twisted, he suddenly caught sight of a small long-ship floating, but tied to trees both bow and stern. Bodies were strewn along the shore, and an armed shield wall faced him from the ship's deck.

The third man from the stern was a giant, and Ambrose smiled. He called out to his old friend. "Well done, Phillip of Wessex! Did you suffer any casualties?"

The big man smiled back. "The bodies in front of you are all Viking, Prince. We have three wounded, but none seriously."

"Excellent, and what about my sun-stone, Weapons-master?"

The big man grinned. "Come aboard, Prince Ambrose."

Ambrose followed Phillip to the stern. The big man threw open an ornate chest that looked like it may have belonged to the Viking captain.

Ambrose spoke. "I see some well-made clothes, Phillip, but I fear that none will fit."

The big man continued to grin. "Look in the deer hide pouch, Prince."

Ambrose picked up the pouch and suddenly felt his heart pounding. He loosened the pouch's drawstring and turned it upside down with trembling fingers. A thin white stone tumbled into his hand.

Ambrose stared with awe. The stone was more precious to him than gold or diamonds. Ambrose had once owned one, freely given to him by a Viking sea captain. It had helped him reach North Africa safely, allowed him to avoid ambush by letting him ride through the trackless expanses of the North African desert, and, he hoped, it had safely guided his friend Hakim across the burning sands of the Sahara.

"God is good, my friend!"

"God rewards the just, Prince."

⚑

As Ambrose, Polonius and Philip led the veteran fyrdmen

over the rise, they spotted the long sought-after column below. The massive column of wagons, infantry and hangers on of all descriptions topped the rise to the West and snaked down into the valley below.

Below Ambrose were the thousands of late-arriving thanes, churls, slaves, cattle and wagon loads of food and supplies that would support the hard riding mounted fyrdmen who had so recently ridden the Long Ride. Together, the force had crushed Viking armies and rebellious ealdormen. Without a strong leavening of battle-hardened fyrdmen, however, the caravan was actually very vulnerable.

Ambrose, Phillip and Polonius watched the slow-moving column for a full minute. Finally, Ambrose raised his hand and signaled the thanes to advance. Ambrose turned to Phillip. "There they are, Weapons-master. Thanks be to God for keeping them safe . . . let's ride!"

The column of armored thanes thundered down the hill and split to either side of the huge convoy. The fighting thanes rode west to spontaneous cheers from the thousands of Saxons, Angles and Jutes who were trudging east. Ambrose waved merrily as he rode past infantry, wagons and entire families on the move. Suddenly he spotted a massive wagon pulled by a double team of oxen. He pulled out of line and drew his horse to a halt in the meadow beside the old Roman road. Polonius and Phillip joined him. Ambrose spoke. "Phillip, is that not Alfred's royal wagon?"

Phillip pointed further west. "And is that not your wagon, Prince?"

Ambrose just stared. "By all that is holy - what are those doing here?"

Polonius smiled. "I think that you may find out quite soon. I see a woman who looks remarkably like your Gretchen pushing her way through the horsemen."

Ambrose grinned in spite of his anger. Dashing across the meadow was his wife and children!

The prince swung down from his saddle and caught three children who were shrieking in their excitement. After kissing and hugging each one, he put them down just in time to have Gretchen leap into his arms. She spoke breathlessly. "Well met, husband! It is good to see you."

Ambrose continued to hold her close. Phillip and Polonius had dismounted and headed for the royal wagons, presumably to look for their own wives. Ambrose spoke.

"I cannot say that it is not a delight to find you here, but you were supposed to stay in the safety of Winchester."

"I thought you were happy to see me."

"Gretchen, I am. For at least the safety of the children, however, you should have stayed where you all were safe."

"Husband, your eldest daughter has had the first bleeding of a woman, and all are the children of a warrior. They must take their chances. Besides, if Guthrum came south, who is to say what part of Wessex is safe? Is he coming by land or sea? If by sea, he can land anywhere he wants. If land, he will be mounted and his army will be capable of riding long distances in a single day. We have seen his warriors do it before."

Ambrose looked at his wife. "Are you saying that since Guthrum can strike anywhere, it does not matter where you go? Do the walls of Winchester count for nothing?"

"Husband, Queen Ealhswith decided to ride to her husband. I could hardly let her go alone!"

"But my love, do you not realize the danger?"

"Husband, here I am surrounded by almost two thousand armed men. Is there a safer spot in all Britain?"

"Don't let the numbers fool you, my love. If Guthrum had caught up with this force, large as it is, he would have torn through these ranks like a hot sax through butter."

"These are fighting men ready to give their lives in defense of their country, Husband!"

"Wife, they are mainly churls and slaves, with a smattering of thanes on spavined mounts who could not keep up with their king. They could never stand up to the Viking skjaldborg."

"Skjaldborg?"

"Their shield-wall."

"Why would they not?"

"My love, the Vikings are all veterans, and they are well-armored. They will charge forward, throwing their spears. As the individual warriors near, they will throw a pair of hand-axes each, shattering many of the Saxon shields or at least weighting them down. Then they will lock shields and move forward. While most will wield spear or sword, some will carry massive double-handed axes capable of killing a man behind his shield. Against such foes, you would have had farmers with no armor, and some using farm tools as weapons."

"Then what good are they to Alfred? Why are they marching to Rochester?"

"Don't get me wrong, my sweet. Some are good archers or slingers, and others have the skills to build sturdy fortifications. If the armored duguos and drengs, the thanes, provide their front rank, the shield-wall, then these men can provide depth and easily deal with any individual Vikings who manage to hack their way through. They can be very effective, but only if they do not have to face the Viking skjaldborg directly."

Gretchen smiled up at her husband. "But you have brought the very armored and veteran thanes they need to reinforce the host."

"You are safe enough now. Until very recently, wife, you were only a short distance from London and were without the armored riders. You very definitely were not safe."

"Poof. That is why the queen brought your old friend Galar and his fifty thanes, along with enough horses to mount everyone in the royal party. We are not fools, husband. We were prepared to abandon the wagons and ride inland if necessary. . . Are you not pleased that you can rest your weary bones in your own wagon tonight?"

"If you are at my side, my love, I do not care if I have to sleep on bare rock."

Gretchen giggled. "We do have three chaperones in the wagon, husband-of-mine - and who said anything about sleeping?"

Ambrose hesitated. "I am confused. On the one hand you are attempting to seduce me, but on the other you tell me that we will have no privacy tonight."

"I did not tell you the happy news, husband-of-mine. Our children were greatly honored just today."

Ambrose looked puzzled. "How so, my love?"

"Queen Ealhswith has invited all three children to sleep with the royal children tonight. They are going to sleep in their king's own wagon."

"I can only applaud the queen's timing - and her generosity. In that case, then it just may be possible for you to seduce me tonight."

Gretchen just squeezed her husband's hand a little tighter. "To seduce you, husband-of-mine, I generally only have to remove one item of my clothing."

Ambrose squeezed back. "Now that is a lie for which you will have to ask forgiveness from Bishop Asser. I am a discriminating man - it depends on what item you remove."

"Then husband, I will gird myself as did Kuralla on the day she took on those two slavers in the Little St. Bernard Pass."

The prince smiled. "Yes, that just might succeed . . . Did Kuralla and Matilda join the queen's caravan?"

"Kuralla was as eager as the queen and me to return to our husband's side."

"And Matilda?"

"She opted to stay at Winchester. She told me that she had enough children. She is afraid of approaching Phillip again. She feels sure that she would become pregnant."

Ambrose laughed. "It is true. He is away most of the time, yet she manages to deliver a child a year. Still, he will be very disappointed.'

Ambrose sighed. 'Let us catch up with our wagon. The column is leaving without us!"

As they walked after the slow-moving wagon, Phillip and Polonius caught up with Ambrose. Polonius spoke first.

"Do you think you could spare me for a few hours, Master?"

"Polonius, I insist. I want you to lie down in your wagon and rest. I am sure that you are exhausted."

Polonius grinned. "Not yet, Prince, but I will be."

"Go with God, my friend."

Phillip spoke next. "My Matilda is not here, Prince. What do you want me to do?"

"Weapons-master, you are welcome to rest. You have earned it."

"You and Polonius will no doubt be occupied for some time. It appears that I will not be. I am restless, Prince."

"Do you want to gather two hundred men and take a mounted column back down the road towards Southwark?"

"Aye, Prince. I will do that."

"If you see any hint of a Viking force, send messengers and I will join you with the rest of the mounted thanes."

"Understood, Prince. May God be with you!"

"And with you, old friend!"

꩜

The great twisting beast crawled up the hills and down into dales. The commanders in the front ranks were looking for a camp site almost before the last of the straggling women and children broke the previous camp. The progress was torturous, but at least the massive column now had veteran fyrdmen to provide the leavening. The reinforced column was no longer a soft target for even a large Viking force.

꩜

It took three days. On the fourth, the ponderous column marched into the dusk. There would be no roadside camping this night. Not far ahead was Rochester and their king. The grueling march was almost over.

Horns sounded in the twilight when the massive column was first spotted. A large column of armored thanes galloped east, to be met by their companions who had ridden east almost a week before.

With laughter and cheers, the supply column reached the open land around Rochester and dispersed until the meadows were overflowing. As darkness fell, the thousands of men and women who made up the majority of Alfred's army lit fires and sat down stiffly on the grass.

The king, climbing the city wall to watch the arrival and deployment, was shocked to recognize his own wagon.

Abandoning all dignity, he raced towards it.

CHAPTER 13

Ambrose Returns To His Brother's Side

King Alfred smiled. "Now, brother-of-mine, tell me more about this mysterious sun-stone I hold in my hand. You have talked of its value for years, but it does not look like much to me. What is so special about it that you value it more than gold or jewels?"

Ambrose replied. "What do you see, Alfred?"

"I see a thin dirty-white stone, brother. I know you told me that it has great power, but how exactly do you make it tell you directions?"

"The Vikings hold it high, say magic words, and slowly turn completely around. When the long side of the stone faces the sun, even if it is not visible, the stone glows a deep blue. A quarter turn to the left or right, and the stone glows yellow."

"Interesting. And it will do this even on a foggy or cloudy day?"

"It will always tell you where the sun is, as long as there is a tiniest hint of blue sky somewhere. It does not even lose its magic until long after the sun has set.

Alfred, I told you that when the Rus tribesmen went south on their expedition against Byzantium, they crossed the entire Black Sea without one single sighting of land. The Byzantines expect trouble from the north. For hundreds of years, vast armies of barbarians have pressed on Byzantium's northern frontiers. The empire has set up an ingenious series of signaling towers that can send a message hundreds of Roman miles in less than a day. With them in operation, it would be impossible to surprise the city of Constantinople."

"Yet the Rus managed it."

"Yes, partly because the Rus have expert navigators, but mainly because of sun-stones similar to the one you hold in your hand. The first inkling the Byzantines had of our presence was when we sailed into the straits just north of Constantinople."

"Then if we left sight of land, you could bring us back to the coast of East Anglia?"

"I do not have the runes that the Viking navigator had that told him exactly what angle to sail, or what waves to look for when he neared his destination, but, yes, I could bring a ship back to the coast even through light fog. I could not, however, guarantee where on the coast we would hit, or promise to keep the ship off coastal rocks."

"You truly have the magic words that makes the sun-stone work?"

"I pray to Almighty God, brother, and the stone seems to work just as effectively . . . Just what exactly do you have in mind?"

I have no wish for Guthrum to discover our presence before we strike, Ambrose. There are many Viking ships coasting north and south past East Anglia, and I would not be surprised if Guthrum posted lookouts on the headlands. One way or the other, I have no doubt that we would be spotted long before we made it as far north as the Stour River."

". . . Unless we sail far out of sight of land and then cut due west."

Alfred grimaced. "Exactly, brother."

The lithe long-ship kept the various headlands in sight as it traveled north. Ambrose was sure they had been spotted a dozen times, but no ship came out to challenge them.

On the third night since leaving Alfred, Polonius and the main fleet, the lookout called out. "Island ahead!"

Most of the crew rushed to the bow. There, lying very low in the water, was the island as promised by their Frisian navigator. He pointed to it.

"There it is. Prince and Lords. It is uninhabited and rarely used as landfall, except by the odd fishing boat."

"Why is it uninhabited, Navigator? The man shrugged. "There

is no source of fresh water. No crops can grow on the rock, but, most importantly, in the winter season, storms and tides have occasionally combined to drive the water right over the island. Those foolish enough to try and live there have been swept out to sea and lost forever."

"And if a storm arrives as Alfred and the fleet are anchored here?"

"The king will not enjoy the experience much, but the summer storms, while they can be severe, have never, in living memory, driven the water right over the island."

Ambrose stared for several minutes. "Then if all goes well, my brother's fleet should arrive here sometime tomorrow, and he should be safe enough against any summer storm."

"Not necessarily comfortable, Prince, but safe enough if the ships are kept in the lee of the island."

"And your fellow navigators can find it as easily as you?"

"We have all used it for shelter at some time, Prince. They will find it."

꡾

The lithe vessel finally broke free of the savage offshore winds and slid smoothly into the relatively sheltered waters of the Stour River. Moving up-river using the power of the rowers, the ship soon approached a natural landing where the crews of some twenty ships had made a temporary settlement. Their ships were beached or tied up nearby. As Ambrose approached, he could feel eyes following his ship's progress, but no one made a hostile move.

A tall warrior clad in burnished armor waved from the shore. The man cupped his two hands and called out to the crewmen. "Where are you from, strangers?"

Ambrose called back. "We are Rus tribesmen who came south to join our cousins in Francia."

"Then why are you here? You are a long way from Francia."

"Our Danish cousins left before we could arrive. We tried to follow the army up the Seine to Francia Orientalis, but the Franks were not very accommodating. They have built some serious fortifications on both sides of the river. They actually had the nerve to try and burn our ship and kill us."

"That explains why you are not with the army in Francia. You have still not explained why you are in East Anglia."

"Our ship is still full of trading goods, and we had no wish to return home without a little adventure, and hopefully not a little profit."

"And so?"

"And so when we heard that some of our cousins had decided to attack Rochester, we were sure that they would need our skills or at least our supplies. Sadly, we again arrived too late. King Alfred was camped on the spot with a very impressive army. He does not seem to like Vikings overmuch. His horsemen almost caught us on the beach, and he sent several Saxon ships after us."

The Dane smiled. "But you obviously escaped."

Ambrose grinned in return. "What chance did a mere three ship-loads of Saxons have against a Rus long-ship?"

"Ah, then you defeated them all in battle?"

"Perhaps after many drinks, that will be the way we remember it. The truth is, however, we rowed until the blisters broke, and then we rowed harder. I have heard of Alfred's offer to any Viking he can catch - six feet of good land and a hemp rope. Or is it six feet of hemp rope?"

"Well, if you had the good sense to bring good Viking ale from home, then you are welcome indeed!"

"We have several kegs of it."

"Then come ashore, stranger! If you bring those kegs, then you will most assuredly be welcomed."

⚐

Ambrose sat in front of the roaring fire and held out his hands to warm them. Although it was summer, the sea breezes brought in dampness and cold, and Ambrose was glad of the warmth.

The tall *hersir* who had earlier called out to him sat across the fire and spoke. "Well, my friend, this is indeed good ale. You may make your fortune in this camp and never have to raise a sword in battle."

"Nevertheless, Captain, my men will be disappointed. They are spoiling for a good fight."

"I am afraid that you arrive too late, Rus. The Odin-cursed Saxons were too strong for us. The stubborn fools did not know when they were defeated. They held their decrepit old walls against wave after wave of our finest warriors. Then, to add insult to injury, their King Alfred arrived out of nowhere at the head of thousands of his warriors - all mounted on swift horses. Saxon magic must be more powerful than we know. His entire army just suddenly materialized outside our fort. Half a dozen raiding parties and a full two dozen of our scouts were out, but would you believe that not one of them managed to get word to us of the arrival of thousands of Saxon Warriors. We were so surprised that we had to abandon our fort and even the fine horse herds that we had brought so painstakingly all the way from Francia. That Saxon bastard even got some of our Frankish treasure!"

"Then what happens to your army now?"

"That is a good question, and one which is being hammered out in council even as we speak."

"But what do you think is most likely?"

"Personally? I think our Francian Army will probably head back home. All of the Saxon kingdoms on this island, but one, have been conquered, but that one, Wessex, is ruled by a wily bastard. He has repeatedly beaten off Viking armies. I understand that he actually organized one army for his summer campaign, and yet another one for the winter. King Guthrum struck hard into Wessex in a winter campaign some years ago, and almost had the West Saxon king by the balls. This Alfred obviously doesn't want that to happen again."

"That is interesting news. How did you learn of it?"

"Red hot iron persuades most captives to speak; even the stubborn ones. Before we were done, they begged to be allowed to give us information."

Ambrose nodded. "So if you can't go south again, then you can always return to Francia."

"You mean return back to Francia with our tail between our legs?"

"Is that so bad?"

"The West Frankland king is a fool, but he still commands an army five times larger than anything we can put together, and you say he is busy building forts to block the Frankish rivers. The other half of our old force is deep in the interior, with the entire Francian Army between us. Our ships give us mobility along the coast, but, with the rivers blocked, we would not have the mobility to venture far inland without our horse herds."

"Which King Alfred now has."

"Exactly."

"Please do not misunderstand. I am pleased to sell all the ale I have to my Danish cousins, but just why is the fleet sitting here?"

"I told you, Rus-man. The jarls still meet in council and send emissaries to King Guthrum. We need time to mourn our dead and treat our wounded. More important, however, we are waiting to see just what Guthrum is willing to do."

"Then there is still hope that the king will go south?"

"We can pray to Odin that he will, but I think his answer will be no. I suspect that you are going to have to look for your fortune somewhere else."

Ambrose waved as his crewmen turned the long-ship into the current. Soon the fifteen ships and the encampment slipped from view. The captain hoisted the square sail to catch the land-sea breezes, and the sleek vessel surged forward. Behind Ambrose was East Anglia, now a Viking land ruled by King Guthrum. Ahead was an island, and if all had gone well, the Saxon fleet.

The ship pitched heavily as it hit the open waters of the German Sea, but the lithe vessel was designed for the open sea and slipped through the rough waters with ease. The landsmen who had been chosen for their language skills found themselves hurling their last meals overboard, while the experienced sailors laughed uproariously.

Ambrose called out to the Frisian navigator. "Are we on track for the island, Captain?"

"Aye, Prince. Note the angle of the sun. We are on track."

Even as the navigator spoke, the lookout mounted on the mast called out. "Island ahead!"

The navigator grinned. "Even better than I expected, Prince!"

༄

The long-ship was rounding the point when five vessels set off from the island in pursuit. Ambrose watched with great anxiety. "I pray that those are my brother's ships!"

Philip shrugged. "If not, we are a Rus vessel, Prince."

"Aye, you are right, Weapons-master."

As the ships approached, the dragon banners of Wessex could be seen flying from the masts. Ambrose heaved a sigh of relief. "Thank the merciful God! It is Alfred's fleet."

As the five vessels fell into formation around Ambrose's ship, the men waved at friends aboard the other ships. The whole flotilla headed for the sheltered beach that served as harbor on the barren island.

༄

Ambrose hugged first Polonius and then his brother. Alfred held him tight in return and spoke. "You go off on far too many crazy adventures, brother-of-mine. I feared for your very life! You do not know how happy I am to see you."

"It was easier than I had expected, Alfred. We even made a good profit on the cargo."

"And what did you learn, brother?"

"There are some ten Francian Viking ships a few miles up the Stour River estuary. They have set up a temporary settlement at a fishing village."

"And Guthrum's men?

There were also some five of Guthrum's ships, but those captains told me that they were probably heading upriver to home as soon as the combined dead have been honored."

Alfred grinned. "Then if we hurry, we just might catch fifteen

Viking crews sitting on the riverbank!"

"They are still tending their wounded and preparing their dead for the pyre. I do not think they will be leaving for at least another few nights."

"What makes you say that?"

"The funeral arrangements are far from complete. And you, brother - was your fleet spotted on its way north?"

"We went far out to sea, Ambrose, as we had agreed. My Saxons obeyed me only reluctantly. The Frisians are master navigators, however, and they steered us by the stars, the sun, and the currents."

"Then you made the trip without incident?"

"Except when the fog closed on us, brother."

"And?"

Alfred grinned. "And the sun-stone worked exactly as you said. My Frisian navigator offered a pound of gold for it!"

"Then you made the island without been spotted?"

"Not entirely. The island is sometimes used by the fishing fleets. We have seized five fishing vessels so far - all Angle. After we explained the situation to the crewmen, they willingly agreed to remain as our guests for a few days."

"Alfred what do you intend to do with them when we leave?"

"When we head upriver, we will release them, with a little Saxon silver. After that, they can tell their new masters anything they want of our little visit. It simply will not matter."

Alfred turned and spoke to Polonius. "Scholar, you heard. Send word to my captains. I want to meet with them at my tent within the hour! We are going to teach the Viking devils a lesson they will not soon forget."

Polonius spoke. "What about Guthrum, Sire?"

"I do not think that the lesson will be lost on Guthrum. It will not harm him to learn that the arm of Wessex is long enough to reach right into his heartland."

PART TWO

In the same year Alfred, king of the Anglo-Saxons, led his fleet, full of fighting men, out of Kent to the country of the East- Angles, for the sake of plunder; and, when they had arrived at the mouth of the river Stour, thirteen ships of the pagans met them, prepared for battle; a fierce fight ensued, and all the pagans, after a brave resistance, were slain; all the ships, with all their money, were taken. After this, while the royal fleet were reposing, the pagans, who lived in the eastern part of England, assembled their ships, met the same royal fleet at sea in the mouth of the same river, and, after a naval battle, the pagans gained the victory
.....Asser's Life of King Alfred

CHAPTER 14

Alfred's Attack on the Viking Fleet at the River Stour

The Frisian captain hurried aboard the king's flagship. He had been summoned, and Alfred was not a man who liked to be kept waiting. The captain bowed to the West Saxon king. "What are your instructions, King Alfred?"

"Jokul, I want you to take the three Frisian ships up-river until you come to the camp that Prince Ambrose reported."

"And when we spot the camp - what then, Sire?"

"Make very sure that you are seen, and then turn in a panic and flee for the open sea."

"The Vikings are like sight hounds, King. If we run, they will give chase."

Alfred smiled. "I am counting on it. We will be waiting around this point with the rest of the fleet."

The Frisian captain grinned. "There will be much treasure aboard the ships, Sire."

"Then fight bravely, Captain. There will be ample rewards for all the men who participate in the taking."

The captain bowed low. "I hear and obey, great King!"

⚐

The lookout, perched precariously on the top of the mast of Alfred's flagship, called out loudly. "Here they come, Sire! Three Frisian ships, rowing hard!"

"Are there any other ships following?"

"Can't see, Sire . . . Yes! I can see one or two. We would have to go out further for me to see clearly. The ones I can see are in hot pursuit!"

Alfred was jubilant. "Yes! Captain, start towards the point -

quietly. I want our presence to be a complete surprise. Polonius, signal the fleet to follow."

The three Frisian long-ships rounded the point at high speed. As soon as they were out of sight of their pursuers, the skilled crewmen quickly turned their ships around. In unison, one bank of oarsmen strained to hold their oars still while the other crewmen continued to row. With the steering oars twisted far out, the three vessels turned quickly in three identical arcs.

Side by side, Alfred and the Frisian ship captain's vessel almost kissed. Alfred stood anxiously on the bow and called out to his Frisian captain, who stood grinning at him.

"That was well and quickly done, Jokul. You are obviously eager to cross swords with your pursuers."

"No sane man wants to go into battle, King, but you took in my people when the Danes overran my land, and I swore an oath to serve you! Suddenly, Jokul smiled. 'But you are right, my King. Our only hope of fortune lies on those ships. Yes, we are eager to board!"

"What did you learn, Captain?"

"There were still thirteen Viking ships at the encampment Prince Ambrose reported a bit upstream. They were beached, but when they saw the Frisian banners and we hurriedly came about, the crews ran for their ships. I think that most of them are coming this way, though probably fully manned."

Alfred smiled in return. "And we are thirty, with double crews. What emblem do they fly?"

The Frisian's grin returned. "Most are from the Francian Viking fleet. The rest fly Guthrum's pennant, Sire. A couple of my crewmen who served at Rochester recognized one of the ships. If you want them, you must hurry. They will be rounding the point soon!"

Alfred turned to his officers. "Polonius, let us try your Byzantine signaling system. Raise the flag to signal attack!"

"Where away, Sire?"

"Dead ahead, Scholar!"

Even as Alfred spoke, the first ship of the Viking fleet came around the point. Alfred paced the deck in his excitement.

"Forget the flag. Signaler, blow the attack! The men will understand well enough."

The captain of the first Viking vessel clearly saw the threat and recognized the on-rushing fleet as enemy. He tried to turn his ship as fast as he could. He turned into the path of several other long-ships, however, causing considerable confusion. Before the Viking ships could complete the turn, the Saxons were amongst them.

The *Leaping Stag* hurtled toward the largest Viking vessel in the front rank. With its built-up speed, it easily caught the enemy vessel. Alfred ran to the bow to take command of the impending battle.

He stood in front of his armored fyrdmen. "Bowmen ready! Shoot! . . . Keep those arrows going. Don't give the heathens time to organize. Phillip, be ready to drop the corvus on my word . . . Now!"

The heavy metal spike at the tip of the portable bridge thudded deep into the rear deck of the Viking vessel. Instantly, the two boats were locked together. The Viking rowers rose from their sea chests and grabbed their weapons, but the Saxon fyrdmen were already pouring over the corvus.

Alfred watched from the lofty position of his own bow. "Throw those spears! Don't let them form up! . . . Left bank of rowers, you're next! Up and over the corvus! Right bank, up and use your bows!"

The Vikings were masters at the sea battle, but they had never faced Polonius' secret weapon before. Before they could form a solid defense, an overwhelming number of Saxon warriors poured onto their deck. The spears and arrows kept coming, even while the Vikings tried to form a shield-wall. Those of their front rank who were not cut down by the missiles faced a swarm of determined warriors lustily swinging battle axes and swords. The Vikings were brave men and veteran warriors, but they were heavily outnumbered and, one by one, they were cut down.

Alfred yelled down to his men. "Finish them off and throw the bodies overboard. Quickly now! I want you back aboard. There are more ships to take! Thane Byram, keep twenty men and sail the Viking ship back to the island."

The **Leaping Stag**, once the corvus had been pulled back to the vertical position, started after a nearby long-ship that was already locked, bow to bow, to a smaller Saxon vessel. The Vikings were almost equal in number, and this time they were driving the Saxons back to their corvus.

Alfred's massive vessel slipped up to the stern of the enemy vessel and dropped its corvus again. His warriors raced over the bridge, led by their king, and attacked the Vikings from behind.

Four men with battle axes, giants all, turned and attacked the newcomers. Their mighty blades cut down the three men in Alfred's vanguard, and suddenly the Vikings faced the king himself.

Phillip thrust himself forward. His blade, almost as long as he was tall, leapt at the first giant.

The giant bearded Viking laughed in contempt, but he was barely able to stop the blow. He saw death staring at him, but he did not hesitate. He raised his axe to swing at the king, but Phillip struck so hard that his blade split the giant's helmet. The next giant, with a bushy red beard and a massive golden *torque* around his neck, was stopped by Ambrose's flickering blade.

The Viking laughed and spoke in Danish. "Today you die, little man! You should have stayed home and grown up."

Ambrose smiled and replied in the same language. "You are very sure of yourself, blowhard. What makes you think you can kill Canuteson of Wessex? Many Vikings have tried, and they are all dead!"

The bearded giant paused in surprise. "You, little man? You are the famous Canuteson the Dane-slayer?"

Ambrose's blade struck a glancing blow against the Viking's armored chest and the man roared. "Today I will rid the world of a spy! Stand still and fight, little man!"

Ambrose took the man's blow on his shield and was almost knocked to his knees, but the man was vulnerable for a second as he was recovering and Ambrose used the moment to drive his blade deep into the man's armpit. The Viking grunted in surprise, stared balefully at Ambrose for a full ten seconds, and then slowly toppled to the ship deck.

Alfred was holding his own against his Viking, but the fourth Viking raised a hand axe to throw at the West Saxon king. Polonius, securely behind Ambrose, yet saw the gesture and threw two of his precious knives. The Viking screamed as one blade penetrated his eye. His axe hit the deck, and then suddenly he was dead. In moments, the Northmen broke. A second ship had been taken.

Alfred climbed back aboard his flagship and looked for more targets, but the fight was almost over. All ten ships that had come out from the camp were in Saxon hands.

Alfred, watching from his flagship, the **Leaping Stag**, was exultant. He clapped his brother on his back.

"Ambrose, we got them! Today Guthrum will rue the day he let his warriors travel south to Kent.

Ambrose nodded. "And what about the three ships that didn't launch?"

Alfred grinned. "Let's go get them! My first thought was to burn any ships left on the shore, but many of our ships are still double crewed. Even with the prize crews out of the picture, we have overwhelming manpower. It should be a simple matter to send enough men ashore to seize the rest of the ships."

"Brother, we will be facing more than three ship crews. Many of the Viking long-ships sailed short-handed."

"We still outnumber them, and who knows what treasures there are on the shore. I say we seize the rest of the Viking ships."

⚑

Alfred's fleet of Saxon, Angle and Jute ships swept further up the Stour's estuary and moved swiftly towards where the remaining Viking ships were beached. Their sudden appearance did not go unnoticed. War horns sounded and Viking crewmen ran for their vessels. There was little time and little that could be done, however. The West Saxon fleet quickly closed the distance, and the fyrdmen on the first vessels either leapt the gaps or ran across the corvuses after the massive planks thudded into the Viking vessels.

As the **Leaping Stag** approached the first of the beached ships, Polonius ordered the corvus dropped. Its sharp spike instantly anchored the flagship to the beached vessel. The Viking crewmen were clambering up the bow while Ambrose led the first of the fyrdmen onto the ship's stern.

The Vikings fought heroically, but the fyrdmen formed a solid shield-wall across the width of the ship, while archers from the high-sided **Leaping Stag** filled the air with steel-tipped shafts. Several other ships landed men a few hundred feet along the shore.

The Danes were being slowly driven back off the ship, but they held their own on the shore. Furious at losing the last of their ships, they threw themselves at the Saxons and the fyrdmen were forced to retreat in disarray.

Ambrose, fighting on the deck of the Viking ship, saw the fyrdmen being forced back up the shore. He called out to Polonius. "Scholar, we need the rest of the men from the fleet ashore as soon as possible. At the moment the men who went ashore are being badly mauled and need reinforcements! Can you get back to Alfred and ask him to signal the rest of the ships to close?"

Polonius called back to the man he had chosen to follow for so long. "Consider it done, Prince."

Ambrose lost sight of his friend as the Byzantine fought his way back to the deck of the **Leaping Stag**. The prince's world swiftly became five feet wide as two burley Viking warriors closed on him. Phillip's great sword cut the first down, and then **Victory-Maker** penetrated the man's chest right through his chain mail.

Almost before the man hit the deck, he was replaced with another bearded warrior intent on sending Ambrose to the Christian heaven. The prince heard, however, the king's signalers blowing the charge.

The Angelisc ships that were beached became conduits for hundreds more fyrdmen and sailors. The corvuses allowed ships to attach themselves to other ships, and soon a steady stream of Saxons was joining their beleaguered comrades on the shore. The force with Ambrose and Phillip finally cleared the deck of the Viking long-ship. The men leapt onto the shore and formed a semi-circle around the ship's bow.

The shield-wall further along the shore swelled with new recruits, steadied, and then gradually managed to move forward. The Vikings fought with all of their energy. It was clear that if the Saxon shield-wall moved them past the three still-beached ships, then their last vessels, too, were lost.

Two Vikings, stripped naked and chanting loudly, broke through their own shield-wall, which receded just enough to let the men sworn to Odin do their heroic deeds. The two berserkers approached the semi-circular formation Ambrose held in front of the ship. Ambrose had seen berserkers before, and he knew the damage they could do. Many of the superstitious Saxons would be afraid to kill them, and thus they would become the victims. Equally important, somewhere behind the Viking skjaldborg, the *boar's snout*, a wedge of warriors, was no doubt forming up. If the Saxon wall broke, then the wedge would suddenly appear, tearing through the gap in the Saxon line. Once the Vikings pierced the Saxon shield-wall, the Vikings would turn and attack the Saxon shield-wall from the rear. Few warriors were able to hold once their formation had been penetrated.

He called out. "Arrows and spears! Don't let those berserkers close on you! Spit them now!"

The two berserkers avoided the spears, but a few arrows thudded into the two men. They didn't stop coming, however. The Saxons shrank away, and Ambrose saw impending disaster.

"Phillip, if we don't stop them, then the line will break! You know what is waiting behind."

The prince and the giant stepped forward to meet the two dreadful apparitions. Dripping blood and arrows, the berserkers lurched forward on sheer mental will.

Phillip moved until he was ten feet in front of his own line. His giant blade started to twirl in circles, until he stepped one more foot forward and his twirling blade intersected with the first lurching berserker. The irresistible swing brushed the Viking's sword aside like it was a twig, and then connected with the man's neck. The Vikings watched in horror as the man's head separated from his body. The headless torso finally stopped its superhuman movement.

Ambrose blocked the second one with his body. He knew that once the man stopped, wounded as he already was, he might not be able to start forward again. The berserker, a bearded giant, swung his axe in a horizontal stroke that was as powerful as Phillip's. Knowing that the power of the blow would snap his own beloved **Victory-Maker** like a twig, the prince rolled desperately backward. Ambrose looked up at the giant approaching him.

The berserker's face was locked in a rictus as he stared at the puny man who had dared to bar his path. He swung his massive axe behind him, preparing for a vertical blow that would reduce Ambrose, armor and all, into a pulp of crushed flesh.

At that moment, Ambrose thrust his **Victory-Maker** forward like a Roman legionary's *gladius*. The sharp point entered the berserker's chest and pierced the man's heart. Ambrose saw the man's death in his eyes, but by an incredible effort of will, the Viking started the crushing swing of his axe. The body finally stopped co-operating, however, and, a look of puzzlement on his face, the berserker slowly lay down on the already blood-stained grass.

Ambrose could see movement behind the Viking shield-wall. The two of them were now hopelessly exposed between the two lines.

"Back, Phillip, as fast as you can! The Viking *svinfylka*, the boar's snout, is approaching. Let's rejoin the line!"

The two warriors backed as quickly as they could, until the shield-wall parted enough to let them join. It was none too soon, for the expected boar's snout of some fifty men burst through the Viking shield-wall.

Chanting 'Odin! Odin!,' the wedge of Viking warriors closed the gap at a run. The Saxon line buckled at the force of the attack, but it did not break. Only the front rank of the wedge could fight, so the Saxons were able to hold, just. Ambrose and Phillip fought desperately, until the dead piled up in front of them. As fyrdmen fell, fresh warriors from the ships jumped ashore, pushed forward and filled any gaps with their bodies.

Even with the reinforcements, the shield-line was barely holding, when the crewmen who had landed along the shore finally broke through the Vikings lines there. Finally, the massive inequality of numbers was beginning to show. The Saxons had by now managed to land their entire force, and they were finally overwhelming the angry Vikings with the weight of sheer numbers.

Suddenly the Viking shield-wall in front of Ambrose broke and the ferocious warriors were quickly transformed into a panicked and running mob. The exhausted Saxons cheered wildly and then started in pursuit.

Before the victorious Saxons had covered more than a few hundred feet, the king's signalers sounded the recall. Ambrose, frustrated, started back and looked for his brother's banner. Spying him on the shore, he made his way to his side.

"Brother, if you had not sounded the recall, we would have sent hundreds more Vikings to hell this day."

Alfred smiled. "Perhaps, brother, but our main task today was to seize the ships, not wipe out the crewmen."

"We were close to doing both, Alfred."

"Perhaps, brother-of-mine, but letting a mob of disorganized Saxons race into unknown country does not strike me as wise. The ships, bought with so much blood, were about to be left unprotected. Our own fleet was about to be abandoned and left unprotected. Last, but far from least, there is a major road along the shore, so Guthrum's Vikings could approach by land or sea. I do not want my crewmen stranded hundreds of miles from Wessex without their ships and under attack by a Viking army."

Ambrose absorbed the logic. "You are right, brother. I have seen armies massacred because the victors of a battle threw away their discipline. I guess it was the bloodlust that made me speak. I was more than a little berserk myself."

Alfred hugged his brother. "Look about you, brother. We have won a battle and seized a fleet. Now all I want to do is get us all back safely to Wessex."

"So what happens next, brother?"

"Once we have all the Viking ships adequately crewed, we will return to the uninhabited island that we rested on last night. There we can determine the seaworthiness of our new ships and deal with our wounded. After that, we will head for home!"

When Ambrose woke, he groaned. The winds had picked up and the temperature had dropped drastically. The rain had started. He wrapped himself in his heaviest cloak and staggered down to the shore.

Both the ships of the Saxon fleet and the captured ships were beached or securely anchored in the lee of the island, but the unprotected waters offshore were roiling. The prince groaned as he looked at the towering waves which hurtled themselves onto the shore in an endless succession.

"Not a great day for traveling, is it?"

Ambrose was startled to hear his brother's voice at his side. He turned to face his king. "I fear for the fleet if we take it out today, brother."

Alfred sighed. "So do I, Ambrose."

"Then we spend another day on this island?"

"I do not wish it, brother. By now, Guthrum must have received word that we are here and what we have done. I can't imagine that he is very happy with us."

"Then you would prefer to travel south sooner rather than later?"

Alfred sighed. "Inland on the rivers, he is not facing wild water the way we are. I have no doubt that he is even now on his way here with every ship at his command. I have no wish to face his entire fleet, Ambrose. We have twisted his tail more than I could have hoped for, plus punished the Francian army. Guthrum will be out for bloody revenge."

"Alfred, I am as keen as you to head south. I think, however, that we would be fools to head out into that. This weather is as bad as the time we lost much of the *Varangian* fleet in the Black Sea."

"Are you referring to the time you told me that the Rus swept down on Constantinople?"

"On the way home, we lost several thousand Varangian warriors, brother."

"You once told me that the Varangian ships were overloaded, did you not?"

"With all the treasures they had taken from Byzantium, plus most of their ships were river boats - much smaller than these long-ships. But, in turn, the Rus were amongst the best sailors I have ever met."

Alfred put his arm on Ambrose's very wet shoulder. "Then let us go find what shelter we can and eat breakfast, brother-of-mine. It appears that we will have a day or two of idleness before we have to lean again on those oars."

The second day was as bad as the first. The waves thundered ashore, and it was clear that to head south through open waters was to commit suicide.

The Saxons buried the men who had died in the night, did their best to make the surviving wounded comfortable, and the Frisian shipwrights, with their Saxon assistants, repaired damage done to the ships in the battle.

On the third day the storm finally blew itself out. Ambrose rose as soon as the sky lightened, and he saw calm water. He called out to his two friends. "Polonius! Phillip! Wake up you sluggards. Today is a gorgeous summer day. Today we can start home!"

Phillip rose quickly and threw a cloak over his shoulders. "If you can wake our Greek scholar, Prince, I will get us something warm for breakfast."

Ambrose had just shaken Polonius awake when the two heard the cry of one of their lookouts. "May the Lord preserve us; there are hundreds of sails to the west!"

Ambrose stood beside Alfred as the two strained to see what was approaching. Suddenly, the wide river mouth was filled with sails.

Alfred rushed out of his tent at the words. He looked to the west and gasped. "May God curse Guthrum and his devils! There are more ships in that fleet than there are fleas on a poxed Viking whore. Phillip! Send the men to the ships on the double. If we do not hurry, then we will be overwhelmed before we get an oar into the water! We have no hope of fighting. I want to at least try and save my fleet!"

"What about the ships beached for repairs, Sire? Some are loaded with treasure."

"Load the wounded. They are the priority. We will just have to abandon the beached ships and whatever else is on the shore."

Ambrose sighed. "It is a shame to leave so much behind, brother."

"We will have to be satisfied with what we took at Rochester and what we have aboard the other vessels. You cannot spend treasure if you are dead. Ambrose, send some men to throw torches into the beached ships. If Guthrum's men take the time to put out the fires, then it just might buy us the time we need to get out of this without losing our entire fleet. I don't actually count hundreds of Viking craft, but Guthrum still might have us outnumbered three to one!"

Ambrose gave the orders and then returned to Alfred's side. "Brother, we must board. We have to get you out of here!"

Alfred stubbornly stood on the shore and stared at his precious fleet as his crewmen manhandled the ships into deep water or cut the anchors. Within scant minutes, the entire fleet was manned and launched. The king finally boarded his flagship as the entire Saxon fleet headed south. Behind them, an even half dozen vessels smouldered on the beach. They were barely in time. Guthrum's avenging ships swept down upon the island. Soon the Saxon stragglers were locked in combat with the Viking vanguard.

Ambrose turned to his brother who stood at the stern of the **Leaping Stag**. "Where are we off to, Alfred?

The king sighed. "South, and as fast as we can. We are a long way from safety."

"And once we reach friendly waters?"

"I have instructed the captains of five ships, plus the **Leaping Stag**, to make for the Thames."

"Rochester?"

"Perhaps briefly. Odda was supposed to take a strong force to Wallingford, but he is probably still in Rochester with the main army."

"What about the rest of the fleet?"

Alfred looked over the stern before he answered. "Those who make it? I told the captains before we started that they were to return to Dover if anything went wrong. I just pray to God that most will make it."

Ambrose was puzzled. "Brother, I understand Dover. It is the main base for our coastal fleet, but why Wallingford? Any ship that goes up the Thames will be trapped and vulnerable. Are you sure that you want to take the **Leaping Stag** so far upstream?"

"I need some ships to ferry supplies and transport my army across to the north bank, and, come spring, I need the crewmen."

Ambrose looked at Alfred. "Come spring? What devilment have you and Polonius cooked up, brother-of-mine?"

"Big-brother, we are going to put together an expedition to take London."

"But what happens in the meantime if Guthrum decides to follow us up the Thames? You could easily lose six of your ships."

Alfred turned to Polonius. "And just what is being done to protect my ships, Scholar?"

"As we speak, Sire, the army is strengthening the fortifications of Wallingford."

Ambrose's faced his Byzantine friend. "Polonius, a fortified burh will protect the garrison, especially if Odda's men are nearby to support them. It will give a haven to the local populace, but it will hardly block the river."

Polonius smiled. "You are right, Prince. The fort **will** protect the twelve *onagers* I am having constructed, however. The onagers, and the several hundred fire pots I have ordered, should do the job quite effectively."

Ambrose smiled. "You play with fire again, my friend. Still, having watched the *Greek-Fire* at work, and your many experiments, I will have to accept that you just might have found a satisfactory solution. Can you be so sure of your onagers' accuracy, however? We both know that to hit a moving ship is not an easy task."

"That is a valid concern, Prince. It has been my experience, however, that, assuming the consistent weight of the missiles and once the ropes have been stretched a time or two, the onagers are quite consistent. It is for this very reason that I have chosen Wallingford. Much of the river is shallow there. We will narrow the channel even further by sinking a couple of our oldest ships in the ship channel. The Viking ships will then have little room to manoeuver. If they wish to go further west, they will have to travel through the gap in single file. If Guthrum's fleet dares the narrows, we will have a hard time missing them. We will have some spectacular Viking ship funerals while the crews are yet aboard."

Phillip interrupted. "Sire, the devils are still closing. What can we do?"

Polonius stood for a few moments at the approaching Vikings and then spoke. "Hakim once told me the trick of catching monkeys in the lands south of the Great African desert."

Alfred turned to Polonius. "Scholar, we are being rapidly overtaken by a vastly superior force. Is this story pertinent to the situation?"

"I think so, Sire."

Alfred sighed. "Then speak on."

"The hunter would drill a hole in a gourd that was just a little larger than a monkey's hand. He would then tie the gourd with a line, and put a favorite nut inside the gourd."

Alfred nodded. "And then what happened?"

"The monkey, being a greedy creature, would reach in and grab the nut. With his hand closed around his treasure, however, the animal could not withdraw its hand. It was then a simple matter to club or net the animal."

Alfred stared over the stern at the approaching fleet. "It is an interesting parable, Scholar, but I am not sure we will have time to speculate for long on its moral."

"Then I will be uncharacteristically blunt, Sire. You must open the fist - abandon the rest of the treasure ships, immediately, or you risk being clubbed or netted. By recalling the prize crews, most of our ships will be double-crewed again, and that just might give us a chance of outrunning the heathens."

Alfred slapped the gaunt Byzantine on the back. "Now **that** I understand, and I fear that you are right."

The king sighed again. "Order the men to abandon the rest of the captured ships and any of ours that are badly damaged. Start fires where possible. We will lose a little time, but the remaining ships should then have enough extra crew that we might be able to out-row the heathen devils."

Phillip nodded. "I will give the orders, Sire."

The orders were passed from ship to ship, and soon each captured Viking vessel approached a Saxon one. The men leapt desperately for the friendly decks, and within minutes, the rest of the captured ships and several Saxon ones were abandoned. Smoke roiled from several of them.

Alfred watched the maneuvering from the stern of his ship. "By the robe of sweet Jesus! Guthrum's men are still catching up! They are almost upon us!"

Alfred turned to the giant Saxon at his side. "Phillip, we are drawing ahead of the rest of the fleet. Tell the captain to drop back! I want the **Leaping Stag** to bring up the rear. Our high sides and deep keel give us a huge advantage over the Viking long-ships."

"Sire, I cannot give that order. If you die or are captured, then Wessex is lost. Whatever you want - you must put your safety first. The entire country is counting on you."

"I am not a coward! You taught me to stand and fight, Weapons-master. I have never run from danger in my life!"

"You must today, Sire."

The king turned to his brother. "Ambrose, will you give the orders?"

"Phillip is right, brother."

"Polonius?"

"You are Wessex's greatest asset, Sire. Only you can hold together all the ealdormen of the empire."

Alfred thought for a moment. Suddenly he nodded decisively. "All right, I see I am outvoted. I will accept what you say, even if I don't like it. You cannot make me, however, totally abandon my men."

Polonius replied. "It has already been decided. The ship

captains will drop back one by one to ensure that your ship is not taken, Sire. Do not waste the mens' sacrifice.

Ambrose spoke. "How about if Phillip and I switch to **Black Arrow**, your courier ship? It is the smallest and fastest vessel in the fleet. We can linger at the rear of the fleet, but will be able to escape from anything the Danes can send after us. Brother, we will do what we can to hold the fleet together."

Alfred stared at his brother. "All right! I will agree only if you and Phillip promise me that you will take no unnecessary risks. I need both of you back at my side!'

The king smiled suddenly. 'After all, I can hardly afford to lose two of the men they sing ballads about."

Ambrose hugged Alfred. "Agreed, king and brother. We will take no unnecessary risks."

Ambrose turned to Phillip. "Would you signal the **Black Arrow** to come alongside?"

"Polonius has already taken care of it, Prince. The **Black Arrow** is on the way."

Ambrose had ordered the **Black Arrow** to approach a drifting Saxon long-ship. Its men had been savaged by two Viking crews, but Ambrose hoped to rescue any sailors not killed outright. It took him back into waters controlled by the Vikings, but he had a double crew and the fastest ship in the Saxon fleet. As the crew were helping some wounded fyrdmen aboard, Phillip called out. "By the Christ's beard, Prince, we are trapped!"

"What in Heaven's name are you talking about, Phillip?"

"Look ahead! There are three long-ships coming out of the channel on the other side of the island, and they are in a position to corner us. The only way out is back, and Guthrum's fleet awaits us there."

"Then we ask for God's forgiveness, old friend, and we fight."

Phillip sighed. "I promised your father I would get you home safe and sound."

"And you have, Weapons-master, a dozen times. You have

also saved my life more times than I can count. Today, we will show the Danes how well Saxons can fight."

The sea wolves approached from in front and on both flanks. Whichever way the **Black Arrow** turned, it would be intercepted. Suddenly, however, Ambrose recognized the sleek black hull that approached from the seaward side.

"Phillip, could that be one of the ships we leased from Sitric Ivarsson?"

"What makes you think that, Master?"

"Look at the angle of the carved dragonhead. I have only seen the one ship with such a rakish angle to the head."

"It looks a lot like it, Prince, and I believe that that is the Lodbrok Raven on the sail. Could it be that the king of Dublin sails with Guthrum?"

"Turn toward the ship, Phillip, and tell the men I want no archers to let fly until I give the command."

"Is that wise, Prince?

Ambrose smiled. "There is death on all sides and we are trapped. What have we got to lose, Weapons-master?"

"Ambrose, the enemy vessels are getting close. Let me tell the archers to start. Maybe we can hit enough rowers to slow the heathens down."

"Not yet, Weapons-master. We do not want to shoot at a possible friend."

Suddenly Sitric's ship swerved and cut off the second vessel. A tall man stood at the bow and waved. Ambrose recognized the man once known as Harold the Frisian, trader in fine jewelry.

Sitric cupped his hands and called out to Ambrose. "It's a good thing I recognized you, Prince Ambrose. Otherwise, we just might have had an unfortunate accident today."

"Even in these present unhappy circumstances, Sitric, it is a pleasure to see you! But are you lost? You are a long way from home, king-of-Dublin."

"I was visiting good King Guthrum when you did something that upset him very much, Prince-of-Wessex."

Ambrose stared ruefully back. "I don't doubt it. So what happens next?"

"You sail home, Canuteson."

"Your friends still look like they want me to stay around for a while."

"If you mean Guthrum's ships, I cannot help you there. You will simply have to out-row them. If you mean the two hounds following at my heels, leave them to me. You are not at war with the mighty Sitric of Dublin, at least at the moment. These are my ships and the captains will obey me or I will stretch their necks in Odin's honor before the sun sets today. You will sail home with my blessing."

"Sitric, again you save my life. You are a good friend and I am in your debt."

"After what you paid to rent my ships for your Irish adventure, you owe me nothing. You made me rich that day, Prince."

"And you gave me back my true love, King."

"Then I am glad, Canuteson. May the gods smile on you today. Row hard - Guthrum is really upset."

"May the Lord of Hosts smile on you too, Sitric Ivarsson."

The crew of the **Black Arrow** rowed long and hard. Slowly, very slowly, the **Black Arrow** caught up with the remnants of the Saxon fleet. Ambrose ordered the captain to pull alongside the **Leaping Stag**.

Alfred called across to Ambrose. "You told me that you would be careful, brother. The last I heard - you were trapped by three long-ships!"

"It's true, brother. Three ships came out of the south channel and cut us off."

"Then how did you escape?"

"We were trapped by Sitric and two of his captains."

"And he let you go?"

"He waved and wished us a good day. What happens now?"

The fleet will return to Dover and lick its wounds, while my squadron heads up to Wallingford."

"Then your plans have not changed?"

"I lost a good part of my fleet, but the army is strong. The defeat has in no way weakened my resolve."

Alfred stared at the pursuing Vikings. Ambrose's ship had caught up, but the vanguard of Guthrum's ships was also approaching. "Ambrose, the extra rowers helped, and several of Guthrum's crews are fighting the fires we set on the abandoned ships, but I fear that we are still not going to escape. The Vikings seemed to have borrowed our tactics. They have stripped the crews off every other ship, and are now able to match us stroke for stroke."

Ambrose looked at the pursuing ships and then towards the open waters to their east. "Alfred, order the fleet to head out to sea – I see fog banks to the east!"

"Brother, we can hide in the fog bank and the Vikings probably will not follow – but we are hundreds of miles from home and our ships will be utterly lost. All fishermen flee the fog banks like the devil is after them."

"We have the sun-stone, Alfred. You used it yourself on the way north."

"We used it to navigate through wisps of fog, brother. What I see to the west is more than I would dare."

"Brother, order the captain to drop the corvus on the ship just ahead."

"That only joins two of us."

"The water is calm and it will give us time to attach the ships together by rope."

"Then you want us to form a continuous chain of ships?"

"Why not? Kind of like a giant raft. We won't lose each other in the fog, and we can put the **Leaping Stag** at the rear. As you yourself said, our high decks give us the advantage if any Vikings are daring enough to follow."

"Not long ago, you forbade me to do just that."

Ambrose smiled. "This time, brother, you can move sufficient crewmen anywhere you want, so that whatever ships the heathens attack, we can achieve overwhelming local superiority."

"Then you intend that we float in the fog throughout the night?"

"Why not – the Vikings are unlikely to follow, and we can always use the sun-stone to find our way back to shore again."

"Ambrose, it is a crazy plan, but is probably our only hope. Order it!"

One by one, each of the remaining vessels dropped their corvuses. As the fog thickened, the exercise was finally complete and the **Leaping Stag** moved into position. Close behind, and catching up since the Saxon vessels had effectively lost their headway – was the first of the pursuing Viking long-ships.

As the fog swirled ever more heavily, the first Viking long-ship closed. Alfred sent messages to the next two ships in the chain. "Tell the captains to keep a skeleton crew each and to send the rest back to the **Leaping Stag**. Go now!"

The combined crews filled the air with an avalanche of arrows and spears. There were so many casualties on the lower decked Viking long-ship that it was forced to veer off.

As quickly as it faded into the fog, however, two more ships began to materialize. Almost like ghost ships, they approached Ambrose's flagship. One started to sweep by the **Leaping Stag**.

Alfred yelled out. "The devils just might manage to break the chain of ships. Polonius, where is your Greek-Fire? Don't let him get by!"

Polonius desperately flipped open his sea chest. He called out. "Phillip, I need your strength! Prince Ambrose, I need fire!"

Within less than a minute, Ambrose had thrown some of Polonius's special powders upon a smouldering log and the fire was set. Phillip swung the rope holding the jar of Polonius' 'Greek-Fire' around and around, until, just as the Viking ship started to disappear in the fog, he let go. The jar flew true. When it shattered however, there were only sullen flames. The Vikings laughed and threw water on them, but the flames were pernicious. The fire just continued to slowly spread.

The hail of arrows and spears slowed the third ship. Finally, like the first, the long-ship backed off. No further Viking ships appeared.

Alfred studied the white fog for twenty minutes before he spoke. "It appears, brother, that they have finally given up."

"The Vikings are intrepid sailors, and some of them, too, have sun-stones, but my guess is that they do not wish to tempt *Aegir* too much near a dangerous coast in a fog. The wise Viking will flee before the fog and make for a safe shore while they can yet see."

Alfred looked puzzled. "Who is this 'Aegir', Ambrose?"

"He is the Viking god of the sea, brother."

"I understood the Viking fear. While the Lord God throws his mantle over us and protects us, yet no Saxon in his right mind ever wants to lose sight of land. What we are doing is terrifying to all of our crewmen. They fear that if we float out too far – then we might fall off the edge of the world."

"Brother – I fear the unknown waters, too. I would be lying to you if I denied it. By doing something that's no Viking would ever expect, however, we have given Guthrum the slip. I have no doubt that his vessels are pushing south just as fast as they can, and looking for us every inch of the way. His captains will not believe that we intend to stay out of sight of land."

"Do we?"

"It is our only chance to survive, Alfred."

Alfred finally nodded. "Then we will have to be careful when we do head for shore. Guthrum's fleet could be waiting."

"With your permission brother, and the help of our Frisian navigators, I intend that we set a course due south. When the navigators estimate that we are nearing the Thames, only then will we turn west. Guthrum will never expect us to stay out so far for so long. He does not think us capable of it."

The fog did not lift, so the progress south was painfully slow. For two days the long chain of ships crawled south.

On the afternoon of the second day, Alfred's captain approached the king. "Sire, we are almost out of fresh water, and the men are both thirsty and scared."

"If necessary, you will cut the ration of water. We are heading south, Captain, and are merely retracing our journey north."

"Sire, then we went through wisps of fog. We have been locked in an unending gray cloud for almost two days now."

"Captain, would you have us give up and surrender to the Vikings?"

"King, the men love you and are sworn to obey you."

"But, Captain?"

"But having been out of sight of land for so long, they fear they will reach the end of the world and fall off."

"Captain, we are between Britain and Europe. We might hit a coast, but we can hardly fall off the edge of the world."

"And then there are the sea serpents, Sire."

"Really? Have we had hints of the presence of terrifying supernatural creatures?"

"Sire, I am your loyal man. We have floated for two days in a mysterious fog, with no sight of land. Even the birds have disappeared. Mysterious splashes are heard out there somewhere in the fog. I am telling you, Sire, the men will follow you willingly into the most hopeless battle, but the fog and the mysteriousness of the last two days are working on the mens' imagination. Soon entire crews are going to cut their ships free and take their chances looking for a familiar coast."

Alfred was angry. "Captain, once an individual ship heads off, the panic will be contagious. We will end up losing much of the fleet either to the Vikings or on the treacherous rocks."

"Sire, I said I am your man. I am just telling you what the men are saying to each other. The fear of the unknown is much greater than their fear of either the Vikings or coastal shoals."

"Or me?"

"They have sailed into fog and the unknown for two days, Sire. They only did this for you."

"Captain, you have been honest and I appreciate that. Phillip!"

"Yes, Sire?"

"Call an urgent conference of all ship captains."

"Sire, we have twenty-one ships in a line, stretched out over a mile."

"The crews will just have to pull the ships together long enough for the captains to climb from ship to ship. I want each of them on my deck within the hour! In the meantime, I will be in my tent.' The king held his stomach. 'Please send Polonius to me, and tell him to bring his medicine."

It took considerable maneuvering, but, one by one, twenty-one captains arrived on the **Leaping Stag**'s deck. They waited impatiently for their king to appear. Alfred himself was not yet on deck.

At last he stepped out and faced the assembled commanders. "Captains, I know that your men are running out of water and the fog and the presence of unknown water creatures have terrified your crewmen. I want you to know we are not lost. My brother is using the same stone that got us as far as the Stour without being detected. Ambrose, what direction are we heading in?"

The prince made a great show of holding the stone high and spinning slowly. At last he spoke. "We are heading due south."

Alfred turned to his Frisian navigator. Gauti, what direction do you make it?"

"Based on the wave action, I would have to concur with Prince Ambrose."

"Navigator, if we drifted off-course, where would we end up?"

"Frisia, Sire, or Francia, or, if we floated north, perhaps Pictland."

"Could we somehow drift off the edge of the world?"

"Sire, the German Sea is surrounded by land or islands. I have sailed every inch of it, and never once did I fall off the edge."

Several of the captains laughed, and the palpable tension was eased. "Navigator, the men heard enormous splashes and saw dark shapes moving not far from our ships. What are they?"

"Sire, the whales breathe air, and must come to the surface every so often. They often come partly out of the water, producing a loud splash. The whale hunters call it breaching."

"Navigator, are these whales a danger to us?"

"I have seen harpooned whales attack the small boats that hunt them, but I have never even heard of an unprovoked whale attacking a ship as large as a long-ship."

Alfred allowed his eyes to slowly scan the group of captains. At last he spoke.

"Captains, you have heard the navigator. The greatest danger we face is if we panic and go racing off in different directions. I need you to go back and talk with your crews. It is imperative that we all stay together."

One grizzled sea-thane spoke abruptly. "My men tremble in fear, King. Fear feeds fear. They are ready to break, and if I try to stop them, they just might tear me to pieces. What is it that you want from us?"

"Captain, I want one more day. Tell the men that if we have not found our way out of the fog and found land by tomorrow at sunset, then each crew may decide for itself what to do, with my blessing."

"And if any ships cut loose before then?"

"I swear before Almighty God that I will hang the captain and every crewman aboard. Their homes will be torn down and their families will be driven into exile. Is that clear enough?"

The captains looked at each other and murmured quietly. At last the grizzled warrior who had acted before as the voice for the captains spoke again.

"We are agreed, Sire. We will hold our men in check for twenty-four hours. After that - each crew will vote and decide what to do on its own."

"We are agreed, captains. Return to your ships. I thank you for your loyalty and your obedience. I will get you home safe and sound."

⚑

The dawn was subdued. The ships were still sailing through a gray mist that muted all colors and severely restricted visibility. Alfred and his advisors stood in the bow and watched both the water and sky ahead. The progress south was painfully slow. Suddenly, Gauti, the Frisian navigator pointed to the water ahead.

"Look, Sire, at the color of the water. The salinity has changed. This is a hint that we are level with the Thames River. It is time to head due west."

The fog was ever-present, but there was a hint of blue sky. Ambrose prayed briefly, then slowly rotated the sun-stone.

Suddenly, the dirty white stone turned a bright blue. Ambrose called out.

"Navigator, the stern is still pointed north. We must turn right."

The navigator looked up from his study of the ripples and the currents. "I concur, Prince.' He pointed due west. 'That way is the Thames."

The ship finally broke out of the seemingly endless fog bank. Ambrose almost immediately recognized the southern bank of the Thames estuary. He turned to his brother.

"Where to, Alfred?"

"Pass the word - the ships can cast off the restraining ropes. The entire fleet will put in to Rochester for food and water. We are close, and at least part of our army is still camped there."

One by one, the ships slipped up the Medway River. Large mounted forces paralleled their progress, but when Alfred ordered his dragon banner hoisted, the riders cheered lustily.

Alfred hugged Odda on the riverbank. "Greetings, you old warhorse! Have there been any problems since I left?"

The old ealdorman finished counting the ships that followed in the wake of the **Leaping Stag**. "Apparently less than you, King. I counted thirty-two vessels when you left, but now I count only nineteen."

"We had a great victory, Odda. We took some thirteen ships – only to lose them all, and more besides, when Guthrum's fleet caught up with us. And here?"

"Very quiet, Sire. As you ordered, I sent reinforcements to Wallingford and Southwark. We found and destroyed one small group of raiders that had been trapped when their fleet fled. They had gone inland, so it took a little longer to find them."

"Has there been any sign of Guthrum's fleet in the last few days?"

"It is funny that you should ask. There were several Viking ships cruising the southern shore yesterday. That is the first that we have seen since they fled north."

Alfred spoke. "Send a strong contingent of coast-watchers out today then, Ealdorman. It sounds as if Guthrum has followed us south."

"Sire - if I may be so bold - if Guthrum's fleet caught you, how did you escape?"

"Thank my brother, Odda. He talked me into something so foolish that even the Vikings would not risk it."

Odda looked confused. "Just what feat of seamanship would frighten the Vikings, Sire?"

"We sailed into the open waters of the German Sea, and then we made for the fog banks."

"King, there is no way you can keep a fleet together in the fog. It is a miracle that the rest of your ships did not end up on the rocks."

"That is the magic, Odda. We linked the ships together by using the corvuses and rope."

"Then you were floating blind and deaf, Sire. No wonder the Vikings didn't follow!"

"One or two ships did. We defeated them."

"But you were still lost in the fog."

"Ambrose found a sun-stone when he took that long-ship last fall."

"I do not know what a sun-stone is, Sire."

"It is a great Viking secret. As long as there is the tiniest hint of blue in the sky, it unfailingly tells you which direction is north."

"That is great magic indeed, King."

"Polonius, how long would it take to put together two onagers and make up a couple of your firebombs?"

"I left most of my chemicals in Winchester. Most of what I left behind should now be at Wallingford. I did bring two wagon loads to Rochester, Sire."

"Excellent."

Polonius looked rueful. "Except that one of my wagon loads

of chemicals burned on the way here from Southwark, Sire. I have the second wagon, however, so the chemicals are no problem. With enough skilled carpenters and adequate supplies of rope – I can have two onagers finished by nightfall."

"Good enough – see to it. Philip, I want a log boom just behind our ships. As well, I want camouflaged platforms for the onagers and a whale-hide rope weighted and stretched across the river five hundred feet downstream from the log boom - where the river is at its narrowest."

Philip smiled. "Are we going fishing, Sire?"

"Aye, Weapons-master. For Viking ships – if they are foolish enough to follow us up the river."

The squadron of Viking long-ships became visible just as the first of the coast watchers galloped toward Rochester. The rider saw the king and his entourage on the river bank and rode directly to him. "They come, Sire. The Vikings!"

Alfred turned to Philip. "Signal the men on the other bank to mount up, and then order the same here. We will escort the Viking ships upriver."

One by one, the Viking squadron sailed into line and started to work their way up the river. The Vikings entertained the Saxon riders by 'riding the oars.' The youngest and most agile warriors climbed far out on the oars and then leapt from one to the next in incredible displays of balance. Even the Saxons could not help but cheer when a warrior completed the entire bank without falling into the water.

Where the river narrowed, most of the vessels came to a halt. One however, impudently pushed on upriver. Several mounted archers tested the range, but the arrows fell short and the Vikings laughed.

The ship continued to nose up river until it struck the log boom that Alfred had ordered constructed. The ship crew began to reverse their stroke, but suddenly a heavy whale-hide rope lifted out of the murky waters. The ship was trapped!

A Signaler blew a single note and the branch walls that hid the onagers were thrust aside. Large stones hurtled towards the trapped ship. The Vikings jeered, but the onager ropes were stretched by the ranging shots, and the stones fell progressively nearer the ship.

The long-ship pushed hard against the rope. A daring sailor tried to snag and cut it. A blizzard of arrows quickly cut him down. Polonius ordered his crews to switch to the precious fire pots. One after the other, they arced towards the trapped ship. First one, and then another, struck the long-ship.

Several of the Vikings risked arrows and tried to flush the chemicals away with seawater. The pernicious flames however, continued to stubbornly burn. The ship was quickly becoming a funeral pyre.

Some of the warriors threw off their armor and leapt overboard. The other ships, careful not to approach the shore too closely, moved up to rescue the swimming Vikings.

Alfred stood on the shore looking across at Guthrum's land, indistinct in the distance. He finally sighed and turned to his assembled commanders. "The commanders of our scouting forays reported that Guthrum's fleet has sailed north. This has been confirmed by our coast watchers. It appears that he has gone home."

Polonius spoke. "That is a great relief, King. I feared that he might try and move up the Thames."

"Is not Southwark and Wallingford ready?"

"Wallingford is ready to stop a fleet. Although Southwark could not easily be taken, the river is much too wide to block unless we hold both banks."

"We will – soon enough. That is our next target."

Ambrose spoke. "What happens now, brother?"

"Now that Guthrum has left, we will send most of the fleet to Dover for the winter, and then the crews can go home. My personal squadron will move to Wallingford."

"And the army?"

"That bears some thinking about. I do worry about Guthrum's fleet."

"How so, brother?"

"He could land in Kent, sail up the Thames to strike directly at Wessex, or land at a dozen places along our southern coast."

"Then what do you propose?"

"We will keep a reinforced garrison here at Rochester. I think it unlikely that the Vikings might return to besiege Rochester, but I cannot leave it to chance."

Ambrose nodded. "And the rest of the army?"

"I want the garrison at Southwark reinforced. If Guthrum comes by road, he will likely want to cross at London. A strong fort, well garrisoned, would be capable of cutting his supply lines and be a threat to his entire force."

Polonius spoke. "And Wallingford, Sire?"

Alfred smiled. I have not forgotten Wallingford, Polonius. It will play a crucial role come spring. For now, I want Odda to take his fyrdmen there and work on the fortifications."

"His men will be exhausted, brother."

"Wallingford is on their way home. He can call up his winter fyrdmen when the summer force goes home. He has more than enough warriors with him to hold the fort if the Vikings launch a surprise attack."

Polonius spoke. "Sire, in a couple of weeks our own summer fyrd is going home."

"I know, Polonius. Make it clear to each ealdorman that I expect the full winter fyrd in place before the summer army is released to return home."

Polonius nodded. "With your permission, I will ask Bishop Asser to help me. With his aid, your instructions should be on their way before the sun sets again!"

⚑

The squadron, led by Alfred's flagship – the **Leaping Stag**, slipped out of the Medway River and headed up the Thames. The ships moved steadily against the current, until the dilapidated walls of London came into view. Curious Vikings met the fleet and paced it westward, even climbing out on the ruined London Bridge as far as they could. They made no hostile moves, however, and the ships docked safely at Southwark. King Alfred inspected his fortress sitting on the south bank and then looked across the river at his island's ancient capital.

"By the beard of Almighty Christ, Ambrose! If we held London and Southwark, and reconstructed that bridge, no Viking would ever again sail this way."

On the following morning, the fleet headed out again into the current. Paced by the Viking riders, the fleet continued west toward Wallingford. The single Viking long-ship that had been tied up at the London dock set out in pursuit.

One by one, the Saxon vessels threaded the artificial narrows directly in front of Wallingford and moved majestically upstream. The Viking long-ship, challenging the Saxons, attempted to follow. A dozen onager arms snapped, and several stones struck the ship, doing some damage, but nothing mortal. The crewmen backwatered desperately, and soon the ship was down-river and out of range. It turned and slipped eastward with the current.

CHAPTER 15

A Thane Loses His Land

Alfred sat on his throne in the open space in front of his Great Hall. In front of him were the assembled thanes, churchmen and ealdormen that made up his force. He stared at one of his fyrdmen for a long time before he spoke. "Thane Pyt, kneel before your king!"

The burly man slipped quickly to one knee.

Alfred continued. "Thane Pyt, I have summoned you before me because we have a great problem."

"Then speak, Sire. As ever, my sword is at your command."

"Thane, your enthusiasm is commendable, but I fear that it comes just a little late. How many hides of land do you hold from me?"

"Some three hundred, my King."

"Such a grant should support some three hundred sailors, carpenters, and their families, Thane."

"It does, Sire, with ease. You have been exceedingly generous."

"And why do you hold so many hides, Thane?"

"I am to build a long-ship and then to hold it and a crew ready for your call, Majesty."

"You should even have enough men left over to farm the land and defend the families in the absence of the ship crew."

"I do, Sire!"

"And what did I order you to do during last Lent, Thane?"

"To bring the long-ship to Dover, Sire."

"And did you do as you were commanded, Pyt?"

"Sire, the crew assembled as ordered."

"Then why did the ship not appear as I ordered, Thane?"

"The ship was not complete, Sire. I hired a full dozen carpenters and put the entire crew to work finishing the ship, in the hope that I would be able to follow your fleet."

"Thane Pyt, that is no doubt very commendable, but why was the ship not complete a full year ago?"

"Silver was short, Sire. The carpenters were busy elsewhere. To be honest, I had no idea that the Vikings would invade."

Alfred leaned forward on his throne. "And what were these busy carpenters building, Thane?"

"I had them build a drawbridge so we could defend the tun more effectively. We are on the coast, and in spite of the coast watchers and the signal pyres, we would be easy prey if Vikings landed unexpectedly. The men would not man the ship until they were assured that their families had at least some protection."

"But according to the latest report from my fleet commander, you still have not brought the ship to Dover, Thane. What else were your carpenters doing?"

The thane started to sweat. "Various things, Sire. They built several houses, I believe."

Alfred suddenly went red in the face. "One house, Thane. Not just any house. You are much too modest. Did they not, in fact, build you a Great Hall greater in size than my royal Great Hall at Winchester?"

Thane Pyt hung his head. "Yes, Sire."

"So let me get this straight, Thane. You hold three hundred hides of land, in exchange for building, maintaining and manning one ship for my fleet."

"Yes, Sire."

"The ship was supposed to be ready for action last summer, it still isn't completed, yet you ordered the carpenters to abandon my ship and build a palatial Great Hall for you and your family."

"A Great Hall, Majesty, such as my rank entitles me to."

The king had slipped into a dangerous calm. "I am left with a dilemma, Thane. Do you want to know what it is?"

The thane's voice could be barely heard. "If you wish it, Your Majesty."

"I must conclude that you are either a fool or a traitor, Pyt."

"I am your sworn man, Majesty! I am no traitor."

"Then I must conclude that you are a fool, and I cannot have a fool in charge of one of my ships."

"Sire, pray give me a chance to make restitution!"

"Very well, Thane. You have served me well in the past and so I will not have your head separated from your body. Here is my judgement. You will take your old place with the young drengs of my Personal Guard. Who knows, you may once again perform an act of bravery and be given land to hold for me."

The man cried out. "I will willingly follow you to the gates of hell, Sire, but I am thane of Ryde!"

"You were thane of Ryde, sir! Now you are a dreng of my Personal Guard - with your head still between your shoulders."

"Your Majesty . . . my family!"

"Your family is lucky to have a brave and free warrior, Pyt.

"But, Sire!"

"I had also considered that a cell in the local monastery would give you time to reflect on the enormity of your crime against your king. If you are not happy with joining the ranks of my young warriors, speak up and I will arrange the alternate accommodations."

The demoted thane hung his head lower. "I thank you, Your Majesty, for your wisdom and your mercy. I will not make such a mistake again."

"Indeed you will not, Dreng Pyt. Next time, I will be forced to conclude that you are a traitor and your body parts will be scattered throughout the realm as a warning to others . . . No, stay kneeling until I give you leave to go . . . Dreng Halig of Tisbury, come and kneel before your King."

A young man, dressed in a battle-dented chain-mail shirt, stepped forth from the crowd of young men and kneeled in front of his king. "Long life, Your Majesty!"

"Warrior, how many gold rings have I given you to date?"

The warrior spoke with pride. "Fourteen, your Majesty."

"Prince Ambrose told me that when three Vikings got behind me in the battle for Rochester, you single-handedly killed two of them. Is this true?"

"The scholar Polonius wounded one and killed the second one, Majesty, with two of his magic throwing knives. I did dispatch the wounded man and killed the third, Sire."

"Warrior Halig, you are an honest man as well as brave. I owe you yet another debt. I think it is time for you to leave the ranks of the drengs. You will travel to Ryde with Pyt here, and you will assume the mantle of Thane of Ryde. Pyt will have one week to move his family out of the Great Hall, and you will, in turn, find a suitable abode for his family to reside in. After that, Pyt will return to the ranks of the drengs here, where he has my permission to march in the vanguard of our army the very next time we face an enemy.

You, Thane Halig, will put every resource at your disposal into completing that ship. I want it finished within weeks, not months. You have permission to hang any man who refuses to cooperate with you in its construction. I will personally pay the *wergeld*. Go now and pack. I am well pleased with you."

CHAPTER 16

Alfred Prepares For The Attack

The Frisian commander stood proudly before his adopted master. "I have fulfilled your commands, King. I have five ships tied up at Rochester. They are all Viking built, and the crews have been carefully chosen. By Lent I will have the ships fully manned and ready."

The tired-looking king looked up from his writing. "Excellent. Here then, are your instructions. Return to Rochester at your own speed. Be sure to visit with your family. At the end of the fourth week of Lent, however, I expect you to be far north of the Thames and preparing to descend on the East Anglian coast. I want you and your men to be very visible and very obnoxious. In particular, I want you to burn all the Viking ships you can find, whether in the water or on the beach. Polonius is making up some jars of his favorite chemicals for you to take."

"Are we just to attack ships, King?"

"You are welcome to land and burn any Viking long houses you can. Kill any Vikings who oppose you. Just be sure to stay close to your ships. Your job is to cause the maximum upset and damage along the coast, with the minimum of casualties. You are but a feint to confuse King Guthrum. I do not want your men to die needlessly."

The Frisian spoke. "You may rest assured, King, that when we are through, there will be messengers killing horses to get word to Guthrum of our incursions."

"Excellent. Try to avoid killing the Angles if you can. Confine your damage to the Viking halls as much as possible."

"I will obey, King, but it is likely that we will stir up a nest of hornets."

"Defend yourself as you must."

"Not only on the land. The jarls will be likely to send a large fleet after us. We may not be able to make it back to your side once the Viking ships are launched."

Alfred smiled. "And that is why I do not expect you to return to Wessex."

The commander only hesitated for a moment. "King, we will sell our lives dearly."

Alfred looked at the Frisian with renewed respect. "Nay, even better - I want you to continue north, raiding as you go."

"We will then be sure to have a Viking fleet between us and home, King. We will not be returning."

"Giric and Eochaid, the joint kings of Alba, have already agreed to welcome and protect you. All you have to do is to reach their sheltering shores."

"There is Guthred of Northumbria, King."

"So? We have no quarrel with him, and in any case, you will not land in his territory. You will stand well out to sea, and neither Guthrum nor Guthred will have any clue as to where you have gone. This is why I have chosen you, Jokul. I need the most skilled navigator I know to pull this off successfully."

The Frisian smiled. "I will obey, King, but I beg you for the use of Prince Ambrose's magic stone."

Ambrose smiled at the man. "It is yours, Jokul, along with my blessings!"

The Frisian seemed deep in thought. "How long do you want us to stay in Alba, King?"

"Wait until *Halegmonath* - holy month - before you slip quietly south. By then, Guthrum should be much too busy to give chase, even if he finds out you are off his coast again."

The big man bowed. "It will be as you say, King."

All remnants of the winter snows had melted, and the current from the Thames was fighting the tide. The fleet of lithe long-ships swung their bows toward the shore in the faint pre-dawn light. Within minutes, hundred of excited West Saxon warriors were scrambling ashore.

Ealdorman Raedan watched with irritation. The crack warriors of the summer fyrd seemed to have forgotten everything they had learned so painfully the summer before. He was an experienced leader, however, having been in more raids than he could count, and he quickly sent his best sub-commanders to organize the men.

Even while the men were being shushed and organized into groups, he called his chief subordinate to his side. "Theomund, I want you to have a ditch and palisade up before mid-morning. If there are Viking forces nearby, it will only be your wall that keeps our ships safe. Without the ships, we are all dead men, trapped deep in Viking lands. Do I make myself clear?"

"Ealdorman, I will obey, but my heart is not in it. I should be at your side, like I have been ever since I was a wee lad and I cleaned your armor for you."

The old ealdorman softened. "The fate of all the ships and men that I command is dependent on how well you do your job. There is no glamor in it, but it is the most important task I can assign you. I need to know that, once I have stirred the hornets, I have a position to fall back to that is secure. Will you do this for an old man?"

"Only if my master promises to take no chances and return safe to my side."

"Theomund, I will do nothing foolish. I am not so sure, however, that I would not as soon die from Viking steel as from this living death they call old age."

Theomund looked stricken. "Come back safe, Ealdorman!"

Even as Raedan spoke, his sub-commanders led the columns of warriors towards the Viking halls at Benfleet, less than two Roman miles across the isthmus and east along the coast. The West Saxon attacks on Viking East Anglia had begun.

CHAPTER 17

Alfred Crosses the Thames

Polonius roused the king just as the first rays of dawn lit the tree tops with a ruddy light. "Good morning, Sire. You asked me to wake you before the sun was up."

King Alfred yawned, stretched, then put his hands on his belly. "Good morning, Polonius. My stomach's churning is telling me that this is a decisive day. I fear that I need a sip of your elixir."

The Byzantine smiled and handed his king a silver chalice. "Here it is, Sire. I made up a dose just in case."

Alfred smiled through his pain, took the chalice and drained it on one gulp. "Thank you, Polonius. This is not a day for me to show the fyrd any infirmities."

"Even a king can be sick, Sire."

"Possibly, my friend, but a king who is perceived to be weak has a relatively short and unhappy life on this island. As my fyrdmen surge forward for death or glory today, they must see a confident king . . . Tell me, what is happening outside?"

"The men are stirring, Sire. Phillip has already roused the commanders. They should have everyone in formation and ready to advance within a single turn of the hourglass."

Alfred swung his feet onto the ground. "Excellent. Are the onagers in place and ready?"

Polonius smiled. "We moved them up just after dark. They are in place along the river and supplied with large quantities of stones, Sire."

"Our main force?"

"There are still hundreds of warriors straggling along the southern roads from Kent to Cornwall, but our main force left Wantage two days ago. Yesterday afternoon they camped about two miles south of here."

"With no fires?"

"With no fires, as you instructed, Sire."

"And today?"

"Odda promised to have the full force here shortly after sunrise. They will move north but stay out of sight of the Viking watchers until you sound the advance."

"And the ships?"

"They were triple-crewed and slipped down-river a little after midnight. The men are even now wading ashore as we speak. The birds . . ."

As Polonius spoke, Ambrose entered the command tent. "Good morning, brother."

Alfred hugged his brother. "Ambrose, you made it back in time!"

"I got in last night after midnight. I could not miss the party today, brother."

Alfred was anxious. "And what about our cousin, Ealdorman Ethelwold?"

"He is encamped just south of the Viking fort at Eton."

"And?"

"And he has had his men parade over and over along the shore for two days before I left to return here."

"And the fires?"

"At least when I was there, each warrior maintained at least five campfires all night long."

"That is good news. He may have finally managed to do something right.'

Alfred spun to Polonius. 'You were about to say something about our feathered friends."

"I am happy to report that two dark pigeons landed beside their coop not a third-of-a-candle-mark past."

Ambrose looked puzzled. "Should I assume that that is significant?"

Alfred smiled. "It is indeed, brother. You were the one who taught me how to communicate with pigeons."

"And what exactly are our little friends telling us?"

Alfred looked very anxious. "It means that our fleet is safely down-river, big-brother, and our crewmen are landing on the north bank. I still worry, however, if Odda has got his main force in place. We will be butchered if we advance across the river and Odda and the main army is not at our backs. We cannot force the river without them!

Polonius, I knew we should have used more pigeons!"

"We could only use ones that were born here, King. We were lucky to find the few we used. Only those born here will return here, Sire. That is their nature . . . and if Odda does not appear, then we can simply postpone the attack."

Ambrose spoke. "Radnor waits outside your tent, brother. I spoke with him on the way in. He assures me that Odda is close and will be in position within the hour."

Alfred, holding his belly again, yet tried to smile. "Thank the merciful Lord! Then with luck, and God's grace, we will be on the north shore of the Thames before noon today."

Ambrose nodded. "And if all has gone well, then the Dover fleet should be falling upon St. Osyth even as we speak. I wonder what Guthrum will make of it all?"

Alfred raised his hands high so the other two could drop his chainmail shirt over his torso. He spoke. "I hope his messengers will tell Guthrum that there is a large army massing just across from Eton, two Saxon fleets loose; one on his eastern coast, and the other on the Thames, and a small force threatening to cross at Wallingford."

"That should confuse him, brother."

"I am merely following the advice of Polonius' Chinese friend, Sun Two. Did he not say 'let your plans be dark and impenetrable as night, and when you move, fall like a thunderbolt?"

Polonius responded. "It was Sun Tzu, Sire, and he was not my friend because he died almost a thousand years ago, but you did quote him quite accurately."

Alfred gave Ambrose a mischievous wink and then spoke. "Then let us thank Sun Cho for his sage advice and break our fast. After that, we can go and fall like a thunderbolt upon the heathen!"

Alfred sat on a carved chair in his tent and chewed on a cold goose-leg. He washed his mouthful of cold roast-goose down with a swig of mead and spoke to Ambrose. "Polonius, Is there any chance that the Vikings know that my thunderbolt is going to strike at Wallingford?"

The thin Byzantine replied. "Guthrum has to know the fyrd has been called up and assumes that it will move against him, but I doubt he knows where we will strike the main blow. The fyrd formed up originally far to the south, at Silchester, and when they moved north, they put out a screen of warriors, both by day and by night.

The local Viking commander has been sending a steady stream of scouts across the river for the last couple of weeks, but I think that we have caught them all. Even now, I have over a hundred sentries posted on every road and path in the region. Even seemingly innocent travelers who stumble across the gathering are being held in custody until after today's attack."

Ambrose spoke. "Could the spies pretend to be answering the summons and so have fooled our scouts?"

"Absolutely, Prince. If so, however, they are now about to find themselves unwilling participants in today's attack. The orders were to let any fyrdmen in, but none out."

"And have any tried to leave again?"

"There have been several. They were turned back, however, and are currently being watched very carefully."

"So we have every reason to believe that the Vikings know nothing about the army Odda is bringing to us?"

"You may be sure, Sire, that Guthrum knows your garrison numbers, down to the last man, but it is unlikely that he knows of either Odda's numbers or even his presence."

Alfred stood up and brushed off some bread crumbs. He smiled at his two companions. "Then what are we waiting for, sluggards? Let's go take London!"

Ambrose spoke. "I am ready for a little exercise today, brother, but what about our friends across the river? Have they been up to much since I left?"

The king replied. "Polonius' Saxon spies tell us that they have recently received some reinforcements. There are now several hundred of them and they have been busily building barriers along their side of the river ford. I do not think that they intend to make it easy for us to cross the river."

Ambrose nodded. "And what are we going to do about that?"

"Polonius' onagers are lined up and ready to fire the moment I give the order, and the best three hundred archers have been issued two full quivers each."

"Brother, Polonius' crews can lob all the rocks they want, but they will do little good against men who have dug a ditch and hide in it, nor will the arrows."

"It will help keep their heads down, brother, while the full fyrd arrives and starts to form up and prepare to drive across the river."

"They had built a palisade and dug ditches before I left, brother. Unless they are led by total idiots, they will massacre our men as they struggle across the river. It is still in spring flood and the current is very strong."

Alfred smiled. "You are right as ever, brother, and that is why I have given the onager crews the task of punching holes in the log palisades. They must be knocked down if we are to have a chance."

"We will still be at a disadvantage, Alfred."

"True brother, but there is more. I was anxious about the pigeons for a good reason. Once the heathens are committed to repelling our waves of fyrdmen, both mounted and on foot, I instructed the ship crewmen to come upriver and fall on their flank. If all goes as planned, they will be rolled up and routed before we suffer serious losses.

In the dawn of the spring day, Alfred's army made ready. A dozen onagers thumped and hurtled their missiles across the Thames. Wallingford's small garrison jogged into position and launched a hail of arrows. The Vikings on the north shore, once the initial shock was over, just laughed and ducked behind their palisades and earthen walls when they saw the rocks and arrows arcing high into the air. The onagers thumped continuously, and the log palisades were repeatedly struck and shattered by the heavy rocks. The Vikings, however, just ducked behind the earthen mounds and raised their shields to protect against the rain of arrows. The Vikings, relatively safe behind their shields and the embankment, struck their shields repetitively and jeered.

Suddenly, however, a single Saxon battle horn sounded in the distance. The small mass of signalmen standing beside the king blew a continuous reply. In response, column after column of armored and mounted warriors exited the woods and advanced to join the lines. The notes echoed over the river again and again, and the column transformed into long lines. The Vikings stopped jeering and just stared. In short order, over a thousand armored horsemen were lined up along the south bank.

To renewed blasts from the signal horns, the first wave of horsemen slipped past the archers and prepared to ford the river. The riders hit the water and the Vikings abandoned their shelters and stood to shoot arrows or throw spears at the Saxons struggling to cross the shallow but fast-moving river.

The first Saxon riders started to fall, when suddenly a tight mass of Saxon infantry came charging along the northern river-bank from the east. The screaming warriors fell savagely upon the spread out line of surprised Vikings. The Danish defenses had been built specifically to block the river ford, and they were very vulnerable to an attack from the rear or flank. As the Vikings turned to face this new threat, the Saxon horsemen started to emerge from the river.

Ambrose, flanked by Polonius and Phillip, urged his horse out of the freezing water. He slipped from the saddle and ran to the palisade barrier that now gaped with openings. When he saw a Viking warrior turn to face attacking crewmen, he hurled his spear. The thin point of the heavy weapon pierced the warrior's mail shirt and the burly Viking screamed in surprise and agony. The three men found a break in the barrier where a shot from an onager stone had snapped two heavy trunks. Ambrose was first through and he stabbed at another distracted Viking warrior with his sword. Several Vikings turned yet again to face the first wave of Saxon attackers, but those that did exposed their backs to the running crewmen.

Brave as they were, the Vikings were heavily outnumbered and had been outflanked. They broke; each man running desperately for the safety of the nearby forest. The horsemen, though tired, scrambled over or around the barriers and then spurred their horses in pursuit. Some Vikings made it, but most died with a spear or sword in the back.

Ambrose stared in wonderment. Phillip had retrieved both of their horses, and the two stood looking at the mounds of dead Vikings. Over two hundred of Guthrum's warriors had died in a matter of minutes. Alfred's thunderbolt had struck and his fyrd was loose in Viking territory.

Ambrose took a moment to calm his horse, still restless and fresh, even after the arduous river crossing. "Alfred, are we going to try a Long Ride for London?"

"I don't think so, brother-of-mine. This time I think that we will move deliberately east with the entire army. I wish to leave no pockets of resistance behind me. I intend to cut cross-country until we hit the north bank across from Hurley. After that we will follow the river east until we hit Eton and then the old Salisbury Road."

"And the fleet?"

"The spring flood will move the ships downstream at a good pace. The ships will go ahead and head downstream to Windsor, where the Dorset contingent should be encamped. Once we reach the opposite shore, the ships can be used to ferry the Dorset men across."

Ambrose grimaced. "You do not want cousin Ethelwold to cross before we arrive?"

"Not on your life! Our Saxon spies tell me that Eton is probably defended. Ethelwold is just stupid enough to take a run at the walls and then promptly surrender. The last thing I need this summer is any kind of defeat. It would be more demoralizing to our warriors than the addition of Guthred's entire army to Guthrum's host . . . Mother-of-God, he might do just that! Polonius!"

"Yes, Sire?"

"The first chance you have tonight - write a letter to Ethelwold. Tell him that if he crosses the river for any reason before I arrive - he will be considered a traitor to Wessex."

"As you command, Sire . . . Do you really want me to put it that bluntly?"

"Ethelwold is not a subtle man. I want there to be no ambiguity about my message."

Ambrose spoke. "What about the Vikings settlements between here and London? The first settlement is just ahead."

"I hope that God will forgive me for what I am about to order. Kill any warrior who you can catch."

"If they surrender?"

"Accept the surrender, then hang them."

"And their buildings?"

"I want every trace of Viking settlement between here and London eradicated. Burn every Viking building."

Ambrose looked at the smoke curling up from the distant Viking farms. "I suspect that if we asked the good scholar riding right behind you, he would quote the great Chinese general, Sun Set, and say something like: 'The best thing of all to do is to take the enemy's country whole and intact; to shatter and destroy is not so good.'"

Polonius immediately responded. "Well quoted, Master, except that the name is still Sun Tzu, and I believe that time and distance has not weakened the great general's message. If all goes as planned, the land we are riding through will be a sub-kingdom or shire of Wessex before the summer is over. Destroying all the buildings will cause serious hardships for the Angle and Saxon thralls. Surely we do not want to leave wilderness where there were once prosperous farms."

Alfred thought for a moment and then sighed. "You are forcing a king to admit that he is wrong, and that is no easy thing for a king to do. You have a point, but I still want my message to be abundantly clear. Tell the commanders that I want no Viking long houses left intact for at least ten miles north and south of our line of march. The rest of the buildings are to be left alone."

"They are to leave alone the barns, storerooms and Saxon homes, even if they are owned or occupied by Vikings?"

"Anything inhabited by a Dane is to be burned, but the other buildings are to be spared."

Polonius spoke. "Sire, many of the Vikings live in former Saxon homes."

"We can help the Saxon thanes rebuild their homes later. For now, I want each and every Viking hall to be burned to the ground."

Ambrose spoke. "And death to all Vikings?"

"Ambrose, you told me yourself that the Vikings laugh at Christian charity and only respect strength. Between you, me and God, such an order goes against my Christian conscience, but I must show Guthrum the strength of our resolve. To do that I have to be as ruthless as a Viking."

"Brother, Guthrum probably holds hundreds of our men captive, taken when he defeated our fleet on the Stour."

Alfred sighed again and looked up at his brother. "I think you are hinting that I will need something to trade if we ever want our men back. By Almighty God, I want to . . . No, you are right . . . Tell the men to take prisoners, as long as it is not at the risk of their lives. Don't ever forget, however, that Guthrum allowed a fleet of fifteen long-ships to reinforce the Francian Vikings at Rochester, brother, while yet others of his people dared to slip across the Thames to raid innocent villages. You, yourself, captured dozens of Guthrum's men, some of whom you recognized. After we seized the Viking fleet that had attacked us, Guthrum came close to destroying my entire fleet.'

"All that I know, Alfred. What exactly are you telling me?"

"If we ever want to be masters of our own land, this king needs to be punished. He has to fear my wrath as much as we have so long feared his.'

Alfred sighed. 'All right. Final orders. Destroy any Viking homes. Capture alive any warriors who wish to surrender, as well as all enemy women and children."

"Alfred, what will happen in the end?"

"We will eventually negotiate again with Guthrum, but we will do so from a position of strength. The Thames will never again be our northern border, Ambrose, and I am determined to control at least the western portion of Mercia. Last, but not least, I want London. It was once the capital of this island, and it will be again."

Phillip spoke up. "What do we do with the Viking prisoners we take, Sire?"

"They should be rounded up and kept captive south of the river. They will eventually become a useful bargaining chip."

"Sire, some of our men will abuse the women."

"If a man risks his life in battle, he expects some reward. Even a king would hesitate to forbid all looting and rape.' He sighed. 'I will, however, have the priests remind the men that such an act is a sin."

Ambrose spoke. "Guthrum will be calling up his army once he hears of our crossing, brother. Are you sure that we would not like to hurry at least a little? It would be a shame if Guthrum beats us to London."

"Once, when the Vikings were a nomadic ravaging horde sweeping across this land, I would have feared a surprise attack as early as late winter."

"And now?"

"Now that Guthrum and his men rule a country, they can not easily gather their forces before planting time is over. I chose this specific time of the year for just that reason. His men are still likely scattered at their homesteads, and if he calls up all of his forces before planting is completed, he risks famine next winter."

"So you think there is little chance of Guthrum beating us to London."

Alfred smiled. "Exactly, plus our entire fleet should soon be returning to Rochester from its raids and preparing for its attack on London."

Polonius was still listening. Finally he spoke. "I think the Viking garrison commanders in London will be greatly disconcerted and surprised to see both our army and fleet arrive simultaneously. The presence of the Saxon fleet means that Guthrum cannot just casually send reinforcements by water. Whatever he sends has to be capable of defeating our entire fleet and dealing with our army camped on the shore."

Ambrose frowned. "But Guthrum certainly has the ships and men to force his way through our fleet, or even destroy it. I guess it remains to be seen if his men could land and force their way to Cripplegate Fort. What is stopping him from trying?"

Polonius smiled. "Time, Prince. London will be ours before

Guthrum can either march his army south or can manage to gather his full fleet and move it so far south."

"I have just three words for you, Polonius."

"And what are they, Prince?"

"'Remember the Stour.' Just how long did it take Guthrum to put together an overwhelming fleet?"

"We were deep in his home territory and the weather worked in his favor, Master."

"You are usually the pessimist, Scholar. We are attacking a Roman-built fortification and we do not outnumber the Vikings by your much-quoted ten to one ratio."

"There are not more than two hundred Danes in the London garrison, Prince, so we are not too far off. Even if they manage to pull in another one or two hundred, we still vastly outnumber the city garrison, and they can only hold Cripplegate Fort, not the entire city. Besides we have the Dorset men waiting to join us at Eton, and a second strong contingent from Kent should be approaching Southwark within the week."

"And if the Danes try to hold the entire city?"

"That would actually be to our advantage."

"Polonius, by what twisted Byzantine logic can you tell me that them holding all the London gates is to our advantage?"

"Master, sometimes I despair over you. You saw the extent and condition of the walls. Trying to hold all the city gates with a small force means the Vikings will be massively over-stretched along those walls.

"And the implications of all that?"

"Several of the gates will be vulnerable to a sudden attack. Their water route is cut off by the arrival of our fleet, and a force of our mounted fyrdmen will cut off the northern roads. Without an open supply route and with relatively little food within their fort, they should not be able to hold out for long. Their only hope is to retreat to Cripplegate Fort itself."

Ambrose nodded. "And if they do that?"

Alfred spoke. "We will set up Polonius's onagers and make life miserable for them. The onagers are stowed aboard our warships, and his famous fire pots are aboard the **Black Arrow**."

"And what about the Angles and Saxons of Lundonwyc? Will they rise up in support?"

Alfred turned to Polonius. "Scholar?"

"Unlikely, Sire. We already have their moral support, and several amongst them have long been our eyes and ears. I suspect, however, that they will attempt to remain ostensibly neutral, at least until they are absolutely sure we can both take London and keep it. Remember, their families are hostage to the Vikings. If we are forced to retreat after they have sent us fighting men, they will be massacred to the last woman and child."

Ambrose nodded. "Then let's go conquer a city, my friends."

The massive column of Saxon fighting men moved ever closer to the former capital of Britain. In its wake, plumes of smoke rose from the ruined halls of the Viking masters. The Danes ran fast, they surrendered, or they died. Alfred left no free Viking warriors in his wake.

There was no serious opposition. A thousand veteran fyrdmen tore through any little groups of Danes foolish enough to stand and fight. Bands of wailing and grieving women and children were soon heading under strong escort to captivity and the south bank of the Thames.

Three Saxon fyrdmen drove their horses mercilessly along the river-bank trail. When they reached Alfred's vanguard, they called loudly for their king. Their horses were lathered and heaving with exhaustion. The three men climbed down stiffly in front of their king. They all slipped to one knee, but the scout commander looked his king in the eyes and spoke directly.

"King, we have just ridden from Eton! The rumors are true. The Danes have built a rough fort, are provisioning it, and are calling in all the local Viking men. I fear that they intend to hold Eton."

Alfred turned to Polonius. "Well, Scholar?"

"The news is not good, Sire, though hardly unexpected. It is, however, the first real sign of organized resistance. If killing them delays us enough, then Guthrum just might make it south to London before us."

"I have no wish to leave a river strong point behind us, Polonius, so we will just have to overrun the fort."

"An ill-prepared attack against a defensive position might cost you dearly, Sire. It will take planning and time if you want to minimize casualties."

"We cannot afford a lot of time, Scholar. It is a good thing that I have been blessed with the greatest military advisor in the country, Wizard, if not the world! Did not Askold of Kiev once say about you that you were the most dangerous man he had ever known? From the leader of a couple of thousand Vikings who managed in a year or two to conquer an empire that took weeks just to travel through, that is a signal honor. Reach deep into your bag of tricks, my friend. We cannot afford to tarry long in front of Eton."

"I note, Sire, that both you and Prince Ambrose generally call me 'wizard' only when you expect a miracle from me."

The king smiled. "You are insightful, Polonius, as ever, but, the truth is, you have never once let me down!"

"Well, Sire, if the Vikings run true to form, they will build their walls with the dirt dug out of their dry moat, and then surmount the wall with a sturdy timber palisade."

"So what ideas do you have, Scholar?"

Polonius looked thoughtful. "I was hoping to save my fire bombs for the Cripplegate fort. The external walls of the fort at Eton will be proof from either rocks or fire, but the interior structures will be timber structures with thatched roofs, or skin tents. That is the Viking way"

"Meaning?"

"Meaning that with enough onagers, fire pots, and kegs of oil, we could rain 'fire and brimstone' upon the Danes. We can turn the interior of the fort into one huge conflagration. Without stone buildings or subterranean rooms, there would be no avoiding the flames and the rocks."

Alfred sighed. "I will send for all the oil I can find. I almost feel sorry for the heathens."

Alfred ordered the massive column to a halt as they passed a knoll less than a mile from Eton. He spoke to the men in his personal entourage. "Phillip, would you please see to the encampment? I want a dry moat and earth wall surrounding that hill. It doesn't have to be to the ancient Roman standards, but I want to be sure of no surprises tonight."

Phillip growled a terse reply. "Aye, Sire."

The army rose with the dawn. Alfred, however, accompanied by Phillip, Ambrose, Polonius, and a small escort of drengs, was already scouting out the Viking fort. The king stared at the Viking walls through some screening trees.

"Well, Scholar, it is as you said. If we did not have the means to bombard the defenders with fire, we would be forced to starve them out."

Ambrose nodded. "I fear, brother, that Guthrum would be in London long before that fort was starved into submission."

"Every day I bless God for bringing this underfed Byzantine to my court. Scholar, the ships float yonder, carrying your onagers. Carpenters stand ready, awaiting your orders. When can you start the attack?"

"Within twenty-four hours, Sire, if you give me enough men."

"You can have every man in the fyrd, Polonius, if you wish them all."

"Then let us get back to camp. We have a lot of work to do!"

The first Saxons neared the walls in the early afternoon. Safe behind large mobile wooden shields, the archers started desultory fire at the jeering Vikings. The Vikings had nowhere near the same number of men, but they had the height, so were able to retaliate. There were, however, few casualties on either side.

Polonius' onagers were moved slowly forward behind more mobile shields, until the ranging shots were consistently dropping within the Viking walls. When a second dozen catapults joined the first, the Vikings just jeered louder. The missiles just arced over their heads, thudding into buildings or into open ground, and doing little serious damage.

As the sun set, Alfred silently signaled large numbers of men to move into the forward positions the archers had set up and which protected the onagers. When all were in place, then a lone signaler blew a long melancholy note. It was the signal that the onager crews had been waiting for. Keg after keg of inflammable liquids arced high over the Viking palisades. When some four dozen kegs had been sent over the walls, then the first of Polonius' fire pots were lit and launched.

Ambrose watched with apprehension. A premature attack on the fort could cost so many casualties that the fyrd might be crippled, yet they simply could not waste much time reducing Eton. He prayed that Polonius' plan would work. Gradually, he noticed more and more light within the fort. Whiffs of smoke became columns, and the brightness kept increasing. The onager crews used long metal spikes to shift the aim of their weapons, or shortened the thongs on the leather baskets. Every third shot was a metal or stone missile.

Ambrose held his sword tight. The clouds over the fort literally glowed with reflected light, so the prince knew that the Vikings were in serious trouble. They could just wait and burn to death, but it was not the Viking way. Only a brave death in battle offered the hope of a glorious existence in Valhalla. A little after midnight, they came. Without a word, over two hundred Danes clambered over their own palisade, leapt into the dry ditch, and charged the onager line.

Alfred's fyrdmen were ready. They ran from their hiding places and did their best to form their shield-wall. The sheer ferocity of the attacking warriors allowed some to bull their way through the Saxon lines, but most of the Danes were trapped by the overwhelming numbers of the waiting Saxon forces.

ℝ

Alfred and his advisors walked slowly through the carnage. A dozen members of Alfred's Personal Guard stood nearby, weapons in hand. Some Viking warriors still lived, and groaned. One Dane screamed shrilly, until one of Alfred's drengs cut his throat. The Saxon dead were carried away reverently, to be buried elsewhere.

The king spoke. "Well, my friends, I am gratified that we won such a quick and easy victory, thanks in no small measure to Polonius the Scholar, but it always saddens me to see the price. I now know why my father really wanted a life of contemplation and prayer."

Ambrose spoke. "It is not over yet, brother. The hardest fighting is yet to come."

"You are right, brother. We will do, however, whatever it takes to keep Wessex free from the Viking vermin who have overrun the rest of this island. I just don't have to like it."

Within three days, the decrepit walls of the old capital came into view. Alfred inexplicably ordered the column to a halt.

"Commanders, we will camp here for tonight. The Danes are not far away, so I expect a marching fort to be erected before anyone starts cooking any meals."

Ethelwold, Ealdorman of Dorset and nephew to Alfred, dismounted stiffly from his horse. "It took the Romans four bloody hours, King, to erect the damned thing, and they were experts at it. We outnumber the Danes five to one. Why do we not just settle for a double guard tonight?"

"Nephew, I worry about you."

"How so, Uncle?"

"You are still a young man, yet it could be that you are getting too old for the responsibility I have given you."

Ethelwold twirled his battleaxe in his hand. "With due respect, uncle, I am at the height of my strength. My vision, if imperfect, certainly allows me to cut down the enemies of Dorset!"

"It is not your eyes that concern me, Ealdorman. It is your ears."

"I do not understand, King."

"It appears that you cannot hear your king. That is a dangerous fault."

The man sighed. "Sire, perhaps you would be more pleased if I undertook to oversee the building of a marching fort."

Alfred smiled. "That is an excellent idea, Ealdorman. You are in charge. See to it, but make sure the walls are a lot less porous than the one you had your men build at Wareham."

"Sire, the man who disobeyed your command at Wareham paid with his life. I issued the orders to kill him myself."

Alfred nodded gravely. "I know you did - before my men could use their hot irons to get the complete story out of him. His death was very convenient, Ealdorman."

As the sun slid above the horizon, one of Alfred's scouts galloped his lathered mount right to the king's tent. "Sire, a messenger was rowed over from the southern shore before the dawn. Our main fleet is in position just below London."

"Excellent. Polonius, would you please pass the word. I want everyone fed, packed up and in formation in exactly one hour. We have a battle to win this day."

Except for the squadron of two hundred riders, which Alfred sent galloping to cut the road north of London, the fyrdmen left their horses behind and advanced in three wide columns toward the decrepit city walls. One column marched towards Aldergate, the most northerly of the western gates, while the other two advanced towards Newgate and Ludgate.

Ambrose marched beside his brother. "Alfred, what makes you think that we can take these city gates? We do not even have siege equipment with us."

"You feel we will need it, Ambrose?"

"It is rare for an army to take a fortified city without some serious siege equipment, or at least numerous ladders and grappling hooks. The onagers won the battle for us at Eton. Today we appear to have neither."

Alfred smiled at Ambrose. "You are right, brother. If the Vikings bravely man their walls, we will have little chance of forcing a gate."

"They are Vikings, brother. You know they will fight bravely. If I may be so bold as to ask, why are we going through this exercise?"

"Brother, they do not have the men to cover all the city gates thoroughly. It's likely that the Vikings will feel it necessary to abandon at least one gate, whether Ludgate, Newgate or Aldergate, and simply retreat to Cripplegate Fort."

"And if they don't?"

"Then we fight."

"And without the ladders and other equipment, our men are massacred. What is the purpose of that?"

Alfred smiled. "Brother, today we are the decoys. While the main army makes a lot of noise and makes the Danes split their forces to cover three separate gates, our sailors are creeping up to the river gates by ship and our horsemen will first make a feint at Cripplegate and then have a try at Bishopsgate over to the east. All we need to do is to take one of the gates. The Vikings simply don't have enough men to hold all of them, and I have no doubt that we can stretch them so thin that we will manage to successfully take one. Once any one of them falls, we are in."

The Danes lined the walls over the three gates Alfred's army approached. They beat their shields with their swords and jeered the West Saxons below, while the latter slowly formed into a shield-wall.

Suddenly, however, a Viking battle horn sounded, urgently. The call was repeated over and over. The Viking heads swivelled and then disappeared. Almost immediately there was a cacophony of shouts and the sound of metal on metal.

Alfred smiled at Ambrose. "I think the sailors managed to land on the river bank. Either that, or our mounted column managed to force Bishopsgate.' He slapped his brother on his back. 'Either way, the battle for the greater fortress of London is about over. Now all we have to do is to destroy the Viking stronghold of Cripplegate

Fort itself."

"Before Guthrum and his Vikings arrive."

"Amen to that."

꙳

The men moved warily forward. Over fifteen hundred strong, the fyrdmen had arrows nocked and bows at the ready. The Danes jeered the attackers from the Cripplegate ramparts, but ducked quickly when vast flights of Saxon arrows were released. The Vikings had their bows at the ready too, but even with their advantage of the extra height, they were unable to match the overwhelming firepower of Alfred's entire army.

Alfred ordered a retreat almost immediately. On his command, the lines of archers retreated out of bow range.

Ambrose stared at the fortress walls. "Alfred, how long do you estimate we have to take this fort?"

"We got here in less than four days. I don't think Guthrum can do much for about another two weeks. It will take him that long to call up his warriors and move them south, assuming that he even sends his army to the right place. With luck, he is marching for the East Anglian coast or what is left of Benfleet."

Ambrose spoke. "Will he come by ship or land?"

"I do not know, brother-of-mine, but I don't think it will make much difference. If necessary, we will send the fleet up past Wallingford for protection, and that would actually free up the sailors to join our ranks. Guthrum cannot begin to match our combined army, whichever way he arrives."

"Will he fight?"

"He is certain to if we have not taken Cripplegate fort."

"So what does Polonius have in mind, Alfred?"

"We will start with the fire pots and flammable liquids again. Most of the Viking structures are wooden, so we will see what we can burn. While we are doing that, Polonius tells me that we will build a tower."

꙳

At Polonius' signal, the twelve arms sprang forward. When the arms hit the strike-plates, the leather thongs attached to the pouch snapped the fire pots high into the air. The missiles arced over the walls and disappeared somewhere within Cripplegate Fort.

The men looked at Polonius for further guidance. He spoke. "You know the drill. Use your spikes to move your onager left just a bit and load up again. I don't want any fire pots left when you are through. Keep varying your aim. You can't burn a building down twice."

"And when we run out of pots, Sir? Will we be able to burn them out?"

"I don't think that we can do what we did at Eton. This is an old Roman fort, not a temporary fort thrown together by barbarians in a few days. The original buildings inside are of stone, and they will be proof against both our stones and the fire pots. Still, when the fire pots run out, you will find rocks. Nice big ones. See if you can give some Viking a major headache. I particularly want stones lobbed in at night. There is nothing like a couple of dozen falling rocks to disturb your sleep."

⚑

The tower rose slowly, just out of range of the Viking archers. On the third day, the tower was complete and two hundred Saxon warriors started to push the construction slowly towards the wall. The Vikings sent their archers to the walls with fire-arrows. Alfred forestalled that move, however, by having his own archers, in much larger numbers, move into range, but behind long wooden shields. Some of the Saxons fell, but the overwhelming firepower of Alfred's men cut down far more Vikings. A few fire-arrows did strike the tower, but the water-soaked and untanned cowhides covering the timbers refused to ignite.

As the tower neared the walls, the Saxon archers stationed on it could see into the fort. Not only did they pour devastating fire into the fort, but they were able to direct the onager fire.

Just before the sun set, Ambrose stared down from the top of the tower into the old Roman fort. Few Viking-constructed buildings were left whole, and the Vikings he could see were forced to shelter in crumpled or burned out buildings. Ambrose knew that as soon as it was dark, the men manning the onagers would launch more showers of rocks. No Viking was completely safe inside the walls, wherever he crawled.

On the third day, Polonius ordered his crew to concentrate on the outer wall. The Roman wall was thick, but, struck with hundreds of heavy rocks in one single location, the wall was slowly reduced to rubble.

The defenders bravely moved forward and blocked the breach with a shield wall, the famous Viking skjaldborg. Shield to shield, they stood, ready for the inevitable assault. Alfred, however, chose not to send his men forward. Instead, the onagers flung their loads of rocks and the archers in the tower loosed thousands of arrows at the Viking shield-wall.

Viking after Viking fell, but the line was constantly renewed and it never wavered. As the Saxons tentatively approached the Viking skjaldborg at the breach, five hundred warriors slipped out of the woods to the north and dragged ladders and long boards towards the now-abandoned northern wall.

The long beams spanned the moat and the ladders were flung up against the walls. Before any Viking warriors even noticed, an unstoppable torrent of Angles, Saxons and Jutes poured over the ancient wall.

Within minutes it was all over. The surviving Danes met the attackers valiantly, but in the ruddy light of approaching dusk, they were ruthlessly cut down.

The main gate of the fortress was thrown open and Alfred strode into his new fort. London was now fully his - until Guthrum came to try and take it back.

CHAPTER 18

Guthrum Arrives and Fights

Ambrose sat on the riverbank and looked across to West Saxon territory. He spoke to Polonius. "I have an idea, Scholar."

"And what is that, Master?"

The prince took a stone from the shore and threw it high over the water. "You will note, Scholar, that this rock sinks immediately."

"Yes, Prince. Rocks generally do. I am not sure I see your point."

"Watch this one." With that, Ambrose picked up a second stone and threw it in a low trajectory. This rock skipped three times before it sank.

"I saw you throw two stones, Prince. Both sank. I still do not understand what you are showing me."

"What would happen if you lined up your onagers behind our shield-wall?"

"If you could get Guthrum's skjaldborg to stand in just the right place, I could punch a very big hole in the line. You saw the power of the stones against Cripplegate's sturdy wall."

"And so?"

"So if the skjaldborg insists on moving forward or back, and they would be incredibly stupid if they didn't, the onagers would be relatively useless."

"Unless you lowered the trajectory of the onagers."

"What would be the purpose of that, Prince?"

"Can you get it low enough that a round stone or iron ball would bounce on level ground, like the stone I just threw?"

"Probably, but the ground would deflect it and I could not guarantee any accuracy."

"But Polonius, does it matter? If the ball bounces along the ground, does it matter where exactly the skjaldborg stands?"

Polonius thought for a moment. "Not, I suppose, if the stone is traveling at sufficient speed."

"Then what would a dozen stones, or, if you added a deeper pouch, fifty smaller round stones do to a skjaldborg?"

Polonius began to get excited. "With your lower trajectory, it might be devastating. With massed fire, we just might punch a thirty foot hole in the Viking line!"

"And if we knew the placement and timing of the hole, could we not send a strong force through it?"

Polonius nodded. "You mean like what the Vikings tried on us up on the Stour River? It's one of their favorite tricks. They tried to use berserkers to open the way for their boar's snout, and if you and Phillip had not managed to cut down the berserkers before they reached our shield-wall, then I have no doubt that they would have broken our line. The technique is often damned effective."

"So the onagers could disrupt the skjaldborg?"

"Absolutely. With that new, lower trajectory, the onagers just might be capable of opening a gap for our own boar's snout."

Ambrose grinned. "So can we do it?"

"I am not sure if I can move the strike-plate enough to lower the trajectory sufficiently, but I will definitely go and try it. It may take a little engineering."

"Then it might work?"

"Ask me tomorrow, Prince. If it does, we will have a nasty little surprise for Guthrum."

ß

Alfred faced his advisors, his brother, and his ealdormen. "Well, members of the Witan, we now know that Guthrum has called up his army and is coming quickly south by road. We can easily hold Cripplegate Fort, but that means we lose our mobility and are cut off from the river. We could try and hold the London walls, but they are very long and in very poor condition. Alternately, we can go meet Guthrum and face him in open combat."

Ambrose spoke. "And why does that seem to concern you, Brother?"

"We should outnumber him by a considerable margin, especially with all the fyrdmen pouring across from Southwark, but we would be foolish not to leave a garrison at Cripplegate, and I have to accept that, man for man, the Vikings may be the best warriors in Angleland. Any battle is a close thing. A few men panic and run or some of your allies turn against you, or the enemy succeeds with some trick, and suddenly our army is in full rout. Saxon shield-wall against Viking skjaldborg, it is just possible that we could lose."

Polonius put up his hand. "Sire, Ambrose and I each had an interesting idea that just might shift the balance in our favor."

"And what magic will you and my brother perform this time, Wizard?"

"First, I am in the process of re-engineering half of the onagers. Prince Ambrose pointed out to me the benefits of a trajectory low enough to throw round metal or stone balls hundreds of feet along the surface of the ground."

Alfred nodded. "And how will this benefit us, Polonius?"

"Sire, our shield-wall stands resolute. Suddenly a dozen onagers hurl their stones over the heads of the West Saxon shield-wall ranks. The stones land short and the Vikings laugh. The round missiles roll forward with irresistible force, however, crushing any Viking who is in their path. The onagers thump again and again, concentrating their fire at a single point until a gaping hole appears in Guthrum's skjaldborg, which we immediately exploit with a hard-driving wedge of our best warriors."

Alfred nodded. "And victory is ours."

Polonius grinned. "It is possible, Sire."

Alfred thought for a minute before he spoke. "Can we do it?"

"I modified one onager to see if it can be done, and it worked. We might have to have our own fyrdmen kneel or lie on the ground, however. In my experiments, I discovered that the flatter the trajectory - the greater the distance the stones will bounce, though ground that is both hard and flat helps greatly."

"By the beard of sweet Jesus, if it works I will make the men dig ditches and lie down in them! Tomorrow we will ride the lands north of London. We must find a position that both protects our flanks and puts the enemy on reasonably level land. And you said that you and Ambrose had a second idea?"

"Yes, Sire. You have seen the value of the Roman throwing pilums before. If we face Guthrum in the open, it is crucial that we degrade his skjaldborg, and nothing does that like a half dozen pilums stuck to their shield in the moments before we close. I would like to have at least two thousand pilums made up immediately.

"Polonius, what exactly do you need for your new feats of magic?"

Polonius smiled. "Victory will not come cheap. I need every smith you have in the fyrd, all the iron you can scrounge or buy, and . . . oh yes, all of your masons and carpenters."

"Masons?"

"We need round rocks of a uniform weight, Sire."

"Is that all?"

"Well, probably five hundred warriors to collect and transport rocks."

"You shall have whatever you need, my friend. This may be the most pivotal battle in my lifetime. Either we push north of the Thames and form a strong united kingdom capable of handling the Danes, or the flower of our manhood will lie dead on the battlefield and the last free Angelisc kingdom will likely fall.

The blacksmiths all gathered in the shop smithy. Polonius picked up two short spears. He held up one in each hand for all to see and spoke. "These are the models I want you to follow. I want a thousand of each, just like these two.

Wade, a veteran blacksmith who was an acknowledged expert in metal work, and had been around so long that he had little fear of his masters, stated what several were thinking.

"Lord, I will make the spears any way you want, but that looks like a clumsy weapon. Let us make you real Saxon spears, with long razor-sharp blades and a cutting edge a foot long.

As he spoke, he picked up another of the sample weapons.

"Look at this, lord. The long metal shaft is good, I suppose. It will make it hard for a Viking to cut off your spear head, but the metal is soft. Look, I can bend it with my bare hand. Let me add some carbon to this shaft, and I will make it more rigid. And this triangular point makes thus useless as a slashing weapon. Why would you want such a poor spear?

Polonius smiled. "You ask a good question, so I will show you. Do you see those Viking shields I hung on the wall over there?"

Wade turned to make out the two shapes in the darkness of the smithy. "Aye, I can see them, Lord."

Polonius handed the old smith a gleaming new Saxon spear. "I want you to throw this spear at one of those targets."

"With pleasure, Lord. Now, this is worthy of being called a warrior's spear. " The old man threw smoothly, and the power of his thick corded muscles caused the spear to bite deep into the target, almost splitting the shield. He turned and grinned at his fellow smiths.

Polonius then handed him the clumsy spear. Now bury this one in the other shield.

The spear flew straight, hitting the shield near its metal boss.

Polonius smiled. "Well thrown. Now can you do it again?" So saying, he handed the smith one more of each weapon.

Wade snorted with derision. Both throws were as accurate, and the smith turned proudly.

"I served my time in the fyrd, Lord. I was thrust into the shield-wall at Edington."

The Byzantine nodded approvingly. "Well done! Now retrieve both shields."

Wade returned with the two heavy shields dangling easily in his gnarled hands. "Here you are, Lord Polonius."

"Now work the spear out of the shield."

"Which one, Lord?"

"One from each shield."

Wade worked the first Saxon spear free, then held it up. "See! As good as new, and the razor edge will put the fear of the Christian God in any Viking I ever met!"

"True, Wade, but what happens if the Viking warrior you throw it at survives your throw and decides to return your spear to you?"

The grizzled smith shrugged. "Well, I guess that is why I carry a shield."

"And how easy is it to remove it from the shield?"

"Easy. Lord. The blade acted as a wedge and split the board it hit. A few tugs back and forth, and it falls free."

"Now retrieve one of the new spears from the other shield."

The smith tried to pull it out, but the long, narrow and triangular shaped point had penetrated much deeper, and the weapon could not be pushed back and forth to enlarge the split in the shield. Finally, when the smith applied more energy, the soft iron neck just bent in his hands.

The smith held the offending spear aloft. "See? The point is too long and thin, and the metal too soft."

Polonius smiled again. "True, master smith, and which spear would you prefer being thrown back at you?"

"That's dead easy. This poor excuse of a spear can't be thrown again until I get a chance to heat it in my shop and beat it straight again."

Polonius spoke. "Ah, so is that an advantage?"

Wade thought hard. "I suppose so, if you do not want the enemy to use your own spears against you."

Now pick up the strap on the shield with the new spear still in it."

Wade looked puzzled, but complied.

"Wade, could you use that shield if you were to rejoin the Saxon shield wall?"

"No Lord. It is too imbalanced. I would have to remove the spear first."

"Which is relatively difficult to do?"

"Aye, Lord."

"What you are looking at, Wade, is a copy of the old Roman pilums. For centuries, every Roman legionary marched to battle with two of those spears across his shoulders. The points are hardened, made of your carboned iron, and the long shafts are of soft and relatively thin iron.

As the enemy closed on the legionaries, first the light version, and then the heavy versions were thrown in volleys. They wounded or killed many enemy warriors, but, equally important, they rendered the enemy shields useless in the moments just before the two lines clashed.

Wade nodded. "And the enemy couldn't return the favor even if they took the time to break off their attack and remove the - what did you call them? - pilums."

Polonius smiled. "Exactly, so, master smith. That is why I want you and the other smiths to follow these models precisely. A Viking shield wall, a skjaldborg, is one of the secrets of Viking prowess. If we can destroy the value of their shields, then we have the advantage and can overwhelm them. You have fought them. You know we need all the advantages we can get."

"You are called a wizard by many, Lord Polonius. Now I see why. This little trick could mean the difference between victory and defeat. I would be honored to make up as many of these as you want, and I will follow your pattern exactly."

Polonius smiled. "Then, my friend, you just might be responsible for the next Viking defeat."

☙

Ambrose entered the king's command tent with a grin on his face. Alfred looked up, puzzled.

"Brother, you look unusually happy for a man who is soon to go into battle."

"That is because, king and brother, I have a little surprise for you."

"The last time you told me that, you brought me pieces of waterlogged wood and made me guess where they came from."

"And were you not happy with the surprise when you learned that they were what was left of an entire enemy fleet?"

The King smiled. "It was, indeed, a delightful surprise. What do we have today? Is it a collection of leaves, or perhaps a lump of coal? I admit, I am curious."

Ambrose replied. "Even better, brother and king. I have a man who has asked for an audience with you."

"Ambrose, hundreds of men petition to see me daily. My chief reeve makes long lists and schedules them to see me as soon as I have free time. Does my brother suggest that I see this man out-of-turn?"

"Your brother recommends it highly."

Alfred sighed. "Then bring him on, brother-of-mine, if you think it is so important. Even a king should not argue with his big brother."

Ambrose called out. "Polonius, send him in."

The curtains parted and a man in chain mail entered the tent. He approached Alfred and kneeled before him.

The king stared at the stranger. The armored figure seemed very familiar. Suddenly Alfred gave a whoop of joy and ran to pull him to his feet and hug his son-in-law.

"Ethelred, what in the name of all that is holy are you doing here?"

"My father-in-law is going into battle. My wife insists that her father needs help. How could I not come and stand at his side?"

"Ethelred, how is Ethelflaed?"

"Your daughter is well, Sire, but very angry with me because I told her that she had to stay behind. She sends her love."

"Tell me truly - did she actually take command of her escort when the Viking raiders attacked her on her journey north?"

"She did, indeed, King Alfred. Although almost half of her escort was killed in the initial attack, she managed to rally the men and use an old ditch as a defensive line. She may just be turning sixteen, but she is truly the daughter of the greatest king in all Britain. It was only her quick thinking that saved any of the escort."

"Then I thank God for his mercies - and the Danes will pay dearly for that little bit of treachery. Ethelred, I did not expect you here. The last I heard, you were hard-pressed by the Welsh. Can you afford to abandon Offa's dyke?"

"In the early winter my faithful wolves drove deep into Wales. We burned several tuns and won three major skirmishes. The Welsh leaders have sued for peace. They have even agreed to accept you as Bretwalda, under two conditions."

"Which are?"

"First you must be victorious against King Guthrum.'

"I pray to God nightly that He gives me the strength to defeat the heathen. And the second?"

"That as Bretwalda you rein in your wild and crazy son-in-law. They want a peace guaranteed by the West Saxon fyrd."

Alfred grinned. "Then Polonius' plan worked!"

"With the gold you sent, I was able to hire enough unsworn warriors that the Welsh stood little chance. The Welsh now see you as their only hope for peace."

"Can you really trust the Welsh to keep their word in your absence?"

"They do not know that I have gone. I have left a strong screen of warriors, commanded by my warrior wife, along the dyke. Besides, the Welsh are busy planting and rebuilding."

"And you have heard nothing further from Guthrum?"

"I have received emissaries. He tells me that I may hold western Mercia in his name, if I send sufficient gold on an annual basis and swear loyalty to him."

Ambrose laughed. "You have to give that man credit. He does have balls. You defeat his puppet ruler and he tries to extort gold from you."

"Prince Ambrose, I am a realist. Eastern Mercia was long ago overrun by Guthrum's warriors, and Guthrum has quite thoroughly subjugated all of East Anglia and Essex. After Wessex beat off his attack, he settled most of his men in eastern Mercia. Without the resources to hold all of Mercia, he appointed a puppet Saxon, who was just happy not to be wearing a thrall's collar, to rule in his name. I believe that he is biding his time, absorbing his conquered lands thoroughly before he comes west for the rest of Mercia. Worse, I have reason to believe that Guthred of Northumbria might have similar interests. Without my father-in-law as Bretwalda, western Mercia will fall, followed quickly by the Welsh kingdoms. Only Wessex has the strength to hold the line against the Viking king. Even if I had not sworn obedience to King Alfred here, and was not son-in- law to him, I would be here. It is the only hope for my people. It is why my fighting men are here."

Alfred was startled. "Then you brought more than a personal escort?"

Ethelred smiled. "I have brought you my finest Mercian wolves, Sire. They are the battle-scarred veterans who both helped me defeat Guthrum's puppet king and then spearheaded my victories against the Welsh raiders last winter."

Alfred smiled in return. "And just how many of these Mercian wolves did you bring with you, Ealdorman?

"I have close to six hundred veteran fyrdmen awaiting my call, King Alfred. I regret that I was forced to leave some two hundred guarding Offa's Dyke and the northern *marches*. The men I brought, however, are the best of the best. All are armored, well mounted, and proven warriors."

Alfred continued to look at Ethelred with great interest. "And just where are all these proven warriors?"

"Less than a single day's hard ride west of here. They but wait for your summons."

Alfred looked at Polonius. "Scholar, you were wondering how to protect our flanks. Would three hundred mounted warriors hidden in the woods on either side of our chosen position be a satisfactory solution?"

Polonius replied. "Perhaps even better, my king, would be to have a strange force arrive on the battlefield just as the main force of Viking warriors are committed. It would be even more effective if Guthrum did not know that Ethelred's Mercians were nearby. We would both break their confidence and outflank them at a critical moment."

Alfred smiled. "Could we really surprise them? Guthrum is no fool, and I have no doubt that he knows our current numbers, probably to the last man."

Alfred turned to Ethelred. "I have a question for you, Ealdorman. Does Guthrum know that you are here with your fyrd?"

"I have left a screen of warriors, albeit thin, along my eastern border, Sire, as well as the Welsh border watchers. On the way here, my wolves rode through the land swept clean by your army. We saw no Viking forces along the way and any individual Vikings we flushed were left hanging from the nearest tree. I must therefore conclude that Guthrum does not know of our presence."

"Excellent. Philip, I want you to send out a strong screen of scouts, twenty four hours a day, until we face Guthrum. Ethelred, you will bring your men here under cover of night. I want the presence of you and your men to be a complete surprise to Guthrum."

Guthrum's outriders were spotted first. The single riders were soon replaced by rank after rank of horsemen heading south. In a seemingly endless column four horses wide, Guthrum's army filled the old Roman road as it snaked over the crest of the hill and into the Thames valley.

Ambrose used his hand as a sun shield and watched the Viking riders advance. Guthrum clearly accepted Alfred's challenge, as his army came on confidently, though it started to spread to match the Saxon line barring the road. Within minutes, the famous Viking skjaldborg was formed, with the horses taken to the rear. Skjaldborg to shield-wall, the two forces faced each other over a five hundred foot gap.

Guthrum's force halted and a pair of mounted riders slipped through the line. The two riders slowly approached the Angelisc lines, while the second man held up a white-covered shield.

Alfred turned to Ambrose. "My eyes are beginning to fail me brother. Is the first man Guthrum himself?"

"I think so. Do you want me to meet him?"

"I guess it should be king to king, but I would like you to join me."

The four riders met half way between the two armies. King Guthrum spoke first.

"I would say 'welcome', Godfather, but you are on my land. If you take your men south across the Thames, then perhaps we could greet each other as friends again."

"And greetings to you, Athelstan. For the sake of our friendship and in the name of peace, I might have managed to forgive your fifteen ships of reinforcements to the Francian Vikings at

Rochester, and perhaps even the sanctuary you provided the defeated invaders. I would have been hard-pressed to forgive the fact that you allowed raiders to cross the Thames River during the winter, but I can never forgive the attack on my daughter as she went north to join her new husband. If not for all that, then I might have been able to welcome my godson today as a friend."

"Go south, Alfred, before I send my warriors to destroy you. I have no wish to fight you, but I will not let you stay on my land. You burned a lot of properties and killed a lot of my men on your march from Wallingford. You owe me a lot of geld."

"Send your warriors, Athelstan, and be damned! No one attacks my daughter and lives! No man attacks Wessex and gets away with it. My brother made that very clear to you last summer."

Guthrum sighed. "The man who attacked your daughter was overzealous, and has already paid with his life. I swear on my holy armband that I did not send him. What more do you want, King of the West Saxons?"

"London. The north bank of the Thames. Mercia."

"Those I will not give you. You will have to take them."

"Then paint that shield red. We have nothing further to talk about, King. Send your warriors forward and we will see at the end of the day who owns London and the rest."

Guthrum looked hard at Alfred, but the Saxon's gaze was steady. At last, the Danish king broke the silence. "So be it, king of the West Saxons."

The proud Viking king swung his horse in a 180 degree arc and rode back to his own lines.

Pounding their shields with their swords and shouting"Odin! Odin!" the Viking line started forward. Ambrose watched the fearsome warriors approach and felt the familiar feeling in the pit of his stomach. These northern barbarian fighting men were not to be trifled with. Even with the extra Saxon numbers, victory was far from certain. The prince prayed that Polonius' magic would be as effective as he promised. Ambrose was already looking westward to see if Ethelred's force was in sight yet, though he knew that Ethelred had been instructed not to break cover until the entire Viking force was committed.

Alfred's Signaler blew a long note on the war horn. Every other fyrdman stepped behind his partner, and the archers raced into position through the gaps. Formed up in two rough ranks, they fired arrow after arrow until their quivers were empty, and then they slipped back behind the shield-wall. The alternate swordsmen stepped back into position, and the line was again ready to receive the Viking warriors. Dozens had fallen in the hail of arrows, but the Vikings stoically stepped over their fallen and continued to advance.

Ambrose turned to Alfred. "When do we spring the first surprise, brother?"

"Patience, brother-of-mine. Polonius will signal for the men to drop, and then we will try the onagers."

Even as he spoke, a long continuous note from a battle horn sounded. A long section of the Saxon shield-wall rank dropped to the ground and almost immediately Ambrose could hear the twang and thud of the tensioned onager arms hitting their padded strike-plates.

The hail of rocks and iron balls fell short of the center of the Viking shield-wall, eliciting hoots of laughter from the advancing warriors. The missiles were on such a low trajectory however, that they bounced and bounced, until they reached the Viking line. Suddenly a half dozen men were transformed into red rag dolls. The Vikings roared their rage, but a second, and then a third volley of man-killing missiles tore through the center of their advancing ranks.

The entire Viking line started to move forward faster, but suddenly dozens of men on both wings were screaming in surprise and pain. They had found the caltrops liberally sprinkled in the tall grass.

The Vikings continued to advance, though now in a foot-sliding motion designed to avoid the vicious spikes hidden in the tall grass. The Saxon front rank scrambled to their feet.

The horns blared a second time, and the fyrdmen grabbed the

newly supplied pilums and launched clouds of them at the slowly approaching Vikings. A few enemies fell, but for the most part, the fierce warriors just raised their shields and continued their advance. Pilum after pilum thudded into the shields, and when the Vikings lowered them, they found they had become awkward and heavy. Just as they slowed to pluck the pilums out, the Anglish fyrd obeyed the new braying and advanced to meet them. The shield-walls came together with a terrible crash, but the Vikings were not ready. The pilums and the barrages of rocks had disrupted their formation.

A fourth note sounded, and the center of the Saxon wall split. Three hundred mounted fyrdmen poured through the gap, each armed with an over-sized spear. They hit the Viking's weakened center and, without an adequate number of Vikings standing to lock shields, the Saxon horsemen had no trouble breaking through.

Ambrose watched with mounting excitement. If the riders were able to turn and attack the Viking rear, then Guthrum was finished. The only cure for so many mounted men behind your ranks was to run for the shelter of trees and then try and regroup. He knew the Vikings were brave men, but panic was contagious. Once some started running, it would be almost impossible to stop the rest.

Alfred was watching carefully. "Damn it, Ambrose, the brave bastards are arcing their line to meet our riders! And look, Guthrum has sent his own riders to try and plug the gap."

"And they are succeeding, brother!"

So the wily king thinks he has countered my move, does he?' He turned and yelled to his signalers. 'Sound the call for Ethelred!"

The horns blared out a new and strident summons, which was answered by a wall of mounted Mercians; erupting from the forest to the west. Alfred smiled. "Now sound the general advance!"

The horns sounded yet again, and the entire host started deliberately forward again, adding their weight to the hard-fighting horsemen. Along most of the line, skjaldborg hit shield-wall, but the Viking center was broken and the Northern warriors were in confusion. As Ethelred's men neared, the Vikings in the wings suddenly realized that a second mounted force, hundreds strong, was sweeping towards their unprotected flank and rear.

The Mercian horsemen started their butchery, cutting down the Viking warriors from behind while Alfred's men countered the

Viking horsemen. As the almost invulnerable skjaldborg began to break up into isolated clumps of Viking warriors, the fyrdmen started to have success against their enemy. The Saxon shield-wall held, and both groups of horsemen drove the Vikings against it. There was death on both sides, and the bravest warriors in the world could not stand long in such a situation. The Vikings nearest the broken center started to run.

Another long blast on the war horn released Alfred's reserve, a force of mounted fyrdmen who followed their comrades through the center. Two hundred more riders spurred into action. Guthrum's reserve of several hundred riders had first ridden to counter the Saxons coming through the Saxon center, and then had rallied bravely to meet the Mercians. There were not enough to counter both threats, let alone Alfred's mounted reserve. The Viking king's skjaldborg had finally collapsed and his men were now running for their lives.

Ambrose turned to Alfred. "Do we order pursuit, brother?"

Alfred held his stomach and grimaced in pain. Ambrose turned when he saw the pain on his brother's face. "Polonius! Alfred needs some of your elixir - now!"

Polonius ran forward and handed to the king a stoppered horn. Alfred took the stopper off and drained the liquid in one gulp. He managed a weak smile, although he continued to hold his belly.

"God has seen fit to test me this day, though He has given me a great victory. There is no standing army left between here and Northumbria. If we crush the remnants of Guthrum's army, then he will be forced to come to us on his knees. Ambrose, in the name of God - order the pursuit!"

Ambrose punched the sky twice with his sword. In response, the signalers blew the attack. It hardly mattered. The Saxons, both mounted and on foot, continued to charge after the broken Vikings.

"Brother, are you all right?"

"I will survive, brother. Polonius' elixir will soon take effect. Go after the heathen devils!"

Prince Ambrose signaled for horses, and he, Phillip and Polonius mounted up and rode after the two forces heading north.

Many of the Vikings made it to the relative safety of the

woods. Those caught in the open by the Mercians and West Saxon riders died by the hundreds.

The killing continued until darkness, when the Saxons finally gave up the chase and headed back to where their King's banner fluttered from the top of the rise.

By firelight, the victorious fyrdmen celebrated raucously or patched their wounds. Exhausted men collapsed on the open ground and slept where they lay.

By dawn, Alfred felt better. Phillip helped him to his feet and the king started a tour of the camp. He was galled with what he saw, and spoke to Polonius.

"Scholar, please find Odda and tell him that I want a proper infirmary for our seriously wounded. I want our dead to be given a Christian ceremony and burial, and I want the less-seriously wounded loaded on our wagons and taken back to London without delay."

"Aye, Sire. I will find him immediately."

"Phillip and Ambrose, would you be so good as to form up a force of some five hundred of our best riders – mounted on our best horses?"

Ambrose spoke. "And what do you want us to do, brother?" went n already

"Pursue Guthrum northward. Harry him. Do not let his forces re-form, but do not fight a pitched battle."

"How far, Alfred?"

"Until he goes to ground. My guess is that he will head for Cheshunt."

Ambrose nodded. "It will be done, brother."

Ambrose's column rode north on the great Roman road at a fast trot. Within hours, they caught up with the worst-wounded Viking stragglers. Some were run down, but most managed to make it into the forest. None surrendered.

By mid-afternoon, the hard-driving column neared the little tun of Cheshunt. The appearance of the Saxon column caused consternation. Viking warriors fled for the shelter of the walls, all the while driving in pigs and horses. The tun gates were slammed shut as the Saxon column neared. Grim-faced warriors lined the battlements.

Ambrose and Phillip stared at the formidable walls. Guthrum's Viking army was trapped, but it was not yet crushed.

Even while the commanders looked, the main gate opened and Guthrum, again carrying a white shield, rode out alone. He rode towards Ambrose and Phillip. Several Saxons started to spur forward, but Phillip's stentorian voice stopped them cold.

Guthrum stopped his horse some ten yards from where Ambrose and Phillip sat on their horses. The Viking king spoke. "Greetings Phillip, Prince Ambrose."

"Greetings, King Guthrum."

"You cannot take my tun with a mere five hundred warriors, Prince."

Ambrose replied. "Somewhere close behind me is the full might of the West Saxon Empire, King Guthrum. We are just the vanguard."

"Prince, tell your brother that he has convinced me to consider negotiations. War between God-father and God-son is a sin against the Christian church."

Ambrose smiled. "I will send your words just as you said them. In any case, he will be here personally in just a day or two. I hope you will understand, in turn, that I am honor bound to kill any Vikings who attempt to leave the tun – until my brother tells me otherwise."

Guthrum nodded somberly. "We will wait inside the walls, Prince."

CHAPTER 19

Alfred and Guthrum Discuss Peace

The two kings faced each other across the conference table. Alfred spoke. "King Guthrum, several years ago you swore an oath to God and on your sacred armband that you would never again invade Wessex. In return, I agreed to let you and your men live. You were baptized in Christ's name, and I treated you as an esteemed ally and friend. I even ceded my land north of the Thames, in order that we could have a lasting peace.

When the Vikings from Francia arrived, I asked for your help. You refused me, and went so far as to allow fifteen shiploads of your warriors to reinforce the Vikings at Rochester, effectively doubling the invasion army. Further, once we had driven out the army, you both provided sanctuary and allowed your men to slip across the Thames to raid our shores. Finally, you sent men to kill my daughter as she rode north to marry Ethelred of Mercia. Tell me now, before God and my witnesses, if anything I have just said is not true?"

"King Alfred, I told Prince Ambrose that I would not raid Wessex, and I kept my word. Although some individual warriors crossed the Thames, I repeat, I did not bring my army south. You know as well as I do that if I had marched south, I could have destroyed your supply column and probably razed half of Wessex before you could have caught up with me. I did not do this, Alfred, because I swore to you that I would not."

"No, you did not, Guthrum, and for that much, I am grateful. Nevertheless, you refused to support me in my time of need."

"You asked me to attack my fellow countrymen, Alfred. You are my godfather and you were magnanimous in victory to me once, yet that was a great deal to ask. My men may have mutinied if I had told them to kill their own friends and cousins."

"Then why did you let your people cross the Thames? We fought, and killed, many warriors from East Anglia. Almost half of the force at Rochester was yours!"

"King, my warriors seek adventure. None received my permission to travel south. None of my dragons sailed with my blessing."

"We counted fifteen long-ships of yours, King! Do you deny that your men crossed the Thames? Do you deny the presence of fifteen of your long-ships at Rochester?"

King Guthrum looked uncomfortable. "It is possible, but, as I said, not with my permission."

"Then you deny that your men crossed the Thames?"

"I told you, Alfred, it is possible. I did not lead my army south, nor send my fleet. You tell me my men were there, but I am not personally aware of any particular Vikings who went south."

"Guthrum, I captured some of your men at Rochester. Later, we captured more raiders on the south bank of the Thames. They were your men! Surely you noticed some of your hersirs and jarls were absent from your council. Did you not miss Olaf-the-One-Eyed and Canute-the Mighty? How about Egil the Little, one of your own Personal Guard."

"Egil is under sentence of banishment, Alfred. He dared to attack your brother when he was serving as emissary and was under my protection. For that crime, I stripped him of his property and declared him outlaw . . . Do you know where he is?"

In reply, Alfred clapped his hands three times. Six burly churls dragged Olaf, Canute and Egil, heavily shackled, into the tent.

Guthrum looked at Alfred. "Why are these warriors in chains? This is hardly the act of a Christian king!"

"These men were caught in the act of piracy, on the south bank of the Thames. Two were captured at Rochester, and Egil here was caught when he attempted to pillage a riverside settlement. By your own law, their lives are forfeited, along with the rest of the captured raiders. Egil's ship, by the way openly flew your pennant when we took it."

"Where are the rest of my warriors?"

"Dead or in chains. I promised six feet of land to any Viking who enters Wessex uninvited . . . six feet and a length of hemp rope. The hundreds of Danes we captured north of the Thames are under guard in Wessex. None survived who were caught south of the Thames."

Guthrum stared at Alfred. "You are a hard king, Alfred.' A half-smile flitted across his face. 'You might have been born a Viking. You are the most ruthless Saxon King I know."

"I am the only Saxon king you know, Guthrum. In fact, thanks to you and your fellow Vikings, I am the only Angelisc king left on the entire island. I try to be clear with my messages. Was I successful this time?"

"Alfred, I accept the evidence. Perhaps a few of my men sought adventure south of the Thames. I repeat - I did not send them, nor did I lead them. You can hardly hold me responsible for the deeds of every individual in East Anglia. This Egil that you hold is a scoundrel and a rogue. He has been hiding from my royal justice.

In fact, in spite of my forbearance, may I remind my godfather that, soon after the Francian Vikings fled north, you brought the entire West Saxon fleet against my people on the River Stour? You looted the ships of men who had done nothing to you, and it was only with the greatest of effort on my part that we were able to seize the ships and cargoes back."

"Guthrum, I had hoped that, under the white shield, we would only speak the truth. Some of those ships belonged to the Francian Vikings, and you know it! The rest were yours, but they had been identified as being present at Rochester. I took the time to identify the ships before I attacked. I had already warned you that I would chase the pirates, wherever they went. You did not respect my borders, Guthrum, so I did not respect yours."

"You attacked blindly, King! You had no idea if they were innocent traders or Francian Vikings. You certainly did not know if it was my men who had been involved."

Alfred turned red in anger. "My own brother landed at the encampment to specifically make sure that they were the guilty parties."

"That fact is not possible, Alfred! No Saxons landed there! The only vessel to visit was a Swedish . . . Rus . . . An ale merchant . . ."

"Who was blond, short of stature, and accompanied by a giant named Edgar."

"By Odin's balls, if that jarl cannot see a Saxon when he is staring him in the face, then I will personally pluck out his eyes . . . All right, I will concede the truth of what you say.

Let us talk of London, Alfred. The garrison there did not cross the Thames, yet you landed far to the west and proceeded to burn every Viking hall along your line of march, culminating in your brazen attack on the garrison at London itself. I remind you now that your fyrdmen still hold my city."

"Guthrum, may I remind you that your army has once again been crushed and the remnants trapped. Essex, Danish Mercia and East Anglia are wide open to invasion."

"It is true that we have lost a battle, Alfred. We are not crushed."

"I accept that you and your men are a tough adversary, Guthrum. You know and I know, however, that just before the harvest season, my army will disappear."

"That is the way of farmers who fight, Alfred. It is the same for the Viking armies whose men live on the land."

"That was once true for Wessex, Guthrum, but it is no more. Before these brave men leave, an entire new army of veterans, fresh and eager, will arrive. And after a winter of campaigning, my original army will return. If you attempt to match that, your people will not have time to reap your crops and starvation will stalk the land come winter."

Guthrum sighed. "What are you saying, Alfred?"

"You cannot defeat me, Guthrum."

"Alfred, I have a fleet that you cannot begin to match."

"I concede that, Guthrum, assuming that you have enough men left to man a fleet when I am through here. In any case, I have a great surprise for you if you attempt to sail up the Thames."

"I know about Wallingford, King. My men watched you strengthen the burh's defenses. They even watched you dismantle your giant catapult things."

"And do they know about Southwark? I have closed more than the upper reaches to you and your ilk. The river is closed at

London."

Guthrum shrugged. "Your southern coast is long and inviting, King."

"True, Guthrum, but you would have to strip your northern garrisons in order to crew the ships. While you play in the south, I will cut through your country like a hot sax through butter, and I will hang every Dane that I find."

"And I would follow your example, but in Wessex's heartland."

"You will do your best to take my burhs, Guthrum, but this time you will find them a challenge. They are now fortified, have permanent garrisons, and they will be reinforced by the thousands of churls who would flee to them the moment your landing is reported. The garrisons, and the signal pyres, but await your arrival."

"I repeat - what are you saying, King Alfred?"

"I concede that it would be very costly for me to take back East Anglia and Essex, but I could do it if I am driven to it."

"You might also bring down the wrath of Guthred of Northumbria and Sitric of Dublin on your head. They would not take kindly to a victorious Wessex on Guthred's southern border. I will concede, however, that I probably cannot conquer Wessex. And so we have a stalemate."

"Guthrum, let us speak truths. My brother has an understanding with the king of Dublin, and I will take my chances with Guthred. If I leave you in possession of East Anglia, there will have to be a new reality."

Guthrum sighed again. "And just what do you envision, King of the West Saxons?"

"The Thames will never again be a highway for your long-ships to invade the heart of Angleland. The north bank, at least near London and upriver, cannot continue to belong to East Anglia.

"If you occupy the north bank, Alfred, and, particularly London, it will be a festering sore continually threatening my country. I cannot accept a powerful Saxon army on the north shore - there will be no natural barrier between Wessex and East Anglia."

"Guthrum, with all due respect, only one of us has an intact army. Nevertheless, I see your point. I will tell you what I will do. I will hold London until it is clear that we have an understanding.

I will have my men build up the defenses. When I am satisfied that the city is well protected, I would be willing to consider transferring ownership of London to Mercia. The ealdorman of Mercia is no threat to you."

"But I control Mercia, Alfred."

"You control eastern Mercia, Guthrum. Your puppet king was killed by Ethelred and western Mercia has been independent for several years."

"Alfred, I am not going to give up western Mercia without a fight. I will raise another half dozen armies to face you, and if that is not sufficient, I will ask Guthred and Sitric to join me."

Alfred smiled. "Your friends from Francia have gone home. You know as well as I do that Sitric will not come south against me. Besides, except for the North bank near London, and the city itself, you will keep what you hold, Guthrum. In return, however, you will guarantee the independence of western Mercia along the borders I am about to propose."

"I recognized the banners of Mercia when that force outflanked us on the day of battle. I can only assume that the upstart, Ethelred of Mercia, has sworn obedience to you, Alfred."

Alfred smiled. "He will rule in his own right, though backed, if necessary, by the Wessex Fyrd."

"And your sprig of a daughter will rule him, if the stories are true. Exactly what boundaries do you envision, Alfred?"

"I had thought up along the Thames, and then up the Lea River as far as its source. From there, straight to Bedford and from there, up the Ouse until Watling Street and along it."

"Tread lightly, King. Some of the land you so grandly claim is my land, occupied by my followers."

"You have not occupied most of western Mercia, so you are not giving up so much, Guthrum. In return, I will recognize your claim to the rest of Essex and East Anglia. Some of what you keep was once my land. If I come north, you will have six feet of land or you will be driven to your ships. Instead, I offer you an honorable compromise."

"And if I agree to this, you will swear to recognize our new borders?"

"I and all my descendants. I will swear this before Almighty God, Guthrum."

"It is true that my warriors are tired and our ranks have been thinned. I think most of my people might accept a peace such as you propose. I will take your offer to my council."

"There is more, king of the Vikings."

Guthrum sighed. "I am listening, king-of-the West-Saxons."

My religious fathers tell me that you do not value the lives of your Saxon and Angle subjects. Henceforth, the wergeld for a subject, be he Dane or Saxon, will be the same."

"The wergeld for a Danish *bondi* is eight half marks of gold, Alfred."

"Then that will be the wergeld for the killing of a Saxon or Angle."

Guthrum shrugged. "It is agreed, Alfred. What else is in your mind?"

"If a Saxon churl or Danish bondi is accused of murder and he tries to clear himself by the giving of an oath, then he must do so before twelve other churls or bondi. If he refuses to take the oath, then he will pay triple wergeld."

"I think I can accept that. What else?"

"As of the day that we agree to this treaty, none of my West Saxons, free or slave, will be accepted into your host, nor will I accept your subjects into my army."

"And if young men, seeking adventure, slip across the boundaries and attempt to join the others' army?"

Alfred spoke. "They will be returned."

"That means that we will not harbor each other's refugees from justice. I have no problem with that. Nevertheless, with a long boundary and less natural barriers between us, there is bound to be trade between our two peoples."

"If our two peoples wish to trade, I would welcome it. They may certainly do so, but both sides must give hostages as a pledge of honorable intentions."

Guthrum replied. "Only thieves and criminals would be unhappy with that."

A brief smile flitted across Alfred's face.

"I agree Are we done?"

"That is the gist of the treaty I am proposing. There will be, of course, a matter of hostages and an exchange of any prisoners. I will have my scribes put it into more formal language, and then I will have it delivered to you."

"Alfred, you ask for a lot of land."

"Most of which you do not even control, and, in return, you will be allowed to march the remains of your army home without hindrance. If you prefer, you can go back and hide behind your walls. Polonius wants to show me some more Byzantine siege techniques and I am curious to try them out."

"Alfred, you have a Christian heart of mercy and yet your fist wears Viking steel."

"What do you say, Guthrum? Do we have an agreement?"

"I am frankly reluctant to have you as an immediate neighbor, but I think that with the proviso that London and that part of the northern bank of the Thames that I do not control goes to Saxon Mercia, I think I can probably convince my jarls to accept your terms. Of course, as well as the prisoners, I will expect blood money for each and every one of my subjects killed by your ravaging army. Further, I will expect compensation for any thralls we are forced to release."

Alfred smiled. "I will accept the condition - if you are willing to pay for all the damage you did when your army last ravaged Wessex. Do you have several tons of gold at your disposal?"

Guthrum laughed. "I will arrange for any captives to be sent south."

Alfred shook Guthrum's hand. "I will return any of your sworn men that I have in captivity."

"And the Francian Vikings you captured?"

"The Francian Vikings did not survive their captivity. Each received their promised allotment of hemp and their six feet of land."

"Do you want to know why I did not come south with my entire army, Alfred? There was great pressure on me to do so."

"I don't doubt the pressure. I assumed it was because you had given your word to me."

"A Viking's word given to an unbeliever has no value."

"I know, Guthrum. That is why I hung your hostages, when you broke your word to me after Wareham."

"You are both brave and ruthless, Alfred. When I give my word to a man I respect, then it has great value. You have proven to be worthy."

Alfred nodded. "And that is why I really hoped you would stay out of this problem, Guthrum. I had no wish to attack you. I always keep my word, however, and you broke yours first."

"Alfred, you would have truly made a great Viking."

"I hope this time we may truly make peace, Guthrum."

APPENDIX I

Glossary of Terms

Aegir: Was the god of the sea. He was a personification of the ocean. He caused storms with his anger and it was said a ship went into"Aegir's wide jaws" when it sank.

Ambat: Female Viking thrall or slave.

Angelisc: The name the Angles, Saxons and Jutes had started calling themselves.

Angleland: The land of the Angles, Saxons and Jutes. England.

Atheling: An Atheling was a royal prince. The Saxon kings were chosen from amongst their ranks by the Witan, or council.

Athelstan, King: When King Guthrum was baptized by King Alfred at Wedmore, he took the Christian name of Athelstan.

Asgard: Odin's hall, where Viking warriors go if they fall bravely in battle.

Boar's Snout: See Svinfylka.

Bondi: Was a truly free and land-holding farmer. From this class came many of the traders and hunters, sailors and raiders.

Bookland: Was land given to individuals or the church in perpetuity. Unlike most land grants, they did not revert back to the king at the death of its possessor. For the church, this was vital, for it could not reach real power with its property only 'on loan' from the current king.

Breeks: Pants.

Bretwalda: A ruler of Britain so powerful that all of the other kings recognize him as overlord.

Burh: A fortified settlement with a permanent garrison. When Alfred was through building these forts, no Saxon was more than twenty miles from the protection of one.

Churl: A peasant. His property was guaranteed, but he had to farm and provide military service.

Danegeld: Is a payment to the Danes so that they would leave the land in peace. It was reportedly first paid in 865 by the ealdorman of Kent.

Dreng: Young warriors who serve as the king's companions. If they serve well, they may be given land and elevated to the status of duguo, or land-owning thane.

Duguo: The proven warriors who have been allotted land by the king. They are expected to answer the king's summons at the head of their own household troops.

Ealdorman: A nobleman next in power to the royal princes. The Saxon kingdom of Wessex was divided into shires, and an ealdorman was in charge of each shire. It was the ealdorman who called out the fyrd, or local militia

Francia Occidental: Is the eastern partition of Charlemagne's former empire. It most closely corresponds with France.

Francia Orientalis: Is the western part of Charlemagne's former empire, divided by the treaty of Verdun, 843.

Frankland: Frankland, or Francia, is the name I use for France.

Frisian: Were sea-faring traders who were located on the mainland coast just south of Viking territory. One of their main cities was Wyk Te Duurstede.

Fyrd: Militias made up of thanes and churls. For every five hides of land, one fyrdman, mounted and armed, was obliged to answer the call-to-arms.

Gladius: A short thrusting sword used by Roman legionaries.

Great Army: The name given to the large Viking army that invaded England in 865. Its leaders included Ivar the Boneless, Ubbi, and Halfdan.

Greek-Fire: A volatile substance that burns fiercely and could not easily be put out. It gave the Byzantine navy a considerable advantage in battle.

Godson: In 878, after the defeat of his army at Edington, Guthrum agreed to be baptized and King Alfred acted as his spiritual godfather.

Halegmonath: This is the ninth or holy month of the year. It is the month of festivals.

Hersir: A minor Viking nobleman.

A **Hide** is a unit of measure. It generally denoted enough land to support a single family. In Alfred's day, every so many hides (generally 5) held meant that you had the obligation to send one armed and mounted warrior to join the fyrd when so instructed.

Holmgang: A duel that followed very specific rules.

Jarls: They were important Viking land-owners, who acted as both priests and judges.

Jutes: The Jutes were, with the Angles and the Saxons, the three major Germanic tribes to have conquered Roman Britain. The empire of Wessex was made up of people from all three of the original tribes.

Khagan: The ruler of the nomadic Khazar tribe who controlled the land along the Dnieper River.

Khazars: A powerful nomad tribe that was quite supportive of trade, and controlled the territory where the Dnieper River enters the Black Sea.

Kiev: was a town just north of the open steppes on the Dnieper River. It was apparently seized by Dir and Askold sometime soon after 860 A.D.; after the death of three brothers who had ruled there.

Kvasir's Blood: Is a term for poetry. Odin was supposed to have stolen the 'sacred mead of poetry' which was brewed from the blood of a wise god - Kvasir.

Leaping Stag: Alfred's flagship, built with Frisian help, it was larger than the Viking long-ships, and with higher sides.

Long Ride or Long Gallop: A technique Ambrose and Polonius used to seize Carnarvon. With multiple mounts, the riders start a fast ride towards the target from far away. By changing horses and posting scouts in advance to ambush any couriers, they attempt to outride any news of their approach, thus achieving complete surprise.

A Long-Ship: Was a Viking sea-going vessel somewhat smaller than a dragon ship. It was up to a hundred feet in length, and carried up to 200 crewmen.

Long House: the Viking Great Hall, where a nobleman or multiple families live together.

Lundonwyc: A Saxon settlement of craftsmen and traders just upstream of the depopulated London.

March: A march is a border region; one that may need to be defended.

Night: The Anglo-Saxons counted time by nights instead of days.

Norse: Norwegian.

Odin: Was considered by the Vikings to be the chief god and ruler of the universe.

Onager: A Roman-style rock-throwing catapult that uses the force of twisted rope to hurl a single beam against a padded cross-beam.

Seven-Night: For the Anglo-Saxons, each day began at sunset. Thus, a week before was a 'seven-night ago.'

Sax: A Saxon dagger.

Scop: An Anglo-Saxon poet or minstrel.

Sigrblot: The first of three Viking celebrations. It took place in early summer and signified the beginning of the warm season.

Shire: The kingdom of Wessex was divided into areas, or shires.

Each was ruled by an Ealdorman.

Skald: professional Viking storyteller.

Skjaldborg: Viking shield-wall formation of overlapping shields.

Sun-Stone: The mineral Cordierite, which can show the direction of the sun on cloudy days.

Svinfylka: or boar's snout. It was an arrow-shaped mass of warriors who would press forward and try to break an enemy shield-wall.

Thane: An Anglo-Saxon warrior who is granted land in exchange for yearly service in the king's army or fyrd.

Thor: The son of Odin and the god of thunder.

Thrall: Male Viking slave.

Torque: A band of metal worn around the neck.

Tuns: Towns.

Ull: The Norse god of archery and the hunt. He was called upon for help in duels.

Valhalla: Is Odin's feasting hall in *Asgard*, where the bravest dead are brought by Valkyries to feast and party until the end of the world.

Varangian: I use it to mean the various Viking tribes that traveled the Russian rivers. The Rus was but one of the Varangian tribes, though it was they who provided leaders for Novgorod, Kiev, and several other towns.

Victory-Maker: Was the name of the priceless foreign-made sword Canute the Dane had given his young thrall when Ambrose was still a captive in Denmark.

Wergeld: Money paid as compensation for injury inflicted on another.

Witan: is the council made up of Saxon noblemen and Church elders. They had the final choice over the selection of each king.

APPENDIX II

The History of Wessex, of Russia, and of Ambrose and his Son and Friends in the Ninth and Tenth Century AD.

Historical facts are in plain text.
Fictional stories in this series and comments are in italics.
Parts specific to this story are in bold.

793: First recorded attack by (Norwegian) Vikings on England.

832-865 AD.: Danish Vikings attack East Anglia, Wessex, and Kent.

838: Cornwall surrenders to Wessex.

845: The king's mistress gives birth to AMBROSE.

849: Alfred the Great is born.

850: Vikings winter in Kent for the first time.

853: Alfred is sent to Rome where he is made a Consul by the Pope.

855: Ethelwulf, king of Wessex, takes his son Alfred to Rome again.

856: Ivar the Boneless and Olaf the White take Dublin.

858: Ethelwulf dies. Ethelbald becomes king.

(Trader of Kiev)
860: *Ethelbert becomes king. Vikings sack Winchester before being driven out of Wessex.* Ambrose and Phillip are enslaved in a raid on the coast of Wessex.

861: *Pope Nicholas sends envoys to Constantinople to investigate Photius' ascension as patriarch.*

862: Rurik, a leader of Varangian Rus Vikings, is invited to rule at Novgorod.
Ambrose, Polonius and Phillip arrive in Sweden after escaping from Denmark. Pursued by their former captors, they hurriedly agree to go south with Rurik and his Rus tribesmen.

863: Dir and Askold, Rus jarls, take over the Slavic town of Kiev. Nb. There seems to be considerable debate about both this date and whether Dir and Askold actually really existed.
After setting up a trading post in Novgorod, the friends join Dir and Askold's force going south to Kiev.

864: The Pechenegs, a savage steppes tribe, attacks Kiev. Only with Polonius' expert help, and the fanatical fighting bravery of the Vikings, do they survive. An attack on the Pechenegs at their most vulnerable point not only ends the siege, but forces the Pechenegs to pay to cross the Dnieper River.

(Emissary to Byzantium)
865: Kent is invaded by a Viking force and Danegeld is paid for the first time to stop the destruction. The Great Army (Danish Vikings) arrives in East Anglia from France. Dir and Askold lead a combined Slav and Varangian force against Constantinople because of a perceived injustice. With both the Byzantine fleet and army away, they manage to do considerable damage, although they

never seriously threaten the city. On the way home, a savage storm sinks many of the Viking and Slav ships. Meantime, Kuralla is kidnaped in Kiev. That there was an attack by Varangians, and a storm, within a few years of this date seems inconvertible. Since the Russian Primary Chronicles set the date somewhere between 863 to 867, I arbitrarily assigned it to 865.

866: Reign of Ethelred in Wessex. The Great Army seizes York. Ambrose and Polonius are sent by Dir and Askold as official envoys to Constantinople. They return north to find word from Kuralla waiting for them. The friends rush north, free Kuralla, turn around, and travel again to Constantinople.

After attempts by Basil to involve them in a plot against the emperor, Ambrose, Kuralla, Polonius and Phillip sail for Wessex. Basil, aware they know altogether too much, sends agents after them.

(Southern Journey)
Basil is told by the Byzantine emperor, Michael III, to divorce his wife so he may marry Michael's mistress.

Bardas plans a sea campaign to retake Crete. Michael has Basil kill Bardas.
Michael adopts Basil and makes him junior emperor.
Ambrose and his friends are captured and enslaved by Muslim pirates operating out of Crete. Polonius' skills allow them to break out of their prison, and they escape to the dubious safety of a Byzantine Fleet. When they realize one of Basil's agents recognizes them and intends to kill them, they flee to Egypt, where they join a caravan heading west.
The Byzantine admiral harries them across North Africa, but Ambrose and his friends do manage to strike back and damage the Byzantine ships. Ambrose then finds a

Muslim slaver to transport them to Calabria. Attacked and hunted, the friends finally cross the border from Calabria to Benevento. Ambrose feels that they are finally safe.

(Journey Home)
The friends start north. Ambrose and his friends pay a visit to Admiral Demetrious in Naples. They escape and make it back across the frontier just ahead of vengeful Byzantine soldiers.

Ambrose makes it to Rome, where he meets Pope Nicholas. He and his friends then head north for the mountain pass to France. They arrive after the pass is closed for the winter, and must spend the winter in Aosta.

867: Aelle, king of Northumbria, is killed trying to retake York.

Basil 'the Macedonian' kills his own sponsor, Michael III, emperor of Byzantium. (September)
Ambrose and his friends survive an attack by assassins, and in the spring they head north into the mountains where they are captured and enslaved. After Kuralla rescues them, they reach France and relative safety. They reach Paris and meet the king. Then they head for Calais and a ship to England. The Vikings, however, are raiding along the coast. Finally, after many adventures, they reach Calais and Phillip finds a captain willing to risk the dangerous crossing.

867: Finally, Ambrose and his friends arrive in England, where Ambrose is welcomed back to the court. Ambrose meets a beautiful girl and falls in love.

(Warrior of the King)

868: The Great Army occupies Mercia. King Ethelred and his brother, Alfred, ride north to support Burgred of Mercia. The Vikings are besieged at Nottingham, but Burgred decides to pay Danegeld. The West Saxons go home.

Alfred marries a Mercian noblewoman - Ealhswith. Ambrose and his companions return north and join the Great Army as spies. After finding out the Vikings are going north, they flee. Ambrose is wounded and nursed by his loved one. The Great Army pursues, and catches up. Strangely, the attack is called off.
Ahmad ibn Tulun, a Turk, is appointed by the Caliph to rule Egypt.
Pope Nicholas the Great dies.

(Gretchen; Future Princess)
Gretchen and her father head south for Wessex and her marriage. She is kidnaped and taken to Wales.
In Wales, Vikings attack the group, and Gretchen is taken to the Viking stronghold of Wexford in Ireland.
Ambrose visits Wexford, but is unable to free Gretchen.

869: The Great Army returns to York in the north for a year. Ambrose attacks the Viking ship carrying his beloved north. They are finally re-united.

870: Danes kill King Edmund of East Anglia, then invade Wessex under the Danish leader Halfdan.

871: Alfred becomes king. After fighting nine battles, Alfred pays Danegeld to buy peace for five years.

873: Ivar the Boneless, 'king of Dublin and York', dies in Ireland. His brother, Halfdan Ragnarsson, becomes king in his place.

874: Edward, son of King Alfred and future king, is born.

(Alfred the Great; Viking Invasion)
875: Alfred takes out a small fleet and routs seven Viking ships. (Nb. For dramatic purposes, I arbitrarily moved this event to the following year, where I tied it in with Guthrum's invasion.)

876: Danes under Guthrum break their word, slip past Alfred and seize Wareham.

877: Guthrum agrees to a truce, but slips away to Exeter, which the Danes fortify.
After a Viking fleet is dashed on the rocks in a storm, the Danes agree to withdraw.
Halfdan Ragnarsson is killed in Ireland fighting Norwegian Vikings.

878: Guthrum, a Danish chief, rides south across the Wessex border in winter.
Alfred at first hides in the forest of Selwood.
A second Viking army, led by Ubbi Ragnarsson and invading from Wales, is defeated in Devon.
As spring approaches, Alfred builds a military camp on the island of Athelney.

Battle of Edington: Alfred's forces meet the Vikings here in May. The Danes break and run to Chippenham. The Saxons blockade the Danes within their fortress of Chippenham for 14 days.
At last Guthrum surrenders and agrees to be baptized.

879: Guthrum takes his retreating army to East Anglia, where the men eventually settle down.

882: Alfred fights a battle against four Danish ships.

883: Halfdan dies. Guthred is recognized as king of Jorvik.

884: Ethelflaed, daughter of Alfred, marries Ethelred of Mercia.

(Alfred the Great: King's Revenge)
885: A Danish army crosses to England and besieges Rochester. Alfred relieves the city before it falls.

885: Later that summer Alfred fights a naval battle at the mouth of the Stour River. He takes all 16 enemy warships.
Guthrum breaks his treaty. He gathers every Viking vessel and attacks Alfred's laden fleet. He wins.
Alfred calls up his entire force and marches on London. He takes it and garrisons the city.

886: Alfred signs another treaty with Guthrum, where he gets London and control over part of Mercia.

889: Edgar, son of Ambrose and Gretchen, is born.

891: Danes in France suffer two serious defeats.

(Alfred the Great; Young Edward)
892: Five thousand Danes land in Kent and seize an unfinished fort at Appledore. A second fleet follows, led by Haesten, and lands at Milton Royal. Alfred arrives with his army, drives Haesten away, and then moves against the Danes at Appledore.

893: Haesten's fleet sails away, to Benfleet, and is eventually joined by the second, larger fleet. The Danes then raid deep into Hampshire and Berkshire. Edward, son of Alfred, inflicts a major defeat, and then chases the Danes across the Thames. After being forced to surrender, the Danes give hostages and depart. The

Danes of Northumbria and East Anglia send two fleets to Dorset as a diversion. Alfred rushes to the west, while Edward marches on Benfleet. Edward wins a great victory.

The Danes gather all their forces and march along the Thames again. They are besieged, break out, gather fresh forces, and try again. Besieged at Chester, the Danes break out yet again and flee to Wales.

Late summer, 893: Edward, Ethelred, volunteers from the London garrison, along with reinforcements from the West Country, gather and march on Benfleet. The Viking army is away raiding, and the Saxons take the town.

All Danes now gather at Shoebury in Essex. They march west to the Severn River. They build a camp at Buttington, in Montgomeryshire. Though besieged, the Danes break out and make it back to Essex.

Early autumn 893: The Danes in Essex march without pausing along the old Roman Watling Road, into Cheshire, where they seize the tun of Chester. Besieged, the Vikings break out yet again, though they suffer heavy losses. They flee to Wales.

Spring 894: The Danes split up and flee back to Essex via different roads.

Winter 894: The Danes sail up the Lea River and build a fort.
London men attack, but are repulsed. Alfred arrives and guards the peasants who harvest the local crops. Alfred then moves his army to the mouth of the river, where he builds twin forts to blockade the Viking fleet. The Danes abandon their ships and ride north and west, to

Bridgnorth in Shropshire.
Athelstan, future king and son of King Edward, is born.

895: In the spring the Vikings sneak back to Essex or move
to Northumbria or East Anglia.
Guthfrith, king of Northumbria, dies on August 24.

896: *Sitric Ivarsson dies.*

(Edward the King)
899: King Alfred dies. Ethelwold seizes two royal estates
and kidnaps a nun. Faced with an army under Edward,
he flees northward. The Danes of Jorvik (Northumbria)
accept him as king.

902: Ethelwold arrives in Essex with a Northumbrian fleet,
and the Danes there submit to him.
The Norse are expelled from Dublin. Ingimund attacks
Wales. Driven out, he settles on the Wirral Peninsula
with the permission of Ethelflaed, since Ethelred is sick.
(While the exact date is in doubt, the most likely year of
this event was in 902.)
Elfweard, second son of King Edward, is born.

(Introduction to 'Ethelflaed, 'Lady of the Mercians')
903: Ethelwold convinces Eohric of East Anglia to join him,
and together they raid Mercia and Wessex as far as
Cricklade and Braydon before retreating. In retaliation,
Edward gathers his fyrdmen and ravages the Viking
lands as far north as the northern fens. He then orders a
retreat, but the Kentish fyrdmen are slow to obey and the
Danes catch up with them on December 13. Ethelwold
and Eohric are killed on the Danish side, while
Sigehelm, the Ealdorman of Kent, falls on the other side.
Both sides suffer serious losses. This is known as the
Battle of the Holme.

(Ethelflaed, 'Lady of the Mercians')   (902 to 919)
905: The Norse under Ingimund demand land and the old
fortress of Chester. When their demand is rejected, they
revolt and besiege Chester. Ethelflaed provides extra
fyrdmen and the garrison is able to hold the Norse off.
Edgar is Kidnaped by Ingimund and Ambrose goes after
his family in Hitchingford.

906: King Edward concludes a truce with East Anglia and
Northumbria, and probably pays Danegeld.

907: Ethelflaed refortifies Chester.

909: Ethelflaed & Edward raid Danish East Anglia and bring
back the body of St. Oswald.

910: The Saxons and Mercians defeat and kill joint Jorvik
kings Eowils and Halfdan II at the Battle of Tetenhall.
Ethelflaed builds the fortress at Bramsbury.

911: Ethelred dies.
Ethelflaed is chosen by the Witan as 'Lady of the
Mercians'.
Edward annexes London and Oxfordshire.

912: Ethelflaed builds two more burhs along the Welsh
border - along the Severn River.
1. Bridgnorth - main crossing point to Wales.
2. Scargeat- location is unknown. Probably upriver north
and west from Bridgnorth.
Edward takes his army to Essex, builds a fortress at
Witham, and receives submission from Essex.
Some of Edward's supporters moves to the burh of
Hertford and work on it.

913: Danish forces at Leicester look west and see two new
burhs: Tamworth and Stafford.

Danes march south to the village of Banbury, joining forces with Danes from Northampton for a coordinated attack. The Angles meet them in battle and defeat the Vikings.

914: Ethelflaed fortifies the largest town south of Danish Northampton - Buckingham.
She builds a fort on either side of the River Ouse.
Danish armies of Northampton and Bedford submit to Ethelflaed's army at Buckingham. Jarl Thurcetel submits.
A Viking army arrives from Brittany, led by Ohter and Hroald. They land in the Severn estuary. They go inland, but the men of Hereford & Gloucester meet them and put them to flight.
The Vikings finally leave in the autumn.
A Danish Viking, Ragnald, seizes power in Northumbria after Tetenhall, and defeats the Scots in the First Battle of Corbridge in 914.

915: This allows Edward to establish a fort at Bedford, directly across the Ouse from the former Danish camp.
Ethelflaed now had a nearly straight line of forts from Chester to Hertford.
There are two gaps. Ethelflaed closes the Mersey gap with several more burhs.
914 - Eddesbury. Warwick.
915 - Runcorn.

916: Edward builds a fort at Maldon.
Ethelflaed sends her army into Wales. An abbot had been killed. The army destroys a town and captures a Welsh king's wife.

917: Ethelflaed signs a treaty with two Scottish kings, both called Constantine, insuring their alliance against Jorvik.
Ragnald is unwilling to face Ethelflaed. He fights the

Scots and Picts again at the Second battle of Corbridge. He wins again but the numbers of his army is cut in half. Edward fights the Danes in the east - Towcester, Bedford, Wigingamere, Tempsford. He kills King Guthrum II at Tempsford and all resistance in East Anglia collapses.
Ethelflaed's troops march into the Danish center at Derby and take it.
All Danish leaders now submit to Edward and accept him as their protector.
They are granted their estates and allowed to live according to their Danish customs.

918: Edward builds a burh at Stamford. The Danes there submit without a fight.
To the west, Ethelflaed marches into Leicester, where Danes surrender without bloodshed, probably led by Danes seeking support against the Norse threat from the west.
The last two Danish enclaves, Nottingham and Lincoln, fall to the West Saxons by the end of summer, but Ethelflaed dies on June 12, 918.

(Elfwynn, Traitor Queen)
The Mercian Witan gives the title of queen to the twenty year old daughter of Ethelflaed - Elfwynn. Ambrose and Polonius kidnap her during the winter. They return to rescue the boys of the Royal School in the spring of 919.

919: Edward calls Elfwynn to his court and officially annexes Mercia.
Edward moves his army to Gloucester and Betlic flees. Ambrose and Polonius chase him northward. They fight on the way, and Elfwynn finally kills Betlic.
Norse adventurer Ragnald storms York and establishes a line of Norse kings.
During his reign he gives nominal allegiance to Edward,

who recognizes his new kingdom.

921: Edmund, son of King Edward, is born.

(Athelstan, First King of England)
924: There is a Mercian revolt in Chester. King Edward is killed at Fardon-on-Dee. Mercia supports Athelstan as king. Wessex supports Elfweard, his half-brother. Elfweard suddenly dies a few months after his father.

925: Athelstan is finally crowned as king. He is crowned at Kingston-upon-Thames, by Ayhelm, Archbishop of Canterbury. This is the first time a Saxon king is crowned with a crown instead of a helmet.

926: Athelstan arranges for his sister Edith to marry Sihtric of York. They agree not to invade each other's territory and not to support the other's enemies.

927: Sihtric dies. Cousin Guthfrith leads a fleet from Dublin to try and take the throne. Athelstan captures York and receives the submission of the Danes. (It is not known if he fought Guthfrith). The Northumbrians are outraged at this usurpation.

July, 927: at Eamont, King Constantine of Scotland (Alba), King Hywel Ddn of Deheubarth, Ealdred of Bamburgh and King Owain of Strathclyde accept Athelstan's overlordship, which leads to seven years of peace. Athelstan is now the first king of all the Anglo-Saxon people.

933: Prince Edwin drowns, possibly after a rebellion where someone called Alfred attempts to blind Athelstan.

934: Athelstan invades Scotland, though the reasons are unclear. Sometime thereafter, Constantine of Scotland marries his daughter to the Norse king of Dublin.

937: The Norse king of Dublin, Olaf Guthfrithson, joins with the Scots and Strathclyde Britons under Owain to invade England in the fall. Ambrose meets with the Scottish king. The opposing armies meet at the Battle of Brunanburh. Athelstan wins an overwhelming victory, though he also takes heavy losses. Ambrose and Polonius die protecting the king.

939: (October) Athelstan dies.

(Edmund, King of England)
939: Edmund is proclaimed king. Crowned in November.

939-940: King Olaf III Guthfrithson conquers Northumbria and invades the Midlands. Conquers as far south as Watling Street.
Olaf marches south from York to Northampton. When that siege fails, he goes on to Tamworth, which he takes by storm. King Edmund besieges King Olaf and Archbishop Wulfstan at Leicester, but they escape by night. Battle is averted when Archbishops Oda and Wulfstan reconcile the two kings and a truce is concluded. Watling Street becomes the new boundary.

941: Olaf Guthfrithson raids Bernicia and dies shortly thereafter. Olaf Sihtricson succeeds him on the Northumbrian throne. He has his cousin Ragnall as co-ruler.

942: Edmund defeats Idwal of Gwynedd.
Edmund reconquers the Midlands.

943: Edmund becomes godfather of King Olaf Sihtricson of York.

944: Edmund reconquers Northumbria.
Edmund drives out of Northumbria both Olaf Sihtricson
and Ragnall Guthfrithson.
Congalach Cnogba, High King of Ireland, sacks Dublin.

945: Edmund conquers Strathclyde, but cedes the territory to
King Malcolm I of Scotland in exchange for a treaty of
mutual support.
Blacaire of Dublin driven out by Olaf.

946: Edmund is killed in a brawl by an exiled thief named
Leofa. Eadred, Edmund's brother, succeeds to the
throne.

APPENDIX III

Treaty between King Guthrum and King Alfred the Great

This is the peace that King Alfred and King Guthrum, and the witan of all the English nation, and all the people that are in East Anglia, have all ordained and with oaths confirmed, for themselves and for their descendants, as well for born as for unborn, who reck of God's mercy or of ours.

1. Concerning our land boundaries: Up on the Thames, and then up on the Lea, and along the Lea unto its source, then straight to Bedford, then up on the Ouse unto Watling Street.

2. Then is this: If a man be slain, we estimate all equally dear, English and Danish, at eight half marks of pure gold; except the churl who resides on rented land and their [the Danes'] freedmen; they also are equally dear, either shillings.

3. And if a king's thegn be accused of manslaying, if he dare clear himself on oath, let him do that with 12 king's thegns. If any one accuse that man who is of less degree than the king's thegn, let him clear himself with 11 of his equals and with one king's thegn. And so in every suit which may be more than iv mancuses. [A money of account representing thirty pence] And if he dare not, let him pay for it threefold, as it may be valued.

4. And that every man know his warrantor in acquiring slaves and horses and oxen.

5. And we all ordained on that day that the oaths

were sworn, that neither bond nor free might go to the host without leave, no more than any of them to us. But if it happen that from necessity any of them will have traffic with us or we with them, with cattle and with goods, that is to be allowed in this wise: that hostages be given in pledge of peace, and as evidence whereby it may be known that the party has a clean back.

(From The life and times of Alfred the Great, by John Allen Giles)

APPENDIX IV

Genealogy

The Lodbrok Family

RAGNAR LODBROK
b. 765, Sweden
d. 845 England

▼   ▼   ▼

IVAR THE BONELESS   HALFDAN   UBBI
b.878 Denmark   d. 877 Ireland   d. 878.
d.873. England.Killed by Odda in Devon.

▼

SITRIC IVARSSON
KING OF DUBLIN.
b. 837
d. 896

The Kings of Wessex

EGBERT
802-839

ETHELWULF
839 - 858

ETHELBALD	ETHELBERT	ETHELRED	(Ambrose)	ALFRED
858 - 860	860 - 866	866 - 871		871
-899				

▼   ▼

(Ethelwold)   EDWARD I

(Alfred chosen over him)

APPENDIX V

ALFRED'S ENGLAND

APPENDIX VI

About the Author

After counseling teenagers and adults for more than forty years, Bruce Corbett retired to concentrate on his writing and photography. To date, he has written a collection of Science Fiction short stories and two Science Fiction novels. The project closest to his heart, however, is his series of well-researched historical novels based on a family of fictional heroes, set in the time of Alfred the Great, his children and grandchildren. **Alfred the Great; King's Revenge**, is the second in the King Alfred Sagas, eighth in the overall series, and starts with the surprise attack by Vikings on West Saxon territory.

These novels are arguably the most comprehensive series of novels ever written based on the time of the Anglo-Saxon Chronicles. A complete description of the various novels, including samples, links and supplementary information, may be found on Bruce Corbett's web site:

www.brucecorbett.com

Bruce Corbett lives in Pincourt, Quebec, Canada. He is an avid landscape and wildlife photographer, and is generally found reading anything historic.

APPENDIX VII

Other Books Released by the Author

In chronological order

HISTORICAL
I. The Ambrose Sagas
1. Ambrose, Prince of Wessex; Trader of Kiev
2. Ambrose, Prince of Wessex; Emissary to Byzantium
3. Ambrose, Prince of Wessex; Southern Journey
4. Ambrose, Prince of Wessex; Journey Home
5. Ambrose, Prince of Wessex; Warrior of the King
6. Ambrose, Prince of Wessex; Gretchen, Future Princess

II. The King Alfred Sagas
1. Alfred the Great; Viking Invasion (formerly #7)
2. *Alfred the Great; King's Revenge* (formerly #8)
3. Alfred the Great; Young Edward   (formerly #9)

III. The King Edward Sagas
1. Alfred the Great; Edward the King
2. Queen Ethelflaed; 'Lady of the Mercians'
                                2023 release
3. Elfwynn, Traitor Queen of Mercia **2023 release**

IV. The Anglo-Saxon Kings of all England
1. Athelstan, First King of England **2023 release**
2. Edmund, King of England.   **2023 release**

SCIENCE FICTION
Bruce Corbett's Speculative Short Stories
The Goldmines of Alpha Centauri   (coming soon)
The Vuorran Pogrom   (coming soon)

The above novels are available worldwide as e-books from your favorite online book sellers, and the paperbacks are available from Amazon and Drafts2Digital.